I0535306

Time Travel Tales

Edited by Zach Chapman

Published By:
Chappy Fiction
1304 Turtle Creek Blvd
Austin, TX 78745
www.chappyfiction.com

ALL RIGHTS RESERVED

Copyright © 2016 by Chappy Fiction
Cover art: Dan McCarthy
Stories copyright © 2016 by the authors:

"Omnipunks" by Brian Trent. © 2016 Brian Trent

"Into The Desolation" by Catherine Wells. © 2016 Catherine Wells

"A Map of the Mines of Barnath" by Sean Williams. © 1992 Sean Williams

"Proceedings from the First and Only Sixteenth Annual One-Woman Symposium on Time Manipulation" by Stewart C Baker. © 2016 Stewart C Baker

"When We Went to See the End of the World," by Robert Silverberg. © 1972 by Agberg, Ltd. Reprinted by permission of the author and Agberg, Ltd.

"Grandma Was a Time Machine" by H.L. Fullerton. H.L. Fullerton © 2016

"The Day it All Went Sideways" by Auston Habershaw. © 2016 Auston Habershaw

"A Murder of Crows" by Brenda Anderson. © 2016 Brenda Anderson

"The Documentarian" by SL Huang. © 2016 SL Huang

"Dragon Father's Wounds" by Tony Pi. © 2016 Tony Pi

"Danta in Black" by Steve Simpson. © 2016 Steve Simpson

"Come One, Come All" by K. Kazul Wolf. © 2016 Kara Wolf

"The Convention" by Rasheedah Phillips. © 2016 Rasheedah Phillips

"Visits (with a Stranger)" by Martin L. Shoemaker. © 2016 Martin L. Shoemaker

"If the Stars Reverse their Courses, if the Rivers Run Back from the Sea" by Alter Reiss. First appeared in The Magazine of Fantasy & Science Fiction in November, 2012. © 2016 Alter Reiss.

"A Switch in Time" by David Steffen. © 2014 by David Steffen. First published in Perihelion Science Fiction. Reprinted by permission of the author.

"The Time Traveler's Accountant" by John A. Frochio. © 2016 John A. Frochio

"Absolute Pony," by Alisa Alering. © 2014 by Alisa Alering. Originally published in Perihelion, January 12, 2014.

"I Only Time-Travel During School Hours" by Desmond Warzel. © 2016 Desmond Warzel

"Not with a Bang," by Rosemary Claire Smith. © 2013 Rosemary Claire Smith

ISBN-13: 978-0692807750

No part of this work may be reproduced or transmitted in any form or by any means, electronic or mechanical, including photocopying and recording, or by any information storage or retrieval system without the proper written permission of the copyright owner unless such copying is expressly permitted by federal copyright law.

For Sarah and John Connor

CONTENTS

Forward by Zach Chapman   6

Omnipunks by Brian Trent   8

Into The Desolation by Catherine Wells   26

A Map of the Mines of Barnath by Sean Williams   39

Proceedings from the First and Only Sixteenth   69
Annual One-Woman Symposium on Time
Manipulation by Stewart C Baker

When We Went To See The End Of The World by   74
Robert Silverberg

Grandma Was a Time Machine by H.L. Fullerton   85

The Day It All Went Sideways by Auston   88
Habershaw

A Murder of Crows by Brenda Anderson   112

The Documentarian by SL Huang   116

Dragon Father's Wounds by Tony Pi   124

Danta in Black by Steve Simpson   139

Come One, Come All by K. Kazul Wolf   167

The Convention by Rasheedah Phillips   174

Visits (with a Stranger) by Martin L. Shoemaker   187

If the Stars Reverse their Courses, if the Rivers Run Back from the Sea by Alter Reiss   206

A Switch in Time by David Steffen   222

The Time Traveler's Accountant by John A. Frochio   234

Absolute Pony by Alisa Alering   241

I Only Time-Travel During School Hours by Desmond Warzel   258

Not with a Bang by Rosemary Claire Smith   268

Forward
by Zach Chapman

What's the oldest time travel tale? Is that even a relevant question? Maybe this book contains the first 20 tales. Perhaps a temporal paleontologist accidentally leaves this book behind after fleeing an angry Tyrannosaurus. Then I can say, Chappy Fiction and these 20 amazing authors started it all! We started the science fiction subgenre that's more present and less fleeting than cyberpunk, post-apocalyptic, or space opera! And you're welcome for inspiring *Timeless*, *11/22/63* and whatever the next big time travel thing is.

Well, I can hope. In the current, non-fossilized Chappy Fiction Time Travel Tales timeline, time travel fiction may be older than you think.

H.G. Wells's *The Time Machine*, published in 1895, only popularized time travel in the science fiction genre. Many stories, myths, and legends predate it. *The Diothas*, *Looking Backward*, and *The Great Romance* were all time travel utopian novels published in the late 1800s. Even *A Connecticut Yankee in King Arthur's Court* came before *The Time Machine*. There are older examples yet: In Dicken's *A Christmas Carol*, Scrooge visits Christmas past and future. One of the oldest Japanese writings, the *Nihon Shoki*, contains a tale of time travel where Urashima, a fisherman, leaves his village to visit an undersea palace. When he returns, 300 years have passed. Similar myths of time travel into the future are depicted in Hindu and Buddhism.

Enough about the past; what about now? The genre is still relevant and as varied as ever. I'm sure some of your favorite films center around time travel. *Terminator 2? Back to the Future?* The classic comedy, *Groundhog's Day*, is an hour and a half of Bill Murray in a time loop. And don't forget one of the greatest psychological horrors, *Donnie Darko*, is a movie about wormholes and time travel. Just last month Tim Burton directed a time travel movie.

My mission for Chappy Fiction's Time Travel Tales was to collect 20 tales, as varied as the genre itself (if you're a time traveler/forward skimmer, see the prior two paragraphs), some humorous, some bleak, some science fiction, some fantasy. Half are reprints and half are new stories. As you read, slip into the past, save the future, discover dinosaurs, and puzzle over paradoxes. Don't be afraid to skip around—this is a time travel anthology after all!

Editor's note:

While America contains a significant portion of the world's English speakers, it ain't the only kid in the pool. These stories come from around the globe and I did not americanize the spellings for any of them.

Omnipunks
by Brian Trent

She had downed three German planes and there was one remaining, somewhere, but her fuel tank was nearly dry and she needed to land. In the midst of the dogfight she had lost sight of the rest of her squadron. Three columns of black smoke were rising from the tiny Italian island below— wreckage from the ME-109s she'd disposed of in the mad, adrenaline-filled contest of life-and-death in the big blue sky. Now, she needed to put down, or her *Dueling Damsel* would create the next smoky column.

Dolores Vincent landed her P-40 Stormhawk in a field of wheat, the husks slapping at the hull as she taxied and stopped a dozen yards from a peculiar obelisk, milky jade in color and several meters tall. A sleepy village lay nearby, although the dogfight had brought out some of the inhabitants; farmers were gathering in a bewildered gaggle, gesticulating to the columns of smoke and her own landed plane.

Dolores hopped out of the cockpit and drew her pistol, wary that some German pilots might have survived their crash… and warier still that they might be robots.

The smoky tang of diesel burned in the back of her throat. Dolores undid her goggles and leather flying helmet. She squinted at the cloudy sky. There had been four *Luftwaffe* scouts; she'd downed three of them. She wondered if the survivor was the kind of man—or machine—who would circle back, guns chattering, to gun her down where she stood.

"Hello there!" she cried to the distant villagers. "I need fuel! Um, *benzina!*"

"Dolores!"

She jumped at the thunderous voice. It had *not* come from the villagers, yet there was no one else nearby.

Dolores Vincent whirled about, scanning the rippling fields of wheat for signs of German automatons.

"Dolores!" the voice repeated, "I require your help."

"Yeah?" she snapped. "Who are you?"

"An entity from beyond time and space."

"Really?"

"Yes," the voice said. "Really."

The voice spoke perfect American English. Still, that flying robot she had battled with over Shanghai last April had bellowed at her in English that had been pretty jake, too.

Dolores instinctively fingered the locket she always wore around her neck. "Where are you? Who are you?" Dolores demanded.

"I am Overlord."

"Never heard of you." She regarded the nearby town, its ancient stone tower and seaside cottages. No way someone could be shouting at her from that distance. Her gaze gradually drew to the curious stone obelisk. It was oddly primitive in its lack of cultural motifs, like a javelin from a prehistoric era. The voice seemed to be resonating from it. But that was impossible, wasn't it?

"Please walk to the obelisk," the voice said, as if reading her thoughts. "You will not be harmed. In fact, we may be able to aid each other."

Dolores gazed at the jutting monument. It was just wide enough to display three sides. Was it a radio transmitter of some kind?

Scanning the skies once more for signs of the remaining German scout, Dolores edged closer to the obelisk. Play it safe, Dad always said, but that was one piece of advice she was never good at following. The thrill of the dogfight was still tapping in her wrists and heart. Her scarf wavered in the smoky breeze.

"Please cross into the circle," the voice instructed.

"Circle?" Dolores noticed that the ground beneath her feet was set with square bricks of the same greenish quality as the obelisk. She was no archaeologist or historian, but the whole thing seemed to exude an ancient presence that seemed out of place for such a rural, insignificant little isle. She wondered at the history of this place. Had some unknown stoneworker toiled here in the earliest days of Rome, carving this marker out of what appeared to be a single piece of stone? She ran a fingertip down its cool, smooth surface and her frown deepened. It felt like metal, but if so, it was unlike any metal she had ever seen.

"I wish to aid you in your war against the Germans," Overlord boomed, "but I have been trapped beneath this needle. Please step into the circle, and I will have others do the same."

"What others, pal?"

"This obelisk is a nexus point through which other people can lend their aid."

"Lend aid to do what?"

"To remove the source of my imprisonment, and release me back into the world. Your enemies, those, um, dastardly Germans, have trapped me on this island."

Dolores halted at the perimeter of the green circle. Still fingering her locket, she said, "I'm a capable dame, but I can't exactly uproot this needle-thing by myself."

"Two other people will assist you."

"I don't see anyone else here."

"They hail from different time periods. The three of you will collaborate across the centuries. In *this* century, I am asking you."

She waved her pistol towards the unoccupied sides of the

obelisk. "So who exactly are these other people?"

Vin¢ awoke in the gloomy hospital room just in time to rip the IV line from his arm and throw himself through the window as the door burst open and two netrunner agents found him. The room was pulped by a storm of microflechettes as he plummeted nine stories through the humid night air.

There was barely time to select HEAL off his aug-menu. He struck the cobblestone hospital grounds and splattered on impact.

Vin¢'s bones were still knitting back together when the netrunners reached the hospital lobby. They spotted him easily enough. Not too many half-naked men wearing hospital gowns rising from puddles of their own blood.

He reached for his pistol. Remembered that he'd left it in Shimizu.

Damn.

Vin¢ somersaulted out of the way as the agents dashed outside and opened fire. Their microflechettes stitched the ground where he'd been. He took cover behind the base of a weird greenish obelisk contained within a circle of equally green stones. Mind racing, trying to keep focus amid the sizzling pain of regeneration, he fingered open his thigh-panel, found the single steel *shuriken* he kept there.

"**Vin¢!**" an unseen voice thundered.

He almost leapt out of his skin. "Yeah?"

"I require your help."

"You require *my* help?" he cried.

One of the netrunners disappeared in a blur of optical camouflage. The man's invisible boots splashed through puddles of blood, so Vin¢ tracked the red prints until they stopped by a recycling bin on the perimeter of the hospital parking lot. Then he flung the *shuriken* into the goon's throat. The weapon's mini-EMP detonated in a brief flash of light, and the bastard dropped, any healing nanonics he might possess melted into slag.

One thug down. One left.

"I said," the mysterious voice repeated, "I require your help."

"Kinda busy. Who are you?"

"An entity from beyond time and space."

"Huh." Vin¢ scrambled to the dead netrunner, nabbed the man's flechette pistol, and fell back to the obelisk. A twig snapped; he twisted, narrowly avoided a stream of weaponsfire, and returned fire on the bodiless muzzle-flash only six yards away. The thug materialized as his camouflage fell away, the biocells on which they depended sinking into the big sleep.

Vin¢ sighed in relief. "Okay, bud. It's only a matter of time before more of these Yakuza netrunners come after me, so cut to it. Who are you and what do you want?"

"You can call me Overlord."

"IFF?"

"What?"

"You a friend or foe?"

"Friend. But there *is* a foe out there. An enemy threatening your world. It's those, um, Yakuza netrunners. They trapped me here. Only *you* can release me."

"Why's that?"

"This obelisk—"

"Is made from a material that's exhibiting unique tachyonic world-line properties," Vin¢ interrupted. "I'd even say it's multi-temporal. Am I right?"

"Yes," Overlord said, sounding surprised. "How did you—"

Vin¢ rubbed his stubbly chin and winked his cybernetic

eye. "Oh, I'm so crammed with tech I probably piss code."

"Nonetheless, you humans perceive time in very limited ways."

"Fuck you."

"Listen to me," Overlord said tersely. "Perhaps we can aid each other? I can only be released through coordinated assistance across history from three different time periods. Three people, all operating in the same place, just from different eras. Will you help and, in doing so, let me help you?"

Vin¢ frowned. "You said three people. Who else—"

Captain Silas Vincenzo stood among the steaming, twitching wreckage of the giant mecha-locust horde and wondered, not for the first time, if they represented a simple factory malfunction, or if this was the latest plot from the nefarious Professor Rogvold "Crimson Khan" Filippovich.

"Can you hold right there?" the reporter for the *Global Gear & Gazette* asked, stooping behind the studio camera to photograph the famous airship captain. Silas' vessel floated overhead, its shadow immense, darkening the fields of wheat and the cozy Italian village nearby. The airship was tethered by docking ropes to the crest of an ancient stone tower, its rope ladder twisting in the wind. It was all terribly out of place for such a remote little island, but then so was the mecha-locust horde that littered the field; Silas had bombed them to pieces before they could leap on their steam-powered serrated legs and do real damage to the innocent villagers.

"Perfect!" the reporter cried, ducking behind the camera's dark cloth. "Hold fast!"

Silas propped one leg upon the nearest steel monster— just one of hundreds which had hopped their way across western Europe on a path of destruction, their black eyes rimmed by rivets, steel mandibles chewing up every crop from Athens to Rome. The reporter emerged from the dark cloth and carried his camera to a new angle.

"**Captain Silas!**" said a mysterious voice.

"I am indeed," Silas said, looking around. Seeing no one, he wondered if this was a mecha-locust communication from the nefarious Crimson Khan. "Who addresses me?"

"I am Overlord. I require your help."

"Require?" Silas frowned and adjusted the feather on his iron airship helmet. "Seems you should make a *request*, rather than start this dialogue off with a demand, yes?"

"I *request*," gritted the voice, "That you lend aid to a battle across time and space. I have been imprisoned beneath the nearby obelisk by, um, the dastardly Crimson Khan!"

"I say! Today is looking rather thick!"

"If you aid me, I can in turn help you with—"

But Silas was already striding towards the obelisk.

The reporter popped up from behind the camera. "Captain Vincenzo? I still need one more good shot..."

Silas drew his brass blunderbuss. To the invisible voice, he said, "What is the strategy, my good sir?"

"Oh," Overlord intoned, "just cross into the green circle and stand there for a bit."

When Dolores reached the circle she hesitated. Her boots stopped short of crossing its perimeter of greenish stone.

"That's right," prompted Overlord. "Step into the circle, please."

"Uh-huh." She felt a burn of anxiety in her chest, and it wasn't just from not knowing where the fourth German plane had gone to. "You know, I come from a long line of heroes. My great grandfather was one of the first airship pilots in history. He defended Europe from the mecha-locust plague and brought the Crimson Khan to justice—"

"Fascinating, but I do require you to enter the circle if I

am to get out of here."

"Sorry. I blab when I'm nervous." Dolores lifted her boot to take another step, halted. "So who else is with us? These people from other times?"

"There's a netrunner aiding us."

"Netrunner? What's that, some kind of fisherman?"

"Please, I require you to—"

"When's he from?"

"The year 2089, but that really doesn't matter. If you would please step into the circle and... wait, where are you going?"

Dolores hopped backwards from the obelisk. "Just a sec." She felt in her pocket for a pen, found only her lipstick, and began to write something on the inside of her aviator scarf.

Carefully, Dolores pried up one of the green cobblestones. She stuffed the scarf beneath it, and set the stone back into place.

Using her pistol's barrel—wincing as she did—she scraped the numerals 2089 onto the stone.

Vin¢ only noticed the faded etching on the cobblestone because his optical augs were in full spectrum mode, amassing and collating data across the entire wavelength of visible light.

2089.

That's what was carved into the brick. The current year of 2089, despite the obvious antiquity of the carving itself. What the hell was going on? Could this day get any stranger?

He pried the stone up from the ground. In the dry recesses beneath it, something was crumpled. Vin¢ retrieved an old scarf; it might have been white once, but now was faded to an aged, brittle brown. Words were written in some kind of red ink:

I'M DOLORES VINCENT. MY GREAT-GRANDFATHER WAS CAPTAIN SILAS VINCENZO, AND HISTORY RECORDS THAT HE DIED UNDER MYSTERIOUS CIRCUMSTANCES ON THIS VERY ISLAND.

Dolores Vincent? Vin¢ scratched his head.

He accessed the city's local web-brain. He ran a search on **DOLORES VINCENT.** The results spooled into his visual field:

Dolores Vincent, American flying ace and veteran of two world wars, pilot of the Dueling Damsel, was murdered by an unknown assailant on a small island off the Italian coast in 1938.

One-hundred-and-fifty-one years ago, he thought.

He prodded the web-brain for info on a Silas Vincenzo, and then once more for **EARLY AVIATOR NONVERBAL COMMUNICATIONS.** No sooner was that data unraveling in his head than he was neuro-texting a message via pulse beam into the obelisk itself, using the thing as a beacon, thumping its tachyonic resonance field in a deliberate pattern he hoped someone would understand.

Dolores noticed the needle pulsate suddenly with a dull, staccato glow and a pinging sound akin to metal reverberating off a sheet of ice.

"What the hell is this?" she asked aloud.

It *almost* seemed like Morse code; the short thumps peppering a sonic scale like electronic crickets to her ears. But it was older than Morse code, representing some style of communication that no one used anymore.

"What are you trying to say?" she asked the obelisk.

Captain Silas immediately recognized the thumping signals radiating from the needle as the Royal Airship Mecha-Locust Tracking Communication Code. He placed his pipe between his teeth and translated aloud from the pulses and clicks and trills.

"'I am Vin¢. It appears that you and your descendent Dolores were killed at the same stone obelisk that you're looking at now. Put simply, you were decapitated. Please take all necessary precautions to avoid this from happening.'"

Silas chewed the end of his pipe. "I say, this is rather disconcerting! Surely no one can sneak up on *me*. My ears can detect a mecha-locust chirp from a good three miles..."

Nonetheless, he chanced to peek over his shoulder.

A hulking green pincer had risen, ghost-like, from the ground and was chopping for his head. Silas threw himself to the ground and the pincer closed on empty air.

He drew up his blunderbuss and opened fire on the pincer.

"Historical records indicate that a blunderbuss was discharged against whatever attacked you," Vin¢ continued texting. *"However, as it's still recorded that you died, perhaps the blunderbuss isn't the most ideal weapon in this case—"*

Silas chanced to peek over his shoulder.

A hulking green pincer had risen, ghost-like, from the ground and was chopping for his head. Silas threw himself to the ground and the pincer closed on empty air.

He hurled his explosive pocketwatch up at the creature—

"Historical records indicate that an explosive pocketwatch was discharged against whatever attacked you. Unfortunately the resulting explosion killed you and injured a nearby reporter. Perhaps your famous blunderbuss is the better choice in battle—"

"Humph!" Silas scoffed after translating the message. "I would never *open* a duel with my pocketwatch! I must have tried the blunderbuss during an earlier effort and, dear me, it failed!"

He spun around just in time to see the green pincer coming for him. It stretched wide, serrated edges glinting in the low light, coming for his neck.

Silas Vincenzo held his ground. He wound back his electric right fist and punched the pincer dead-center at the joint.

Dolores finished scribbling on her scarf:

I'M DOLORES VINCENT. MY GREAT-GRANDFATHER WAS CAPTAIN SILAS VINCENZO, AND HE WAS ATTACKED BY A MYSTERIOUS ASSAILANT ON THIS VERY ISLAND. HOWEVER, HE ENDED UP UTILIZING THE ELECTRICAL COIL IN HIS ARTIFICIAL RIGHT HAND TO DEBILITATE HIS ATTACKER AND ESCAPE THE CIRCLE.

Dolores sensed movement. She leapt aside as pincers rose up behind her and slashed for her neck. She hit the ground, tucked into a roll, and was back on her feet as a forest of new claws sprang up from the earth, snipping, intent on separating her head from her neck.

"Why are you attacking us?" she demanded, retreating to

the cover of the obelisk. "What exactly did we do to you?"

Overlord's voice seemed to come from everywhere at once:

"I arrived on this world when your people were only scavenging apes! *I was a god on a world of beasts!* You all groveled before me! You were mine to control and command!"

Three claws darted for her. Snip! Snip! Snip! Dolores bobbed and wove like a prized pugilist, and the breeze of their gyrations whipped over her head.

The ground erupted, disgorging a wild tangle of tendrils like thorny vines. Dolores had no time to react to this new threat; the tendrils entwined her legs, clashing and tearing through her pants. She was abruptly yanked against the obelisk, and she cried out as her back impacted the solid stone.

The eyestalk twisted around to glare into her face.

"I could have ruled this world!" the voice thundered at her, "Even with my vessel shattered around me from impact, I was unstoppable. Your spears and clubs could not harm me! *Nothing* on this world could have harmed me."

"Something did," Dolores taunted, thinking of the obelisk she was being strung up against. "Or was it some*one?*"

"One of you little apes trapped me! He used a shard of my own ship to stake me to this spot... he dared to grab it in his furry hand and run me through, burying me here for all time!"

Dolores couldn't move her legs, her body effectively pinned against the obelisk. But her arms were still free, and she suddenly knew what she needed to do. She snapped open her pistol and emptied out her bullets; they tinkled to the cobblestone at her feet. Grabbing the locket from around her neck, she snapped it from the necklace. She fingered open the case, and extracted a single bullet. A *special* bullet. A family heirloom that had passed to her from Silas Vincenzo himself.

"A caveman primitive defeated the great interstellar conqueror?!" Dolores taunted, trying to stall the decapitating claws.

"*He got lucky!*" the monster roared petulantly. "That one ape got *lucky*—"

Vin¢'s optical augs detected a frothing disruption in the temporal wavelength, like something bubbling up from the depths of the ocean. Claws! There were terrifying claws reaching for him across the gulf of time! And behind them was something else, a hideous eye-stalk like something off a mutant lobster.

He tucked and rolled aside as the monster erupted into his time period. He tried darting back to the safety of the hospital, or anywhere outside this strange circle of cobblestone, but a forest of alien appendages shot up from the ground, containing him within its deadly circle.

He was trapped.

And yet... so was the monster.

His augmented vision was reading more than just the creature itself. It was tallying data on the obelisk, and the mounting conclusion could not be denied: the obelisk was pinning straight through the center of the monster, staking it like a vampire to the earth. It was still dangerous, yet decidedly constrained. Someone, sometime, had succeeded in driving this multi-temporal material into the monster's body...

"I'll bet it was an ancestor of mine!" Vin¢ said aloud. "Isn't that right? Whoever trapped you here is someone from my own bloodline! It can't be a coincidence that the three people you lured here are all related! Someone from the ancient past—someone from my lineage—figured out that ordinary weapons were useless against you, so they grabbed a piece of this obelisk... a piece of your own starship and..."

"—and in touching that ship," Dolores said to the eyestalk, "something in the material seeped into his body, into his very blood... and therefore..."

Into me and my bloodline! My family and this devil united in eternal, cosmic enmity!

The veins on the eye bulged and twitched like snakes.

"Any hope I have to escape is thwarted by your bloodline!" Overlord hissed. "Every time a chance arrives, one of your blood defeats me! My only hope is to extinguish you from this wretched little planet! Then this world will be mine again!" The feelers tightened their grip. Dolores suppressed a scream as the thorns perforated her thighs. She almost dropped the special bullet.

But she didn't.

Her trembling fingers inserted it into her pistol's chamber with a neat, satisfying click. She raised the pistol and pointed it at the alien eye.

The eye swiveled to regard the weapon.

"Bullets?" Overlord taunted, and gave a scratchy sound that might have been laughter. "I am immune to your primitive steel and brass and copper and—"

"How about electricity?" Dolores snapped.

Before the beast could respond—before the horror of comprehension could fill its hateful, cyclopean stare—she squeezed the trigger.

The eyestalk instantly whipped backwards, flailing like an out-of-control firehose. The blinded creature screamed—a sound unlike anything she'd ever heard, like a chorus of separate agonies resonating across the ages. The thorny feelers shook her loose; she fell, collapsing into a bleeding heap at the base of the obelisk. The earth trembled beneath her.

She remembered Dad's advice, the day she entered the service: *My prayers and love go with you, Dolores, but they may not be enough. Take this bullet with you and keep it on your person at all times. Silas Vincenzo insisted that electricity had once saved his life. I had this bullet made special for you. Keep it in this locket, and look to it when all other options are exhausted.*

The monster continued shrieking and flailing around her. Dolores dragged herself out of the circle while the claws vanished back into the ether, abandoning this time period. She reached her Stormhawk, grunting as she pulled herself to her feet and bandaged her wounded legs. A moment later, a townsman arrived with a tank of diesel and helped her refuel the plane.

May the winds of Fortune stay with me and my bloodline, she thought proudly.

Above, the distinct droning of an ME-109 began to rise. Dolores squinted to the sky and spotted the last of the German squadron, circling high to the southwest.

"Oh yeah," she whispered. "You and I weren't finished yet."

She pulled herself into the *Dueling Damsel* cockpit and returned to the heavens.

Silas, sitting in his leather study at the age of eighty-two, used his quail feather-pen to scribble a set of instructions into his Last Will and Testament:

It must be told to every descendant of my bloodline that a terrible devil is on this world, and that electricity is the remedy. May the Lord's mercy protect us through the eons!

Now it makes sense, Vinç thought as the blind eyestalk flailed

22

around like a useless hydra neck in front of him, its claws snapping and grasping uselessly. *The tattoo on my arm, the one I had since childhood. The one showing a little electric volt. I never knew my parents or family lineage, but they clearly knew something about this strange fate we're all caught up in. An electric volt giving me a clue that just might save my life…*

Vin¢ called upon the last charge of his biocells, and selected BURN off his aug-menu. Then he aimed his fingers at the freakish monstrosity around him.

White electricity forked out from his nanonics and assailed the alien creature. Overlord shrieked wildly, an ululation that rippled along the frequencies and temporal corridors of the universe. Then the nightmarish apparition retreated, faded, sank away into whatever hellish Limbo it had been consigned to untold ages ago.

The cobblestone square was silent once again.

Vin¢ reached into the pocket of his hospital gown and retrieved a cigarette. Using the very last of his biocell's energy, he lit the butt and took a deep drag.

What a fucking day, he mused, retreating into the city. He blew smoke through his nostrils and, as uncharacteristic as it was, found himself grinning.

May vectors of quantum entanglement continue to preserve my family's *awesomeness*, he thought.

The night's rain had dressed the lemon trees and soft wheat in jewels of moisture as Caterina Vincentius glided down with her waxen Icarus wings from the stone tower. She landed, awkwardly but with a satisfied laugh, near a strange green obelisk that jutted up from a circle of green stone. Her mechanical wings squealed as she lowered her arms, its bronze underframe retracting like a fan.

From the tower, Master Leonardo squawked, "Caterina?

Did it work? Return here at once and we can discuss! You cannot go up against our rivals unless you are fully equipped and trained with my inventions!"

Caterina playfully flapped her wings; the springs and cogs wheezing in their joints. She thought, too, of the vellum illustrations in her master's candle-lit workshop, of the strange potions and clockwork beasts, the incendiary bombs and spring-loaded grapples. Their enemies would never expect such ingenuities… or that an insignificant peasant girl would be wielding them! She twirled around in merriment.

"Caterina!" a mysterious unseen voice cried.

The woman gasped. Her and Master Leonardo were supposedly the only occupants of this island! Had the House of Salviati sent an assassin after her? Did they know of the Medici plot?

"Hello?" she replied awkwardly.

"I have come to you in a time of great need, mortal," the voice said. "Will you let me help you?"

She edged towards the odd needle in its prison of cobblestone. "Who are you?"

"An enemy to the, um, Salviatis."

"Oh?"

"Come forward, and I shall tell you more!"

Caterina ignored Master Leonardo's shouts. So *this* was the day, she thought, feeling her heart pound with fierce purpose and resolve. The Vincentius clan had long told tales of an evil presence on this island. The legend had been circulating since before Rome sprouted upon her seven hills.

May the Fates guide and protect me, she prayed, and advanced to the obelisk.

Brian Trent's speculative fiction appears in a wide range of publications including ANALOG, Fantasy & Science Fiction, Daily Science Fiction, Apex (2013 Story of the Year Reader's Poll), Clarkesworld, Escape Pod, COSMOS, Strange Horizons, Galaxy's Edge, Nature, The Mammoth Book of Dieselpunk, Pseudopod, and numerous year's best anthologies. He is a Writers of the Future winner and a 2015 Baen Fantasy Adventure Award finalist. Brian lives in New England, where he works full-time as a writer and screenwriter; his dark historical fantasy series RAHOTEP debuted with Igneous Books and is available on Kindle. His website is www.briantrent.com.

Into The Desolation
by Catherine Wells

I know when I see her that she's headed into the Desolation. I mean, why else would a middle-aged woman carry a single huge backpack and check into a run-down motel on the edge of the Event? Probably put all her money into a fancy dunerunner with all kinds of equipment that won't do her much good once she crosses the boundary. I glance out the front window, but I don't see any dunerunner.

Her look says I'm right, though: that even, unwavering look of someone with their mind made up. Someone whose family tried to talk her out of this. I watch her come up to the desk, make one sweep of the lobby with her eyes, then fasten them on me. "I'd like a room, please."

A low, strong voice. Polite, but not deferential. Lines around her eyes, a couple from her nose to her mouth , all soft. Mousy brown hair with strands of gray. "One night?" I ask.

"Yes."

"Fifty-three dollars, cash only."

She sheds her backpack and looks down at the index card I slide across the desk. One eyebrow goes up. "No computers?"

"Not this close to the boundary." The Desolation screws with magnetism, and makes computers unreliable. At least, the kind of computer we can afford.

"Ah." She fills out the card, hands it back. Imogene Glass, someplace in Nebraska, phone number that probably doesn't work here, but my mom insists we get one. Then she fishes in her backpack for the cash.

"Second floor okay?" I ask.

"Fine." She's looking me over now, and I know what she sees: a raw kind of kid, mostly bone and gristle. Messy black hair, a couple of zits, didn't bother shaving this morning. Why should I? I'm stuck behind this stupid desk all day while Mom cleans the rooms, does the laundry. She hands over the cash. "So, when am I?" she asks.

"Plus Seven," I say. "Most of the time. We get brown-outs, but we always come back. If you stay in town, you'll go back to the world you remember." She doesn't plan to stay here, though. Why else would she come? I slide her a key — brass, because magnetic key cards get wonky, too. "Out the door, right, first staircase. Room 214."

"Thanks." She picks up the key, hesitates. "Is there a grocery store close by?"

"Couple of miles." I look at the backpack resting against her thigh, and I see it's one of those internal frame packs. I wonder how far she plans to carry it. "The military surplus just down the street carries a lot of camping supplies. Dried food, MREs, if that's what you're looking for."

Her lips twitch, almost a smile. "I suppose you get a lot of folks here headed into the Time Wastes."

Now I know she's not local. No one near the boundary calls it that. We call it the Desolation. Sure, the terrain is mostly desert, and there wasn't a whole lot there before the Event, but all those jokes about the "sands of time" and people who cross into it being "Time Wasters" — Not funny, not here. Not when you've seen the people who come back. If they come back. I kept track for a school project once: 37 percent. That's how many don't come back from the Desolation.

But I don't tell her that, because I'm sure someone else has, and it's not my problem anyway. I just tell her, "Not as many as we used to." Even the scientists don't come as much.

Her eyes are a pale blue, and they look at me as if they

can see through to my brain. "You know anyone?" she asks. Wondering if it's personal for me.

I look right back. "Everybody knows someone."

She lets it go and I like her better for that. I hope she's one of the 63 percent. She hoists her pack with one hand, then hesitates. "What's your name?"

"Abel."

"How old are you, Abel?"

"Nineteen."

"So you were...twelve, when the Event hit?"

When time shattered like a stoneware plate hitting a tile floor. When chunks of the world lurched back ten years, or fifty, or maybe just a couple of months. When it became dangerous to cross the boundary, because out there it was still happening. Is still happening. "Yeah," I say. "I was twelve."

She's looking at me like she wants to ask a question but isn't sure she should. I keep staring back, and she takes that as permission. "Did you lose anyone?"

"Grandparents." That's partly how they figured out the boundary, by finding the places no one came out of, places you could no longer reach by telephone or satellite. Places that, if you drove to them, they were somewhen else. "They lived about twenty miles in. My dad tried to find them, but..." I shrug. "The whole town was gone. Who knows when it landed." What my dad found looked like something from before Columbus.

"And your dad, he...."

"Went over on a Thursday, came back four hours later on a Sunday." She lets out a breath, like she's relieved he made it, until I add, "The first time. The second time...we're still waiting."

And like that, the lines on her face deepen and her eyes dull, and she hasn't even crossed the boundary. But she doesn't say "I'm sorry," and I like her better for that, too.

Instead she straightens up, hoists the backpack onto a chair this time and shrugs into it. "Which way is the military surplus?"

I nod to the left. "I can sell you bottled water, too, if you need more. Wholesale." Mom will laugh at that—I'm the one always gives her a hard time for selling supplies at wholesale.

Imogene hesitates, and I can see she wants to ask me something else. I think she wants to ask if I'm interested in coming along when she crosses. But she just says, "Thanks," and goes out the door.

I sit there for a while, tapping her index card on the desk and wondering who she thinks she's going to find. If you don't count the scientists, most crossers are looking for someone, a relative or something. Sure, some just want to see what's out there, for the hell of it, because why wouldn't you want to bounce around in time if you could? Mostly young guys, mostly on foot with a buddy or two, egging each other on. Funny thing is, those guys come back more often than not. I didn't write that up for my school project, it's just something I noticed. Why you cross into the Desolation shouldn't have anything to do with whether or not you come back, so I didn't collect data on it. It was a school project, it had to look scientific.

But I did notice. And the ones who come back… Is there a scientific term for "screwed up"? Nevermind, I don't need one. Everyone around here knows how people are when they come back.

There's all different ideas about what caused the Event. The scientists talk about exotic matter and quantum mechanics and string theory. One suggested our sun went supernova in the future and created a rotating black hole with ripple effects back through time. I doubt they'll ever figure it out. Around here, folks like to talk about meteorites and alien technology and a secret supercolider built under the Four

Corners area. Right. Tell me why you'd try to build anything underground in that rock.

I hear my mother back in the office on the phone, so I quickly start writing Imogene Glass in the log and make it look like I'm working. In a few minutes she comes out front. "We get a customer?" she asks, looking over my shoulder.

"Yeah," I say. "Some lady with a backpack. I put her in 214."

My mom's shoulders droop, like they always do when she hears someone else is going into the Desolation. But she never tries to talk anyone out of it. To do that, she'd have to talk about my dad, and she still can't, not without crying. It's been four years. Sometimes I'll catch her staring toward the Desolation, and when she sees me watching she just gives a little shrug and says, "Maybe tomorrow, huh?" And I say, "Yeah, maybe tomorrow." But I haven't believed that for a while.

There's a pattern, see, and I can't quite put my finger on it. It has to do with things that shouldn't matter, things like why you're going, and how big a smart-ass you are, and maybe if you know what you're doing or not. I'm not sure. Some people cross over two or three times and they still seem mostly normal. Like the scientists. And others... My dad was gone three days the first time—four hours for him—and he was never the same. His eyes kept drifting in that direction, like the magnetized needle you float in a cork in that dopy school experiment. And he kept telling us what he found, over and over again, like he was stuck in a loop. "The river had water in it," he kept saying, like that baffled him. For all his life—for all his dad's life, I guess—the river has been dry most of the year.

"Gus Patel called," my mom says. "He still wants to buy this place, I don't know why."

He wants to buy my mom, is what he really wants.

30

Thinks buying this motel is the way to get her, and she'll work for him for free after that. Probably thinks I will, too. "So sell it," I say, "and move to Dallas." My sister went to Dallas as soon as she finished high school. She lives with my aunt.

Mom turns to look at me, surprised. "You want that?" she asks. "You want to go to Dallas?"

I shrug. "Not particularly." If I wanted that, I'd have gone a while ago. Enrolled in junior college. Of course, that would leave no one to help my mom run the motel. Which wouldn't matter, I guess, if she sold the place to Gus Patel. "But I would if you wanted to."

She shakes her head like I know she will. "Not yet," she says. She still believes. Then she straightens up and smiles. "Listen, I'm going to work in the office for a while. I can keep an eye on the desk if you want to go out for a bit."

She doesn't have to ask me twice. I'm out the door before she can change her mind.

I meet Imogene Glass coming down the stairs, no backpack. "Headed out?" she asks me.

"On my break," I say, like I was a paid employee entitled to a break.

She smiles. "Yeah, I had a family business. Farming. My kids used to harass me about wanting their coffee break."

"How many kids?" I ask.

Her smile dribbles away like rain down a gutter. "Three."

"They try to talk you out of this?"

"Two of them did."

I almost ask about the third but decide not to. Instead I say, "I'm going over to the surplus store to see my friend Ronnie, if you want me to show you where it is."

The smile almost comes back, not quite. "Sure."

I forget my legs are longer than hers, but she keeps up

without any problem. She must be used to walking. "Where's your car?" I ask.

"Back in Nebraska. I came by bus."

The bus station is three miles from here, at least. "So you're going to walk in."

"That's the plan."

I nod, glad. "People who walk in have a better chance of walking back out."

She turns and lifts an eyebrow like I just spoke in Mandarin.

"I did a project in school," I say. "Who goes over and who comes back. When you leave out the scientists, people who walk in are more likely to come back than those who drive."

"Are they." She's watching me and I pretend not to notice. I still think she wants to ask me to come along. "Maybe they run out of gas," she says. I don't mention all the extra fuel cans I've seen packed in with their gear. Then she shakes her head and grins. "Speculation. We can't exactly ask them why they didn't come back, can we?"

I laugh. I like Imogene.

"Why did you factor out the scientists?" she asks.

"They all drive, and they mostly all come back." At the beginning, lots of them went in, loaded with equipment. Measuring this and that, mapping, making notes. The first ones came back with screwy stories and screwier readings. I guess time doesn't like to be measured. They drew up a chronograph with wavy lines and arcs showing where it was 1943 and where it was 1552 and where that blended into 1911 or roughly 1200. But then others came back and said no, no, that was all wrong, it was 1873 in this spot, not 1911, or it was just after the volcanic eruption of eleven-something. And that's when they figured out the area was still unstable.

Where I am, when we first got tossed around by the

Event, cable went out because the satellites disappeared for a while, and then it came back, and then the stars shifted like God hit the fast-forward button, and when Mom tried to phone her sister in Dallas there were no cell towers east of El Paso. We found out later the whole world was like that, but different in different places. Maybe we were in the 1800s for a while, but Kentucky was shifted into the Bronze Age, and California had Japanese balloons from World War II show up—it was just all mixed up, everywhere. After a couple of days, though, that passed and in most places things settled back to normal, if you don't count the World Clock reading 21:15 when the sun was at high noon over Greenwich, and some cities being a day or two off compared to others. By the end of the week, nothing was jumping around anymore.

Except in the Desolation.

"Did you know more scientific missions went out of here than out of any other point along the boundary?" she asks. "I wonder why that is."

"We're close to the Interstate."

"Oh. I suppose." We're at the surplus store then. "The study you did—was your father in it?"

I glance sideways at her. "It was just a school project," I say. I don't tell her I've been keeping it up for the past three years.

Inside the surplus store, two guys are arguing and Ronnie is watching them. One wears jeans and a flannel shirt, the other wears desert camouflage. Jeans has a frame backpack he's trying to sell to Ronnie. "Come on, it's brand new," he says.

Camo Dude is in his face. "Dustin, what the hell are you doing?"

Jeans—Dustin—turns to Camo Dude, face red. "I said I'm not going!"

"We made a pact, man—"

"And I'm breaking it!" He turns back to Ronnie. "I paid two and a quarter for it last week."

"You got robbed," says Ronnie. He likes to pick fights. It makes him a lousy salesman.

Camo Dude grabs Dustin by the arm. "I thought you wanted to see for yourself! I thought you wanted to see if it's all a hoax. Or jump back in time and see if everything they taught us is a lie!"

Dustin yanks his arm away. "I don't care if they lied. I don't care if all of history is a hoax. You saw that guy. You want to end up like that? Not me."

Camo Dude is sweating, and the store is air conditioned. He tries again. "That guy? He was probably nuts to begin with."

"Yeah, well, you're nuts to begin with, so what do you think is going to happen to you?"

Camo Dude pulls back like he's been slapped. Then he ices over. "You want everyone to know you haven't got the balls to go through with it?"

Dustin nails him with his baby blues. "Think of it as a gift. You're off the hook, and you can tell everybody I was the one who didn't have the balls." He turns back to Ronnie. "I'll take a hundred and a half for it."

Ronnie says, "I don't buy used stuff."

"Dustin, come on, man." Camo Dude is pleading now. "Don't hang me out like this."

"A hundred and a quarter," says Dustin. "And you can keep all the stuff in it."

"I'll give you fifty bucks," says Ronnie.

"There's more than fifty bucks in supplies in there!"

Ronnie shrugs and turns to Imogene. "Can I help you, ma'am?"

"I'll help her," I say, steering Imogene over to the dried

food aisle.

She starts looking at the different packages, but I don't think she's all that interested. "Your father drove in, didn't he," she says.

"Both times."

"Who's the crazy guy?"

I glance toward the front where Dustin is walking out with his backpack, Camo Dude still shouting as he follows. "Never saw him before," I say.

She laughs. "No, not him. The guy they met. The guy who scared them."

I shrug. "Could be anyone. They're all a little different when they come back. Some more than others."

"Even the scientists?"

"Who can tell?"

She laughs again. "My husband was a scientist. An agribotanist."

Was. I shouldn't even ask. "He know you're going?"

"He hasn't cared in a long time." She's holding a package of tuna hotdish, just add water and heat over a campfire. "We lost a child. Our son."

"In the Event?" I ask.

"No, he drowned. In a swimming pool." She puts the tuna hotdish back; I didn't think she really wanted it. "I had sent him out to stay with my brother for a week, play with his cousins. I was taking a cruise with some girlfriends. He was six." She blinks rapidly, brushes at her face. "Something in my eye." Then she straightens up. "You know, I probably have enough supplies. I was really hoping for a little fresh fruit to eat in my room. I don't know what I expected to find, really, but—" She waves a hand at the display. "It's not here." She turns and starts out of the store.

I follow her, forgetting I said I had come to see Ronnie. I don't really like Ronnie all that much, but he's still around.

Not a lot of options in this town. "Wait," I say. "You said you sent him out to your brother—out where?"

We're outside the store now, walking past Dustin and Camo Dude, who are standing by a jeep, still arguing. She's walking fast, and it's several steps before she answers. "Albuquerque."

That's well into the Desolation. I get cold, like maybe the sun just went behind a cloud. "You think you're going to find him."

"It's a million to one shot, I know. But if I stay here, it's a million to zero."

I feel like Camo Dude, and I don't know why. I don't want her to do this. "You think you can save him?" I ask. "Because you can't change anything, you know. The people who come back—they say it's like being a ghost, when you're there. All they can do is—"

"Watch," she says. "I know, I read the accounts."

"You want to *watch?*"

"No!" She's still walking fast. "No, I just want to see him once more. Before."

"That's what you say now. But when you see him—when you're there—" I try again. "You can't change anything. It's that whole Grandfather Paradox, and you can't—"

She stops short and I almost run into her. "How do you know I can't?" she says. "How do you know I can't save him? We know the people who came back couldn't change anything, but *what about the people who stayed?*"

And then, *click*. It all comes together for me, all the non-scientific data I wasn't really collecting, and I realize: That's why they don't come back. They go over to *do* something. To see someone, to change something, and either they don't find it—or they don't come back. I grab Imogene's arm and pull her around to face me. "You won't come back," I say.

Her face is hard at first, angry, but then it changes.

Softens. Her eyes search mine and she says, "What makes you think I want to come back?"

It hits me like a punch in the gut. *She doesn't care. She doesn't care if she comes back.* And it's like she just stuck a key in my chest and unlocked something deep inside me. What's the worst that could happen? I mean, really—what's the worst? I get stuck in some other time? I'm already stuck in *this* time. Wherever I wind up—whenever I wind up—that's where I'll be. And what I do there, that's up to me. See, I don't have any agenda. I'm not locked in.

I turn and run back to where Camo Dude is driving away, leaving Dustin on the sidewalk with his backpack. I pull out my wallet and point to the pack. "I'll give you a hundred bucks," I say. "That'll get you a bus to somewhere." It'll get me somewhen.

Imogene is waiting for me, and I can see from her face that she doesn't get it. I realize she never actually asked me that question. Maybe it wasn't her question. Maybe it was mine. So I shoulder the backpack. "Could you use some company?" I ask.

She blinks, but then her face relaxes. She even smiles a little. "Sure."

I'll tell my mom I'm going to El Paso. Or Gainesville. Or South America—just so she won't wait around for me. I'll tell her she should sell the damn motel and get on with her life, because Dad's not coming back, and that's okay. Not everyone you love has to come back.

Maybe I'll come home someday. I'm not going to find my dad, or my grandparents, or anything like that. I guess I'm going to find me. We head back to the motel together and I feel light, like I could float out of town and into the Time Wastes. And then I laugh. Time Wastes. I'll be a Time Waster. Maybe it is funny.

Catherine Wells is the author of numerous novels and short stories of speculative fiction, including Beyond the Gates, Mother Grimm, and the Coconino trilogy. In 2016 she received the Analog Reader's Choice Award for Best Novella for "Builders of Leaf Houses." Ms. Wells holds a Master of Library Science degree from the University of Arizona and has been both a science and technology librarian and a medical librarian in Tucson, Arizona. She is married with two grown children and enjoys hiking and choral singing. For more about her work, visit www.catherine-wells.com.

A Map of the Mines of Barnath
by Sean Williams

The Manager of the mines was a small, grey man named Carnarvon, wiry with muscle and as tough as old boots. A slight accent betrayed his off-world origins; one of the older colonies, I thought, or perhaps even Earth. He was sympathetic in a matter-of-fact way, as though my position was far from unique.

"What was your brother's name?" he asked.

"Martin Cavell. Do you remember him?"

Carnarvon shook his head, tapping into a terminal. "No, but his records should... yes. This'll tell us something."

I tried to wait while he read the file, but impatience soon got the better of me. "What happened?"

"It seems he took a three-day pass to the upper levels, then chose to continue deeper when the pass expired." Carnarvon skimmed through the file to the end. "Your brother died on the fifth level."

"How?"

"The exact details are unknown. There was no body, no witnesses, and no inquiry. Assumption of death is automatic under these circumstances."

"A pretty large assumption, I would've thought."

"Nevertheless."

He seemed quite content to leave it there, but ten thousand kilometres of travel prompted me to dig deeper.

"Would it be possible to see the place where he died?"

"Possible, yes, but..." He looked at me oddly. "You don't know the mines, do you?"

"No. This is my first time here."

"Nobody's said anything?"

"I only flew in this afternoon." It was my turn to look puzzled. "Is there something I should know?"

Carnarvon shook his head slowly. "You wouldn't believe me if I told you."

"So show me. Or have me shown. You don't have to take me personally—"

"No. I'll take you. It's been a while since I went all the way." He looked around the office, eyes itemising the contents one by one until they finally came back to me. "If you want a Grand Tour, I'll give you a Grand Tour."

"Thank you." His capitulation was both unexpected and total; he made me feel slightly guilty for inconveniencing him. "As soon as I find out what happened to Martin, I'll be out of your hair, I promise."

"That could take longer than you think."

"I'm in no hurry."

He sighed and called his deputy into the office. "I'm going Down, Carmen," he told the woman. "You're in charge until I get back."

They shook hands gravely and I thought for an instant that she was about to say something. But she didn't. She just watched as we left the office, her eyes filled with something oddly like grief.

Carnarvon led me to an elevator shaft, handed me a hardhat and a dirty blue overcoat. He looked around the surface level—at the swarming clerks and technicians, at the administration buildings and bulk-transport containers—and shook his head a third time.

"Let's go," he said wearily, and hit Down. The cage door closed and the floor fell away.

The Mines of Barnath are the biggest in known space, and rumoured to be inexhaustible. Discovered a century ago, they have turned our previously struggling, pastoral world into a major mineral exporter. The five thousand people—according to the unofficial tourist brochure—who work its seven levels are capable of extracting over a million tonnes of any given ore per month, plus the same again in refined materials, most of which is exported off-world.

Yet, strangely, the mines are completely independent of the rest of the planet, like a distant country or a very large corporation. Visitors are rare, especially to the deeper levels, and the flow of information to the world outside is often restricted, as it was regarding my brother's fate. But the official policy on the surface is to let the *status quo* remain. The fate of the planet depends on a constant if not large supply of Barnath metal—so while ore comes out of the upper shaft any situation, no matter how unusual, can be tolerated.

Carnarvon, if he was aware of his awesome responsibility, didn't let it show.

"We don't get many people here," he said, pausing to light a cigarette. "Usually from off-planet—those who have heard rumours and want to check for themselves. Most are satisfied with a few pamphlets and a quick tour of the upper levels."

"What about Martin?"

"He was an exception, like you."

I nodded, allowing him the point. "What about the other miners, then?"

"A handful—the ones called 'skimmers'—live nearby. Drifters and no-hopers, usually. They only go as far as the third level, where we do the refining. More permanent miners work the deeper levels. The deepest ones never come Up at all."

"So some actually *live* down there?"

"Of course. They're the ones that work best."

My surprise was mild but genuine. This was a rumour I

had heard and dismissed as unlikely. I had never been in a mine before, but the thought of crawling for any length of time along what I imagined to be cramped, poorly-lit tunnels made me feel claustrophobic.

"Why?" I asked.

Carnarvon looked me in the eye, studying my reaction with interest. "Surface people from 'round here, apart from the skimmers, don't work below ground because they're afraid of the mines. They're scared that if they go inside, they'll get caught."

"Gold fever?" I joked.

"No." There was little humour in Carnarvon's eyes. "*Caught.*"

I waited, but he did not explain further. If he was trying to scare me off, or warn me, it didn't work. I had come too far to be deterred by vague superstitions.

The cage rattled to a halt. The doors swung open and Carnarvon waved me ahead. "After you."

I nodded, and entered the mines.

ONE & TWO

The sparsely populated first and second levels are almost identical, and usually regarded as a single unit. These were what greeted the first settlers, when they discovered the mines and sent the first of many expeditions into the depths of the planet. Carved from the bedrock, at five hundred and seven-fifty metres respectively, the two upper levels were found to be empty of ore and life, little more than half-submerged tunnels littered with rubble and dirt. That they had been fashioned by ROTH—Races Other Than Human—was obvious, however. Mankind had not been on Barnath long enough to begin such an ambitious project, let alone subsequently abandon it. Another species had therefore established the mines, emptied them of all valuable minerals and left.

Or so it appeared at first.

When I arrived, new tunnels were being carved by skimmers in a half-hearted attempt to reopen the upper levels. The air was full of dust and the screaming of pneumatic and sonic drills. The weight of the rock above and around me was almost palpable—a feeling compounded by the stifling half-light. Flickering electric arcs swung from carelessly-looped cables draped along the tunnels. It was unexpectedly hot and uncomfortably damp. In some tunnels, it almost seemed to be raining.

Jean Tarquitz, the supervisor of the upper levels, greeted us as Carnarvon showed me around. She was an attractive woman, although filthy, grimed with moisture-streaked dust. When Carnarvon explained that we were heading on a Grand Tour, she looked surprised.

"Why?" she asked, staring at us both with naked curiosity.

"I've been topside long enough," Carnarvon explained, "waiting for an excuse to come back Down." Even I, who had known him little more than an hour, could tell that his casual words hid a more complex reason. "I thought it was about time."

"And you?"

"Looking for my brother."

There was both amusement and pity in her pale orange eyes as she snorted disdainfully and waved us on.

My tour of the first level passed quickly. Tarquitz accompanied us to the second, which had little new to offer, and bade us farewell as we re-entered the shaft to the third. A load of processed ore climbed past us, deafening all those nearby with the sound of labouring machinery.

"The Director has been active in the lower levels," she

said. "I've heard rumours—"

"I know," said Carnarvon wearily. "We'll be careful."

"If it comes for you," she asserted, "it comes regardless of care."

"I haven't forgotten."

"Who's the Director?" I asked, but Carnarvon merely shook his head and motioned me into the cage.

"Take your time," said Tarquitz.

"I will," Carnarvon replied, and the doors closed.

The lift fell, swaying gently from side to side, and although the first two drops had lasted little more than sixty seconds each, this descent took at least ten minutes.

THREE

The third level held the first of many surprises to greet the settlers. Its heart is an enormous chamber as large as five Old Earth cathedrals stacked one on top of the other, criss-crossed by ladders and pipes and startlingly well-lit—a brilliant contrast to the upper levels. Its walls are orange and thickly-veined. The air is full of the rumbling of machinery and echoing explosions. Huge ROTH artefacts, inactive for the most part, cling to the walls and ceiling; some are mounted like stalagmites on the 'floor', around which cluster the refineries brought Down a piece at a time by human settlers. Green-clad miners swarm like ants along the walls and walkways, issuing from the myriad tunnels that lead deeper into the earth.

"How many people work here?" I asked, left almost breathless by the sheer scale of the chamber. Too large to be fully comprehended in even a series of glances, it provoked a feeling of vertigo so powerful as to dull the mind.

"On this level, something like six thousand. Most of them in side-cuts rather than the actual core. Your brother was one of them, for a while."

I shook my head. The figure didn't make sense. It was larger than that which I'd received earlier regarding the total population of the mine, and there were still four more levels to go—but I chose not to pursue the matter then and there. I supposed that I'd misheard him through the constant noise echoing in the chamber.

I tried to imagine Martin working here, and failed. We had spoken briefly before his departure for the mines, but he had said nothing about intending to seek employment. Just a holiday, he had said, to satisfy his curiosity. What had happened, I wondered, to change his mind?

The lift ends halfway down the chamber.

We stopped there to procure water bottles, to exchange a handful of words with a taciturn attendant, and to admire the view. Huge ore-lifters floated past us—up, full; down, empty. Carnarvon informed me that protocol forbade us taking such a direct route to the base of the third level. Between the midway point of the third level and its rock floor were only ladders.

"Nothing else can truly do this place justice," he said, and I believed him.

By then I had an inkling that the Grand Tour was far more than a quick circuit of faces and off-cuts—hence Carnarvon's initial reluctance to take me. I was glad that I had no-one waiting for me above ground.

It took us three hours to reach the base of the chamber and the first of many way-stations. We rested there for an hour or so, meeting a few of the deeper miners—called 'moles'—who were heading Upwards for a stint in the refineries and, ultimately, the surface. They were uniformly dirty, but only two thirds were pale-skinned. The rest were deeply tanned, which I found strange. All shared a peculiar dullness of stare, a hybrid of world-weariness which I later learned was called 'miner's eyes'. As though nothing more could surprise them, they regarded the world with patient, cynical scepticism.

I asked them about my brother, but received only quizzical stares in reply.

"Tourist," explained Carnarvon patiently. Some laughed openly; others touched my shoulder in sadness, and went to sit elsewhere.

"Why is everyone so...?" I struggled for the word, but couldn't find it.

"Unconcerned?" suggested Carnarvon, a wry smile twisting his rubbery features. "If they are, it's because they know something you don't."

"Which is?"

"Don't ask now. You'll—"

"I know, I know. I'll find out later."

His smile broadened. "Exactly."

When we had rested, Carnarvon showed me some of the machinery that fills the third level. The purpose of the ancient ROTH mechanisms eluded me then, just as it has eluded human researchers for one full century.

Then it was time to enter the Shaft, the central column that plummets downwards through the four remaining levels. The cage was three times as large as the lift by which we had previously descended. Low benches lined two of the walls.

A crowd of miners spilled from the cage, dressed in unfamiliar white uniforms. They stared at us, but said nothing. When they had gone, Carnarvon turned to face me.

"The journey really begins here," he said, on the threshold of the cage. "If you want to turn back, it's not too late."

I shook my head. "I need to know what happened to Martin."

"Why?" He seemed genuinely unable to understand.

"Because he was important to me," I said. "Am I in danger?"

"Yes." His honesty was both dismaying and thrilling. "Everyone who enters the mines is at risk—and the deeper, the more so."

It was my turn to ask: "Why?"

But Carnarvon, waving me inside, refused to answer.

He stood silently by my side as the cage fell, not meeting my stare. Five minutes passed without a word spoken by either of us. If Carnarvon didn't want to talk, I wasn't going to make him.

Then, after fifteen minutes, the floor lurched, and I felt momentarily light-headed. Only then did Carnarvon speak, as though we had passed some unannounced barrier.

"The last time I passed this way was twelve years ago— heading Up from the fifth level, swearing that I would never come back." He took off his hardhat and slicked back his wiry, grey hair. "But part of me always knew I would, one day. And the same part knows that there's no going back this time. You only get out once. If you return, the mines have you forever."

I studied him closely. If this was a confession, then I failed to comprehend it. "Caught?" I asked, using his own word.

He laughed softly. "Well and truly. I hate this place, but I love it too. And the people that work here, mad bastards that we are."

His attention wandered back to his own thoughts. Reluctant to let the silence claim us again, I asked him a question that had been troubling me for some time:

"Why are we the only ones going Down?"

Carnarvon laughed again. "You noticed? Good. If you can answer that question, my friend, you'll be one step closer to grasping the truth about the mines."

And he would speak no more until the cage bumped to a halt and we stumbled from it.

FOUR

Imagine a grey plain at midnight, rippled in a series of low, undulating hills and valleys. The plain is in complete darkness, except for an area as large as a small town illuminated by powerful, white spotlights. In this lighted area sits an open-face mine, hacked into a hillside like a weeping sore. It is so dark in this place that nothing else can be seen: no stars, no horizon; just one patch of brilliant light and a slender line rising upwards into blackness.

Take the plain and bury it four thousand metres underground in a chamber so large that the walls and ceiling are invisible.

And this is the fourth level.

A faceless technician handed me a pressure-suit. A clumsy outfit of rubber and carbon-fibres, it stank of sweat and grease, as though worn by thousands of people in its lifetime. Puzzled, I followed Carnarvon's lead and shrugged into it, leaving my outer garments in a locker. I felt oddly light, and wondered if the air had a higher oxygen content than I was accustomed to. Carnarvon led me to an airlock and cycled the pair of us through.

"Poisonous atmosphere," he said via the suit radio, explaining the suits if not the sight that lay before me.

I watched as cranes swung and powerful vehicles unloaded their burdens beneath the spotlights. The miners swarming across the face looked like dark animals in their grey suits—hence, I supposed, the nickname 'moles'.

"What are they mining for?" I asked.

"Here, iron ore," replied Carnarvon. "There are other faces nearby cut for strontium and uranium."

I hunted for a reference point, some means of guessing the size of the space around me, but failed.

"How big is this level?" I asked, admitting defeat.

"Bigger than you think, I promise you."

We headed through the gloom towards a row of huts, where Carnarvon introduced himself to the level supervisor, a portly man called Stolle whose suit resembled a blowfish with stumpy arms and legs. Still dazzled by the strangeness of the fourth level, I was content to let them do the talking.

"I remember you," said Stolle to Carnarvon, squinting through his plastic visor. His voice was liquid with static. "Two years ago—three, maybe?—you worked here for a while."

"Twelve," corrected Carnarvon.

"Christ." Stolle winked at me dryly, as though sharing a joke I failed to understand. "Time flies down here."

"Any news of the Director?" asked Carnarvon.

"It's out there," said the Supervisor, shrugging. "Definitely out there. We've lost a few on this level, but not many. Usual story. That, and the rumours of an eighth level, are about the only things we can depend on down here."

He invited us to join him for a drink, but Carnarvon explained that we were tired. This wasn't a lie, as far as I was concerned; my watch told me that eight hours had passed since my arrival at the mines, and my eyes were thick with fatigue. So Carnarvon made excuses, and we bunked down in a crowded dormitory wing with a dozen off-duty moles, clipped by airhoses to a communal tank, our radios silenced.

Thus I spent my first night in the mines of Barnath: in a rubber suit, breathing air that stank of *human*, wondering what the hell I was doing. And when I dreamed, it was of Martin walking ahead of me along a dark, stone tunnel, forever out of reach.

A dull explosion woke me an unknown time later. When we stumbled out of the wing, a new hole had been added to the scarred hillside. The ever-present glare of the spotlights seemed brighter and the ceaseless activity of the open-face mine more feverish than before.

We dined on pre-processed slop in one of the few pressurised compartments of that level. The moles around us eyed us curiously, and it was a moment or two before I realised what it was that distinguished us from them. It was, quite simply, that we were talking. On the fifth level, where communication is only practical via intersuit radio, casual conversation is discouraged. Even in the mess-hall.

"How much further?" I asked Carnarvon, regardless. The night's sleep had left me irritable, rather than refreshed. I was impatient to make some progress on my quest to find Martin.

"Forever and a day, as they say." He glanced at me in amusement. "You still think you'll be leaving here in a hurry?"

"Why shouldn't I be?"

"Because these are the mines of Barnath, my friend. They're not like anywhere else. Where you come from, everything's the same—it never changes, it'll be there tomorrow, forever. But here... if the Director doesn't get you, then you're caught anyway."

I put down my spoon, appetite forgotten. There was a new strength in Carnarvon's eyes that bothered me, left me feeling like an intruder, unwanted. His stare was almost a challenge, defying me to unravel the riddle of the mines on my own.

"Who is the Director?" I asked, pacing my words deliberately.

Perhaps he saw the growing frustration in my eyes, and the anger that lurked behind it. Or he too was tired of his own guessing-game. Either way, he also put down his spoon and finally began to explain, after a fashion.

"The Director lives in the mines," he said, "or else it's an integral part of it. Either. We don't know much about it, except that it can go anywhere, any time it wants to. We don't even know where it goes between appearances—I've never heard of it being seen topside—but we always know when it's been."

"'It'?" I asked. "I thought you were talking about someone in particular. Your superior, perhaps."

"No. One of the early explorers coined the name, for whatever reason, and it's as good as any other."

He paused, watching me closely, waiting for a response.

"So what is it? A machine?"

"That's certainly possible. The mines aren't human-built. The ROTH made them; the ROTH left them here for us to plunder. Maybe they switched on some sort of security system before they left, and the Director is its enforcer." He shrugged. "But few people really believe it's an alien artefact."

"Then *someone* must know about it, surely?"

"Just think for a second, before you jump to conclusions. It should be obvious. What if the ROTH *didn't* leave? What if they're still in here, somewhere?"

I stared at him. "Are you suggesting that the Director is an alien?"

"That's the most popular explanation. More than one ROTH, perhaps. No-one's seen it and lived. All we know is that it takes people working in the mines—usually the best, most talented. Those it comes for and doesn't take, it kills."

"You're kidding."

Carnarvon shook his head gravely. "It's no joke down here. Deeper still, it's positively morbid. Live in the mines for a while and the fact starts to get to you. You're always wondering if it'll come for you, and if you'll be taken when it does."

"I never heard any of this before."

"Of course not. The Mine looks after itself. Hardly anybody who comes this deep leaves again. Those few who do leave hang around the surface for a while, and then go back Down. The Director is all part of the lure and the trap of Barnath, you see. No-one knows *where* it takes the ones it doesn't kill." He picked up his spoon and attacked his breakfast viciously. "That's why I'm here. The mystery has me hooked."

"And me? Why am I here?"

"To find your brother, of course."

"Did the Director take *him*?"

Carnarvon paused between mouthfuls. "If you meet it, you can ask it yourself."

I pushed my bowl aside and sealed my suit.

"Going somewhere?" asked Carnarvon, amused.

"Outside," I said. "I need to think."

I shouldered my way through a crowd of miners and headed out into the darkness. The face of the cut was hidden behind a low hill; the only light came from reflected haze and a crooked line of beacons strung across the grey-green dust that served for a floor on the fourth level.

I squatted on my haunches and regarded the empty view for a long while. It was like sitting on the face of a starless moon. I didn't hear Carnarvon approach.

"Time to go," he said, putting his hand on my shoulder. "Coming?"

I raised my head wearily.

"You say Martin disappeared from the next level?"

"Yes, the fifth. That's what the records said, anyway."

"Then I'm coming. At least that far."

Even through the visor I could see his sceptical smile, curled like a question-mark as though he doubted my motives.

"He's alive," I insisted. "I can feel him."

"If you say so."

"All I want to do is find him and take him home. Is that so difficult?"

Carnarvon helped me to my feet, and we trudged back to the Shaft building. I expected to don our old clothes, but we didn't.

"Pressure suits from here on," he explained, as we waited for the cage to reach our level. "Just in case."

The cage rattled to a halt and the doors opened. I regarded the interior with foreboding. Carnarvon didn't hesitate, however, so I reluctantly followed.

The cage dropped downwards. Again I felt that strange sensation of giddiness half-way, but this time my companion chose to remain silent for the rest the journey, lost in thought.

FIVE

I was definitely lighter when I stepped from the cage. The disembarkation bay was an enormous room, sterile-white and brilliantly lit. Behind me, six identical airlocks opened into the wall; we had entered the chamber via the second from the right. A large section of the floor was transparent, and Carnarvon gestured that I should look down through it.

It took me a minute or so to find a sense of perspective. The view was surreal. Great blue sheets of energy slashed and hacked at something I couldn't quite identify. A hill, I thought at first; then a mountain. It wasn't until I realised that the dots drifting over the surface of the object were ore-lifters—themselves so huge they made men look like specks—that I guessed the incredible truth.

Trapped within the mines, orbiting slowly beneath my

feet, was an entire planet.

"That's impossible," I breathed, as bolts of stupendous energy sheared free continent-sized chunks of rock. My vantage point was high—at least thirty thousand metres—and the view spectacular.

"I know," said Carnarvon, "but we're mining it anyway. And it's not that large, really—barely the size of Mars. Completely dead, of course, and metal-rich. It'll keep the mines active for a century or two at least."

My gaze wandered from the planet, across the roof of the incomprehensible chamber. Giant habitats clung to the naked rock of the 'roof' like shellfish, upside down. Huge docking grapnels awaited ore-lifters ferrying material from the scarred surface below. Everywhere I looked, there were men and women in white pressure-suits, crawling like flies over an unimaginable carcass.

"How many?" I asked, almost afraid of the answer.

"Two and a half million," replied Carnarvon, and I swallowed. I had in mind the unofficial government estimate of five thousand, which now seemed ludicrous in the face of what I was seeing.

"Surely someone must have noticed?"

"To date, no-one has." Carnarvon unsealed his suit, crooking the helmet over his forearm like an old-timer. "As I said, people this deep rarely leave."

"But still, they had to come from *somewhere*—"

"Exactly. A few, like your brother, come from the surface, drifting down through the levels over the years, but that still leaves us quite a large number short of the real population of the mine."

"Where, then?" I had a vision of the miners raising families, which I immediately discredited. Only an idiot would have children in a place like this.

"We may never know the full answer to that question,"

said Carnarvon. "Some miners come Up from the deeper levels without ever having gone Down in the first place."

I studied him suspiciously, wondering if he was playing me for a fool. He wasn't. He was deadly serious.

But he had to be lying.

I too shucked my helmet and breathed the air of the fifth level. It tasted faintly electric, and of the population that had breathed it before me. I could still feel the weight of rock around me, defying the view through the window at my feet. A planet *within* a planet...?

I turned away from the sight. It was too much.

"Come on," said Carnarvon. "We have to log ourselves in." He took my arm and led me along the bay, towards a corridor. The narrow passageway ended in a desk.

A clerk behind a computer terminal greeted us patiently. "Names?" he asked.

Carnarvon gave him mine and added, "Skimmer," when asked for my profession. The ease with which my identity had been redefined did not escape me: from quester to tourist to skimmer in less than two days. Had something similar happened to Martin? The clerk handed me a white, plastic ID card, which I absently tucked into a ziplock pouch.

Then it was Carnarvon's turn. The clerk accepted the title, "Manager," with little sign of being impressed.

"When?" he asked, tapping at the keyboard.

"'45 to '55."

"We had your predecessor through here last year," said the clerk. "He lasted a month."

"Taken?"

"Killed." The clerk handed him a red card which Carnarvon stuck to the front of his suit. "You have a fortnight's grace, you and your friend, after which you'll have to find work."

"Of course," said Carnarvon, not at all fazed by the

apparent insubordination. "Thank you."

He commandeered an electric cart and drove me deeper into the habitat. Occasionally we passed a circular window in the floor, reminding me that beneath my feet lay not the earth my apparent weight suggested, but empty space and then something far more remarkable.

"You'll probably be asking yourself the same questions I asked when I came here." Carnarvon smiled at me sympathetically as he drove. "I was a fusion technician from Earth, so the first thing I said when I looked out that window was, 'How do you pay your fuel bill?'" He chuckled self-depreciatingly. "It wasn't until two years later that I learned where the energy actually comes from."

"And where does it?" I croaked.

"Deeper still," he said. "The next level powers the entire mine. The ROTH were far more advanced than we are. All the equipment in this chamber and the sixth were just lying around, waiting to be used. So we used it. We didn't have to understand how it worked."

Memory prompted me to ask: "I thought there were seven levels?"

"There are," he said, but I could draw him no further on the issue of the last. Instead, he described life in the fifth: the way most of the mining on the planet is tele-operated; how the miners spend nearly all of their time in the ceiling habitats, only venturing to the surface to deal with circumstances that cannot be handled by automatics or remotes. The energy-lances are directed from a cluster of habitats in a segment of the level that has been designated North, coinciding with the magnetic field of the planet.

It was there, I learned, where Martin had worked. When I asked to be taken there first, Carnarvon smiled grimly.

"You haven't grasped the scale yet, have you? It'll take at least three days to get there by cart; one if we can requisition a shuttle."

The corridor widened, became a busy thoroughfare. Miners in clean uniforms walked or drove by on unknown errands, and I watched them in silence, trying to remember what the surface—'home,' I reminded myself—looked like.

But I couldn't. It was too far away.

Carnarvon pulled us to a halt outside a small door.

"Clothes, food, and rest," he said. "And then we keep going."

I nodded numbly, and let myself be led inside.

Standard uniform on the fifth level is a white, cotton one-piece, fitted with numerous pockets and pouches. The outfits are comfortably simple—almost spartan. The food, however, is an order of magnitude better than that of the previous level, being the product of hydroponic gardens scattered across the 'roof'.

"The ROTH left them, too," said Carnarvon as we ate our way through real vegetables and soy-base steak.

"And the habitats?"

"Yes." Carnarvon smiled wryly. "They were more like us than we give them credit for, most of the time."

"What do you mean?"

"Well, everyone down here regards the Director as almost god-like," he said, "when it's probably just a ROTH that eats the same food as us, and stands only a little taller."

I finished my meal in silence, bothered by that thought. I put myself in the shoes of those first colonists, stumbling upon this tremendous cavern and its contents. What had they imagined they'd found? And why hadn't research teams descended upon the mines from all corners of the inhabited galaxy?

I knew better than to ask for answers to these questions. All I could do was wait until the truth became clear on its own, however long that took.

When we'd finished our meal, Carnarvon drove us to a transport dock, where we caught a shuttle halfway to the Northern quadrant. The stubby craft swooped low over the planet below, granting me an unequalled view of the mining operations taking place. From this angle, the sprawl of habitats above resembled a colony of small, white mushrooms suspended from a distant ceiling—or a world of sealed cities, turned inside-out.

As we left the shuttle, a party of miners came towards us through the airlock umbilical. One of them called for my attention as he approached.

"Cavell, you old bastard, where've you been? It's been ages, and you still owe me for Carole."

"I'm sorry," I said, staring at him. He was short, grizzled, and completely unfamiliar. "You must be thinking of my brother. We look the same."

"No," he said. "I remember you. We worked—"

One of his companions nudged him in the ribs.

"Oh, right," he said. "You're on your way Down." He reached out for my hand and shook it. "The name's Donahue, anyway. I guess I'll meet you later."

He entered the shuttle with his workmates. The doors closed on his smiling face, shutting out my confusion.

"What the hell?"

"It happens," said Carnarvon. "You'll get used to this sort of thing."

"I don't *want* to get used to it." Mental exhaustion—too many riddles in too short a time—was taking its toll. "I just want to find out what happened to Martin and get out of here."

"A little more patience." Carnarvon smiled: a mixture of amusement and sympathy. "Not far now."

We took another cart the rest of the way, through a

network of evacuated tunnels that criss-crosses the roof of the sixth chamber. Like insects, we crawled for seven hours along this hollow web, inch by strange inch, while the world-within-a-world turned implacably below us.

Above the unnamed planet's North pole, vast forces crackle through the dust-filled vacuum. Enormous bolts of static electricity split the nether sky, and the habitats echo with thunder. Martin's old home, amidst all of this, trembles on the edge between stone and fire—just as many homes did, and still do, on this level.

A security officer showed us Martin's file. It stated that he had worked in the habitat for no less than two years.

"There must be some mistake," I said. "He's only been missing for six weeks."

She handed me a photo. "Is that him?"

I looked carefully. The man in the hologram was older than I remembered, but definitely Martin.

"Yes, it is," I admitted, grudgingly. "But how do you explain—?"

"We don't," she said. "We just accept."

Carnarvon took the file from her, winking. "Come on," he said to me. "Let's go see where he was taken."

I followed him out of the administration building, hating the curl of amusement I saw in his profile. With the end of my quest in sight, the last thing I wanted to hear was more nonsense.

"This is crazy," I stated.

"Sure," he agreed pleasantly. "But blame the ROTH if you have to blame someone."

We headed to a nearby building, where the files told us Martin had lived.

"He left his room at midnight," read Carnarvon. "Going to meet a lover, apparently."

We followed a series of corridors, all equally unremarkable, until Carnarvon brought me to a sudden halt.

"The cameras tracked him as far as here, then lost him."

I looked around. The corridor was empty and featureless. There was no sign that anybody had passed this way at all, let alone died here.

"What else does the file say?" I asked, staring at the blank, polished floor.

"Not much. Martin turned a corner, walked four steps and vanished. The general consensus, as you guessed, is that the Director took him."

"Where?"

"No-one knows." Carnarvon put a hand on my shoulder. "I'm sorry."

I shrugged his hand away. "I don't believe you're telling me everything."

"Of course not. But I don't know everything, do I?"

"Bullshit." His flippancy annoyed me, fuelled my growing frustration. "This has been one long cover-up right from the beginning. You told me I'd understand when I saw the fifth level. Well, I'm here and I've seen it but I still don't understand. Why can't you just tell me?"

"I—"

"My brother's disappeared, for God's sake!"

"Look around you. Can *you* understand what's going on here? No-one can. Your brother was taken in full view of a security camera and it saw nothing. Four steps—zap—gone. Where? If I knew I'd tell you, I swear. We lose something like three hundred people a year under similar circumstances, and nearly triple that many are killed—"

"So why doesn't somebody do something?"

"Such as? What do you suggest? This has been happening for one hundred years; if something could have been done, we would have done it already."

"So close the mines."

"We can't. They're too productive. And the odds of the Director striking is statistically insignificant, anyway. You've more chance of dying on the surface."

I felt caged in, and wanted to strike something. "You're lying."

"Not at all—"

"You think you can palm me off with false records and insanities—"

"If you'll just calm down—"

"No! I refuse to believe that Martin is dead. He's down here somewhere and I'm going to find him."

I turned on my heel and walked angrily away.

"How?" Carnarvon called after me. "You're not the first to have tried, you know!"

I ignored him. Grief, anger, and a sense of betrayal fought for control of my mind, clouding my thoughts and judgement. I knew that Martin was alive somewhere; I could feel it in my bones. I wasn't going to let the matter go so easily. Martin would have done the same for me, I was sure, had our roles been reversed.

I wandered the corridors, losing myself in the maze of the habitat, not caring if Carnarvon followed. Ten minutes passed before I regained my senses and realised that I was alone. When I did, I set out to begin my own investigation.

I was allocated a room near his and started asking questions.

No-one could give me hard facts about my brother. Few people remembered him, as though years had passed since his disappearance. One even went so far as to suggest that it *had* been years, but I dismissed her as a liar, part of the conspiracy keeping me from the truth, even though she insisted that she had been his lover.

My two weeks of grace passed quickly and fruitlessly, spent for the most part in mess-halls and recreation facilities, always asking questions. The citizens of the fifth level, although sympathetic, were victims of the same passivity to fate espoused by the security officer who had shown me Martin's file. I despaired of ever learning the truth, but for the wrong reasons: I wondered what Martin had done to warrant such a thorough white-wash of his sudden departure.

And always, everywhere I looked, was the strangeness of the mines, the sheer improbability of it all, from the planet below to the habitats above. I felt overwhelmed by odd details gleaned from the people I interviewed: the way power was beamed by maser from the south 'pole' rather than sent along cables; the slag-pit, an apparently bottomless hole in the 'ceiling' that was used to dispose of waste materials; the odd discrepancy between the mass of minerals extracted from the planet and that which arrived on the surface of Barnath, the latter being roughly one-sixth of the former; and the cluster of ROTH artefacts on the planet itself, which, although active, seemed to serve no other function than to send bright sparks of ball lightning hurtling around the sundered crust. But I refused to submit to the disorientation; I vowed that I would remain undistracted until I knew the truth. My life on the surface was waiting. I had to find Martin and bring him back, no matter how long it took.

So great was my blindness that I disregarded what was staring me in the face: that, in order to comprehend what had happened to Martin, I would first have to comprehend the Mines themselves, a task for which I was both physically and mentally unprepared.

It wasn't until I met a man called Azimuth, a well-tanned mole from the sixth level, that I learned what fate was really awaiting me.

I happened across him in a bar on the North-east

quadrant of the fifth level—a dirty man, dressed in his stained undersuit from further Up. He recognised my face, and came to join me at my table.

"I remember you," he said. "You came here looking for your brother, right?"

"That's right. Do you know anything about—?"

He laughed, anticipating my question. "No, no. I never met him. But I heard about you on the news circuits topside, before I came here."

I frowned. "When was that?"

"Well, let me see, now. I came here five years ago, and I'd heard the story six months before that. Five and a half years, then. Sure, that'd be about right."

I must have gaped at his words, for he laughed again at my confusion.

"You haven't noticed yet?" he asked, misunderstanding. "Time is all fucked up down here. You arrived, what...?"

"Fourteen days ago," I forced out.

"And I'm in my sixth year, with the Director's grace. Topside, it could've been centuries. You never know how long until you look."

Azimuth didn't stop there, but I hardly heard what he said. According to Martin's records, he had worked in the Mines for two years—a fact I had initially dismissed as ridiculous. If time really was askew deep in the mines—a possibility I could not discredit, given the other wonders I had already witnessed—then the obstacles facing me were greater than I had imagined. But there was still hope.

I forced myself out of my daze. "The newscast," I said. "What did it say?"

Azimuth hesitated. "You sure you want to know?"

I gripped him firmly on the arm. "Tell me."

"All I remember is the headline: 'Brothers separated, then reunited by death.' Very tragic. I don't know whether that helps you, or makes things worse, but there you go. You wanted to hear it."

I gaped incredulously. Reunited, I echoed to myself, by *death*?

He obviously interpreted my stunned silence as a sign of comprehension and barrelled upwards from his seat, chuckling deep in his belly. "Be seein' you, maybe."

When he had gone, I regarded my drink with despair, thinking dull, slow thoughts. The truth was like a heavy weight—the weight of miles of solid earth—settling upon my shoulders.

When my glass was empty, I wandered 'home', alone.

That evening, I tracked down Carnarvon. He was still in the Northern habitat, easily reached by internal vidcom.

"I've been waiting for you to call," he said. "I knew you would."

I hesitated for a moment, balanced on the edge of total acceptance. When the words eventually came, it didn't sound like me speaking:

"Who did *you* lose?"

"My wife." His voice was even; his eyes reflected the sympathy I offered, unwanted. "It took me a month to realise I'd never find her by looking. When I tried to escape back to Earth by one of the other Shafts, I ended up on Barnath, where I decided to stay. For all the years I've been Manager, I've been waiting for someone like you to bring me back."

"And here we are."

"Yes. Here we are. Looking without finding again."

The silence claimed us again. I had only one question left.

"Do you want to come with me?"

"Sure." He smiled. "The Grand Tour isn't over yet."

We met the next day and logged out of the fifth level.

The Shaft accepted our pressure-suited bodies indifferently, and we dropped like stones into the depths of an impossible earth.

SIX

The sixth level opens onto the fiery face of a sun.

Our period of grace had expired. I found work as an energy-scoop operator, and met the man called Donahue who had greeted me in the embarkation bay of the fifth level. He didn't remember me, of course, but we quickly became friends. He helped me adjust to the artificial gravity of B station and taught me everything I needed to learn about my new job. It wasn't long before my tan was as deep as his, and my acceptance of the impossible almost as automatic.

The sixth level does that to you. It overwhelms, it terrifies, it can even drive a person mad. But those who make it this far and stay for any length of time tend to have been a little crazy in the first place.

Carnarvon's time as surface Manager served him in good stead, even though the post was irrelevant to the deeper levels. He worked in administration, somewhere in the heart of the central gravity-platform. We met once a week to discuss our progress.

Progress where? It didn't matter. We were both marking time before the inevitable.

Then, six months after Carnarvon and I had entered the mines, he didn't show for our weekly meeting. I dug around for information and eventually learned that the Director had come for him during the week. His body was never found.

I waited a month before moving on. My link with the surface had been severed; there was no point staying any longer than I had to. As though I had oscillated until then from a stretched rubber band, I suddenly found myself cut free. I started to fall.

The level supervisor was sympathetic.

There was only one way left to go, at the very end.

SEVEN

The cage opens and I float into a transparent sphere nearly one hundred metres across fixed to the base of the Shaft like a bubble on a straw. There is no-one present to watch or to censure me as I drift through the zero gravity, press my face against the surface of the bubble and stare outwards.

My eyes adjust eventually. Instead of darkness outside the bubble, I see stars.

Stars...

The Shaft ends here. There is no Downward path any more—only Up, and Up, and Up. Forever.

There appears to be no way to leave the bubble, but part of me wonders what would happen if I could. Could I travel through space and re-enter the mines from above, thus completing a strange loop of navigation?

Even here, it seems, there are no answers. There are only questions—and me, staring ape-like at the sky. What could be stranger than this? Like the first colonists, I have stepped into the alien Mines of Barnath and found everything I didn't expect: space beyond comprehension, time in disarray, resources without end, and...

I suddenly realise what *else* the first colonists found, what prevented word from spreading across the galaxy, and what halted the scientific jihad aimed like an arrow at the heart of the mines. Only one discovery could have been sufficient:

People. People have always been here, wandering twisted loops through time, crossing and recrossing, occasionally colliding. They greeted the first explorers of the deeper levels, and integrated them seamlessly into a pre-existing society. Later arrivals were likewise assimilated, lured by mysteries and wonders in abundance, by a curiosity so great that not even the threat of death deterred them.

Whether the mines themselves are from the future or from the distant past, or whether they exist entirely beyond time, doesn't matter. Nothing here is certain, except that humanity has moved in and has therefore been here forever, entangled in some unknowable cosmic scheme.

Maybe the ROTH never existed at all. Even the Director might be human, with a purpose of his own.

My skin crawls, as though across an incomprehensible distance I am being watched.

On the heels of that thought comes an impatience, a need to move—in any direction. Time is passing around me like the heavy surges of a deep sea. A minute here might be a million hours on the surface, for all I know; or a heartbeat a whole lifetime. I want to travel, to be taken further. *Now.*

But the Director will come, I remind myself, only when it comes. Not before. Of that I am reasonably certain, if nothing else.

My ghostly reflection stares back at me with Martin's face—the face of my other half, my twin. A not-so-distant light in the alien starscape moves like a tear down the face of my reflection. I sense that he is waiting for me, wherever he is.

Sean Williams is an award-winning, #1 New York Times-bestselling author of over forty novels and one hundred stories, including some set in the Star Wars and Doctor Who universes, and some written with Garth Nix. His latest series is Twinmaker, a "philosophical marathon" (Locus) that takes his love affair with the teleporter to a whole new level. He lives up the road from Australia's finest chocolate factory with his family and a pet plastic fish.

Proceedings from the First and Only Sixteenth Annual One-Woman Symposium on Time Manipulation
by Stewart C Baker

Hello, and welcome once again to the first and only sixteenth annual one-woman symposium on time manipulation. This year's theme is "Collapsing Space; Expanding Time." Our speakers, as we all know, are Dr. Mirai Keiko (iterations 1 through 16).

All presentations are to have been held in the hotel's ballroom earlier this morning from 9:00am to 9:55am. If you are unfamiliar with the theory of simultaneous time-space n-breaks we ask that you attend the pre-symposium workshop delivered by Dr. Mirai Keiko (iteration 16) from 7pm to 10pm tomorrow evening at the excellent sushi bar across the street (*saké* is on us). We especially encourage those of us who are earlier iterations to attend.

Recordings of each presentation have been made available on the symposium website along with this message. Please *do not* view the recording for your own presentation until after you have delivered it—pre-cognitive fugue states don't help anybody.

We thank you for your careful attention to these instructions, and look forward to having already seen how we will all work together to advance the research and practice of time manipulation.

Dr. Mirai Keiko (iteration 9), chair

Dr. Mirai Keiko (iteration 13), vice chair

Session Title: "As I Was Already About to Will Have Just Finished Starting to Be Saying...": Conjugation and Simultaneous Time-Space N-breaks

Presenter(s): Mirai, Keiko (iteration 13)

Abstract: As Adams & Streetmentioner (1980) make clear, verb tenses during time travel can be confusing. Time-space n-breaks exacerbate the problem by at least a factor of twenty, as one must discuss not only what is/has/will (be/have been) happen(ed/ing), but what is/has/will *not* (be/have been) happen(ed/ing) in other iterations of the same time-space locale. Despite this, I argue that the use of simple present is best in most cases, for obvious reasons.

Session Title: "How Many Time Manipulationists Does it Take to Change a Light Bulb?" and Other Questions of Quantity

Presenter(s): Mirai, Keiko (iteration 7) & Mirai, Keiko (iteration 12)

Abstract: We present a new model hypothesizing that, despite the arguments of Mirai & Mirai, the maximum possible number of simultaneous n-breaks before time-space ceases to cohere can be no greater than 12. We also present a new model hypothesizing that, despite the arguments of Mirai & Mirai, the maximum possible number of simultaneous n-breaks before time-space ceases to cohere can be no greater than 15.

Session Title: What Happens When There is No 'When'? Theoretical Consequences of Stretching Time-Space to Breaking Point

Presenter(s): Mirai, Keiko (iteration 8); Mirai, Keiko (iteration 10); & Mirai, Keiko (iteration 11)

Abstract: We present some consequences of having too many simultaneous n-breaks in time-space. Amongst these are: recurrence, perpetual superposition, recurrence, cause ceasing to follow effect, recurrence, Ovidian transmogrification, and recurrence. In some rare cases, effect

70

may cease to follow cause instead, and events may recur.

Session Title: Towards a Novel Approach for Penetrating the N-break Barrier

Presenter(s): Mirai, Keiko (iteration 4) & Mirai, Keiko (iteration 2)

Abstract: We posit that mirrors, when placed in strategic locations around the area used for time manipulation, can increase the possible number of simultaneous n-breaks indefinitely without danger. We prove our findings by reconfiguring the ballroom to hold an infinite number of iterations.

Session Title: *if you are reading this you must get help*: Consequences of Stretching Time-Space to Breaking Point

Presenter(s): Mirai, Keiko (iteration 14); Mirai, Keiko (iteration 6); Mirai, Keiko (iteration 15); Mirai, Keiko (iteration 4); & Mirai, Keiko (iteration 16)

Abstract: This study explores the conclusions of Mirai, Mirai, & Mirai in greater depth by *if we have succeeded you will find this message in the proceedings please help us we no longer know who we are or where we are or*, rather, we posit that superposition is by far the most likely consequence compared to Ovidian transmogrification and *if we are us or me and me and me and me and me in endless combinations fighting for control* mirror-related trickery of Mirai & Mirai. Such tricks risk *of a body that none of us owns this endless pain this limitless confusion if you do not stop it it will spread and spread and spread oh please if you are there if anybody is there please help us our only chance is if you can* [abstract truncated: exceeds maximum length]

Session Title: The Mirai Effect: Limitless Iterations in a Compact Space.

Presenter(s): Mirai, Keiko (iteration 5); Mirai, Keiko (iteration 5); Mirai, Keiko (iteration 5); Mirai, Keiko (iteration

5); Mirai, Keiko (iteration 5); & Mirai, Keiko (iteration 5)

Abstract: No abstract is available for this paper. Video footage shows six hundred years' worth of otherworldly screaming condensed into fifty-five minutes, while flickering abominations dance around/through/inside an impossibly large stone obelisk. The final five minutes of footage do not show the conference room, but a montage of beach scenes, the tides rising and falling in cadence with the fervor of the screams as inexplicable shapes swim through the shallows.

Session Title: The Effect of Pre-Cognitive Fugue State Hangovers on Time Manipulation

Presenter(s): Mirai, Keiko

Abstract: No abstract is available for this presentation. Video footage shows Dr. Mirai stumbling into the deserted ballroom five minutes late, downing two aspirin with a bottle of water. She taps on a tablet, then appears to watch something on it. "*What* am I just about to will have been already said?" she mutters. "That doesn't make sense." She shakes her head and pinches the bridge of her nose between her thumb and forefinger, then looks around the room, apparently just noticing that it is empty. Something that she sees outside the camera's field of vision surprises her, and she jumps backwards, cracking the mirror. There is a flash, and the remainder of the footage shows only the ballroom, devoid of light and life save a softly flickering glimmer in the broken mirror behind the podium. From somewhere far away comes the cry of a solitary loon, the rustling and flapping of wings.

Stewart C Baker is an academic librarian, speculative fiction writer, and occasional haikuist. His fiction appears in Writers of the Future, Nature, and Flash Fiction Online, among other places. Stewart was born in England, spent time in South Carolina, Japan, and California, and now lives in Oregon with his family—although if anyone asks, he'll usually say he's from the Internet, where you can find him at infomancy.net

When We Went To See The End Of The World
by Robert Silverberg

Nick and Jane were glad that they had gone to see the end of the world, because it gave them something special to talk about at Mike and Ruby's party. One always likes to come to a party armed with a little conversation. Mike and Ruby give marvelous parties.

Their home is superb, one of the finest in the neighborhood. It is truly a home for all seasons, all moods. Their very special corner of the world. With more space indoors and out...more wide-open freedom. The living room with its exposed ceiling beams is a natural focal point for entertaining. Custom-finished, with a conversation pit and fireplace. There's also a family room with beamed ceiling and wood paneling...plus a study. And a magnificent master suite with twelve-foot dressing room and private bath. Solidly impressive exterior design. Sheltered courtyard. Beautifully wooded ⅓-acre grounds. Their parties are highlights of any month. Nick and Jane waited until they thought enough people had arrived. Then Jane nudged Nick and Nick said gaily, "You know what we did last week? Hey, we went to see the end of the world!"

"The end of the world?" Henry asked.

"You went to see it?" said Henry's wife Cynthia.

"How did you manage that?" Paula wanted to know.

"It's been available since March," Stan told her. "I think a division of American Express runs it."

Nick was put out to discover that Stan already knew. Quickly, before Stan could say anything more, Nick said, "Yes, it's just started. Our travel agent found out for us. What they do is they put you in this machine, it looks like a tiny teeny submarine, you know, with dials and levers up front behind a plastic wall to keep you from touching anything, and they send you into the future. You can charge it with any of the regular credit cards."

"It must be very expensive," Marcia said.

"They're bringing the costs down rapidly," Jane said. "Last year only millionaires could afford it. Really, haven't you heard about it before?"

"What did you see?" Henry asked.

"For a while, just greyness outside the porthole," said Nick. "And a kind of flickering effect." Everybody was looking at him. He enjoyed the attention. Jane wore a rapt, loving expression. "Then the haze cleared and a voice said over a loudspeaker that we had now reached the very end of time, when life had become impossible on Earth. Of course, we were sealed into the submarine thing. Only looking out. On this beach, this empty beach. The water a funny grey color with a pink sheen. And then the sun came up. It was red like it sometimes is at sunrise, only it stayed red as it got to the middle of the sky, and it looked lumpy and saggy at the edges. Like a few of us, hah hah. Lumpy and sagging at the edges. A cold wind blowing across the beach."

"If you were sealed in the submarine, how did you know there was a cold wind?" Cynthia asked.

Jane glared at her. Nick said, "We could see the sand blowing around. And it looked cold. The grey ocean. Like winter."

"Tell them about the crab," said Jane.

"Yes, the crab. The last life-form on Earth. It wasn't really a crab, of course, it was something about two feet wide and a foot high, with thick shiny green armor and maybe a dozen legs and some curving horns coming up, and it moved slowly from right to left in front of us. It took all day to cross the beach. And toward nightfall it died. Its horns went limp and it stopped moving. The tide came in and carried it away. The sun went down. There wasn't any moon. The stars didn't seem to be in the right places. The loudspeaker told us we had just seen the death of Earth's last living thing."

"How eerie!" cried Paula.

"Were you gone very long?" Ruby asked.

"Three hours," Jane said. "You can spend weeks or days at the end of the world, if you want to pay extra, but they always bring you back to a point three hours after you went. To hold down the babysitter expenses."

Mike offered Nick some pot. "That's really something," he said. "To have gone to the end of the world. Hey, Ruby, maybe we'll talk to the travel agent about it."

Nick took a deep drag and passed the joint to Jane. He felt pleased with himself about the way he had told the story. They had all been very impressed. That swollen red sun, that scuttling crab. The trip had cost more than a month in Japan, but it had been a good investment. He and Jane were the first in the neighborhood who had gone. That was important. Paula was staring at him in awe. Nick knew that she regarded him in a completely different light now. Possibly she would meet him at a motel on Tuesday at lunchtime. Last month she had turned him down but now he had an extra attractiveness for her. Nick winked at her. Cynthia was holding hands with Stan. Henry and Mike both were crouched at Jane's feet. Mike and Ruby's twelve-year-old son came into the room and stood at the edge of the conversation pit. He said, "There just was a bulletin on the news. Mutated amoebas escaped from a government research station and got into Lake Michigan. They're carrying a tissue- dissolving virus and everybody in seven states is supposed to boil their water until further notice." Mike scowled at the boy and said, "It's after your bedtime, Timmy." The boy went out. The doorbell rang. Ruby answered it and returned with Eddie and Fran.

Paula said, "Nick and Jane went to see the end of the world. They've just been telling us about it."

"Gee," said Eddie, "We did that too, on Wednesday night."

Nick was crestfallen. Jane bit her lip and asked Cynthia quietly why Fran always wore such flashy dresses. Ruby said, "You saw the whole works, eh? The crab and everything?"

"The crab?" Eddie said. "What crab? We didn't see the crab."

"It must have died the time before," Paula said. "When Nick and Jane were there."

Mike said, "A fresh shipment of Cuernavaca Lightning is in. Here, have a toke."

"How long ago did you do it?" Eddie said to Nick.

"Sunday afternoon. I guess we were about the first."

"Great trip, isn't it?" Eddie said. "A little somber, though. When the last hill crumbles into the sea."

"That's not what we saw," said Jane. "And you didn't see the crab? Maybe we were on different trips."

Mike said, "What was it like for you, Eddie?"

Eddie put his arms around Cynthia from behind. He said, "They put us into this little capsule, with a porthole, you know, and a lot of instruments and—"

"We heard that part," said Paula. "What did you see?"

"The end of the world," Eddie said. "When water covers everything. The sun and the moon were in the sky at the same time—"

"We didn't see the moon at all," Jane remarked. "It just wasn't there."

"It was on one side and the sun was on the other," Eddie went on. "The moon was closer than it should have been. And a funny color, almost like bronze. And the ocean creeping up. We went halfway around the world and all we saw was ocean. Except in one place, there was this chunk of

77

land sticking up, this hill, and the guide told us it was the top of Mount Everest." He waved to Fran. "That was groovy, huh, floating in our tin boat next to the top of Mount Everest. Maybe ten feet of it sticking up. And the water rising all the time. Up, up, up. Up and over the top. Glub. No land left. I have to admit it was a little disappointing, except of course the idea of the thing. That human ingenuity can design a machine that can send people billions of years forward in time and bring them back, wow! But there was just this ocean."

"How strange," said Jane. "We saw the ocean too, but there was a beach, a kind of nasty beach, and the crab-thing walking along it, and the sun—it was all red, was the sun red when you saw it?"

"A kind of pale green," Fran said.

"Are you people talking about the end of the world?" Tom asked. He and Harriet were standing by the door taking off their coats. Mike's son must have let them in. Tom gave his coat to Ruby and said, "Man, what a spectacle!"

"So you did it, too?" Jane asked, a little hollowly.

"Two weeks ago," said Tom. "The travel agent called and said, Guess what we're offering now, the end of the goddamned world!

With all the extras it didn't really cost so much. So we went right down there to the office, Saturday, I think—was it a Friday?—the day of the big riot, anyway, when they burned St Louis—"

"That was a Saturday," Cynthia said. "I remember I was coming back from the shopping center when the radio said they were using nuclears—"

"Saturday, yes," Tom said. "And we told them we were ready to go, and off they sent us."

"Did you see a beach with crabs," Stan demanded, "or was it a world full of water?"

"Neither one. It was like a big ice age. Glaciers covered everything. No oceans showing, no mountains. We flew clear around the world and it was all a huge snowball. They had floodlights on the vehicle because the sun had gone out."

"I was sure I could see the sun still hanging up there," Harriet put in. "Like a ball of cinders in the sky. But the guide said no, nobody could see it."

"How come everybody gets to visit a different kind of end of the world?" Henry asked. "You'd think there'd be only one kind of end of the world. I mean, it ends, and this is how it ends, and there can't be more than one way."

"Could it be fake?" Stan asked. Everybody turned around and looked at him. Nick's face got very red. Fran looked so mean that Eddie let go of Cynthia and started to rub Fran's shoulders. Stan shrugged. "I'm not suggesting it is," he said defensively. "I was just wondering."

"Seemed pretty real to me," said Tom. "The sun burned out. A big ball of ice. The atmosphere, you know, frozen. The end of the goddamned world."

The telephone rang. Ruby went to answer it. Nick asked Paula about lunch on Tuesday. She said yes. "Let's meet at the motel," he said, and she grinned. Eddie was making out with Cynthia again. Henry looked very stoned and was having trouble staying awake. Phil and Isabel arrived. They heard Tom and Fran talking about their trips to the end of the world and Isabel said she and Phil had gone only the day before yesterday. "Goddamn," Tom said, "everybody's doing it! What was your trip like?"

Ruby came back into the room. "That was my sister calling from Fresno to say she's safe. Fresno wasn't hit by the earthquake at all."

"Earthquake?" Paula asked.

"In California," Mike told her. "This afternoon. You didn't know? Wiped out most of Los Angeles and ran right up the coast practically to Monterey. They think it was on account of the underground bomb test in the Mohave Desert."

"California's always having such awful disasters," Marcia said.

"Good thing those amoebas got loose back east," said Nick. "Imagine how complicated it would be if they had them in LA now too."

"They will," Tom said. "Two to one they reproduce by airborne spores."

"Like the typhoid germs last November," Jane said.

"That was typhus," Nick corrected.

"Anyway," Phil said, "I was telling Tom and Fran about what we saw at the end of the world. It was the sun going nova. They showed it very cleverly, too. I mean, you can't actually sit around and experience it, on account of the heat and the hard radiation and all. But they give it to you in a peripheral way, very elegant in the McLuhanesque sense of the word. First they take you to a point about two hours before the blowup, right? It's I don't know how many jillion years from now, but a long way, anyhow, because the trees are all different, they've got blue scales and ropy branches, and the animals are like things with one leg that jump on pogo sticks—"

"Oh, I don't believe that," Cynthia drawled.

Phil ignored her gracefully. "And we didn't see any sign of human beings, not a house, not a telephone pole, nothing, so I suppose we must have been extinct a long time before. Anyway, they let us look at that for a while. Not getting out of our time machine, naturally, because they said the atmosphere was wrong. Gradually the sun started to puff up. We were nervous—weren't we, Iz?—I mean, suppose they miscalculated things? This whole trip is a very new concept and things might go wrong. The sun was getting bigger and bigger, and then this thing like an arm seemed to pop out of its left side, a big fiery arm reaching out across space, getting closer and closer. We saw it through smoked glass, like you do an eclipse. They gave us about two minutes of the explosion, and we could feel it getting hot already. Then we jumped a couple of years forward in time. The sun was back to its regular shape, only it was smaller, sort of like a little white sun instead of a big yellow one. And on Earth everything was ashes."

"Ashes," Isabel said, with emphasis.

"It looked like Detroit after the union nuked Ford," Phil said. "Only much, much worse. Whole mountains were melted. The oceans were dried up. Everything was ashes." He shuddered and took a joint from Mike. "Isabel was crying."

"The things with one leg," Isabel said. "I mean, they must have all been wiped out." She began to sob. Stan comforted her. "I wonder why it's a different way for everyone who goes," he said. "Freezing. Or the oceans. Or the sun blowing up. Or the thing Nick and Jane saw."

"I'm convinced that each of us had a genuine experience in the far future," said Nick. He felt he had to regain control of the group somehow. It had been so good when he was telling his story, before those others had come. "That is to say, the world suffers a variety of natural calamities, it doesn't just have one end of the world, and they keep mixing things up and sending people to different catastrophes. But never for a moment did I doubt that I was seeing an authentic event."

"We have to do it," Ruby said to Mike. "It's only three hours. What about calling them first thing Monday and making an appointment for Thursday night?"

"Monday's the President's funeral," Tom pointed out. "The travel agency will be closed."

"Have they caught the assassin yet?" Fran asked.

"They didn't mention it on the four o'clock news," said Stan. "I guess he'll get away like the last one."

"Beats me why anybody wants to be President," Phil said.

Mike put on some music. Nick danced with Paula. Eddie danced with Cynthia. Henry was asleep. Dave, Paula's husband, was on crutches because of his mugging, and he asked Isabel to sit and talk with him. Tom danced with Harriet even though he was married to her. She hadn't been out of the hospital more than a few months since the transplant and he treated her extremely tenderly. Mike danced with Fran. Phil danced with Jane. Stan danced with Marcia. Ruby cut in on Eddie and Cynthia. Afterward Tom danced with Jane and Phil danced with Paula. Mike and Ruby's little girl woke up and came out to say hello. Mike sent her back to bed. Far away there was the sound of an explosion. Nick danced with Paula again, but he didn't want her to get bored with him before Tuesday, so he excused himself and went to talk with Dave. Dave handled most of Nick's investments. Ruby said to Mike, "The day after the funeral, will you call the travel agent?" Mike said he would, but Tom said somebody would probably shoot the new President too and there'd be another funeral. These funerals were demolishing the gross national product, Stan observed, on account of how everything had to close all the time. Nick saw Cynthia wake Henry up and ask him sharply if he would take her on the end-of-the-world trip. Henry looked embarrassed. His factory had been blown up at Christmas in a peace demonstration and everybody knew he was in bad shape financially. "You can charge it," Cynthia said, her fierce voice carrying above the chitchat. "And it's so beautiful, Henry. The ice. Or the sun exploding. I want to go."

"Lou and Janet were going to be here tonight, too," Ruby said to Paula. "But their younger boy came back from Texas with that new kind of cholera and they had to cancel."

Phil said, "I understand that one couple saw the moon come apart. It got too close to the Earth and split into chunks and the chunks fell like meteors. Smashing everything up, you know. One big piece nearly hit their time machine."

"I wouldn't have liked that at all," Marcia said.

"Our trip was very lovely," said Jane. "No violent things at all. Just the big red sun and the tide and that crab creeping along the beach. We were both deeply moved."

"It's amazing what science can accomplish nowadays," Fran said.

Mike and Ruby agreed they would try to arrange a trip to the end of the world as soon as the funeral was over. Cynthia drank too much and got sick. Phil, Tom, and Dave discussed the stock market. Harriet told Nick about her operation. Isabel flirted with Mike, tugging her neckline lower. At midnight someone turned on the news. They had some shots of the earthquake and a warning about boiling your water if you lived in the affected states. The President's widow was shown visiting the last President's widow to get some pointers for the funeral. Then there was an interview with an executive of the time-trip company. "Business is phenomenal," he said. "Time-tripping will be the nation's number one growth industry next year." The reporter asked him if his company would soon be offering something besides the end-of-the-world trip. "Later on, we hope to," the executive said. "We plan to apply for Congressional approval soon. But meanwhile the demand for our present offering is running very high. You can't imagine. Of course, you have to expect apocalyptic stuff to attain immense popularity in times like these." The reporter said, "What do you mean, times like these?" but as the time-trip man started to reply, he was interrupted by the commercial. Mike shut off the set. Nick discovered that he was extremely depressed. He decided that it was because so many of his friends had made the journey, and he had thought he and Jane were the only ones who had. He found himself standing next to Marcia and tried to describe the way the crab had moved, but Marcia only shrugged. No one was talking about time-trips now. The party had moved beyond that point. Nick and Jane left quite early and went right to sleep, without making love. The next morning the Sunday paper wasn't delivered because of the Bridge Authority strike, and the radio said that the mutant amoebas were proving harder to eradicate than originally anticipated. They were spreading into Lake Superior and everyone in the region would have to boil all their drinking water. Nick and Jane discussed where they would go for their next vacation. "What about going to see the end of the world all over again?" Jane suggested, and Nick laughed quite a good deal.

Robert Silverberg is an American author and editor. He has won four Hugo Awards and five Nebula Awards. He has been publishing in genre magazines and anthologies for over sixty years and his works have been translated into forty languages. His most famous works are *Dying Inside*, *Nightwings* and *Lord Valentine's Castle*.

Grandma Was a Time Machine
by H.L. Fullerton

Forward is the same as back, my grandmother's voice whispers in my ear. She said this before she started the forgetting so it must mean something, but since she only had my ears to fill with her wisdom, most of it spilled onto the floor. I was not a sponge, but a mop.

When I visited her in the home, she asked who I was. I told her, Clark, your daughter's son. Her pupils were unfocused; she stared elsewhere, maybe forward, most likely back, watching life unfold on some giant, unseen screen. She smiled and patted my hand. Said, "You haven't been born yet. You must wait your turn." I think of this as I build my time machine.

Forward is the same as back. She repeated it often—nearly every day if the nurses can be believed—while she withered to ashy bone. *They're like babies at this age*, I overheard a nurse tell an orderly. *Big, ugly babies*. He grinned at her, no bark, all bite. Hands and teeth and helpless. I hurried to my car, outdistancing my fears, slamming doors on them. On Grandma.

I made you a necklace, you threw it away.

History repeats itself. Is this the same adage? To reach the past, must you stride first into the future? Are all mistakes frozen in amber, perfectly preserved indents someone will one day wear around her neck?

I left your ring in the church's offering plate. There was nothing else to give.

I add another photo of you to my time machine. It is held together with tears and duct tape. A collage of family treasures: a blue baby blanket; Grandma's mother's rocking chair—it will be my conductor's seat; the silver tea pot; your father's walking stick; bones from family pets I dug in the yard to find. Here's Duke and Lady and a skull from a cat named Baby. A scrap of calico dress, a plastic green army man, an undarned sock, an ancient electric bill, a skein of tangled yarn that once played cat's cradle, a collection of mismatched spoons, a forgotten report card, and an old rubber galosh—to ground the rest. Still, it does not work. I rock and rock, knees chest high, and nothing changes but the hour. This then is the future. Perhaps Grandma was wrong. Perhaps I must forget to remember.

My mother is a story my grandmother tells. Camilla at six, finger-painting daisies on the driveway. Camilla at ten in her Easter dress. At fifteen, in tennis whites. Married at 21 and gone by 25.

How did you lose yourself so completely? When you pushed me into your mother's arms, did you know it was forever?

My wife left me, too. "I want something more," she said, and for a moment, she was you, handing me over to Grandma with a small red suitcase and a half-drunk juice box. But Grandma was gone and then so was she.

Forward *is* the same as back. Of this, I'm certain. That to fling oneself into the future will catapult one back to the beginning. Not erase all mistakes, but make them soft and pliable; impressionable sap once again. I take my time machine apart, rebuild it. Not chronologically, but haphazardly. You, me, her, him—all of us mothers and daughters and fathers and sons mixed up and overlapping. I find the pattern, repeat it. Cover the completed construct with discarded juice pouches, silver side out. It is shiny like magic and distorts like time. I sprinkle Grandma's ashes over it, first light like snow flurries, than furious like splattered blood.

I am ready to ride. To age. To follow Grandma into the

forgetting times. I climb in, ducking my head. Things rustle, like mice in the attic. I harness myself into the rocker with straps from car seats of babies I'll never know.

I rock. Things shudder. Time jerks. My skin sags, sports spots like those my grandmother's wore. My eyes cloud. My scalp balds; strands of hair—white, silver, gray!—fall to the floor. It's working. I'm speeding into the future.

I take a deep breath and brace myself for the coming recoil when forward slams into back. I imagine us, together, painting daisies on the driveway, under Grandma's watchful eyes. Soon, now, soon. I'll tell stories about you.

H.L. Fullerton writes fiction—mostly speculative, occasionally about grandmothers; uses words instead of emoticons; likes semi-colons and the occasional interrobang; might be in trouble with prepositions; loves lists and bullet points; believes apostrophes are commas gone wild; may have dangled a participle or two; binge reads while watching television; and is sometimes published in anthologies such as Crime & Mystery; Writers of the Future, Vol. 32; Triangulation: Beneath the Surface; and Mysterion.

The Day It All Went Sideways
by Auston Habershaw

Killing myself was starting to get difficult. I was running
out of poison, for one thing—just two more bamboo needles
coated in shellfish toxin—and after that I was either going to
have to break my neck, toss myself off a building, or resort to
using a gun. None of those would be low key, you know? The
last thing I needed was to draw attention to myself.

I put a finger on the blinds and pressed down. Outside
was 3rd Avenue in Midtown, Manhattan—dirty Model Ts
and Model As jostling with trolley cars and delivery trucks, a
sea of men in hats and overcoats, heading to work. A kid on
the corner was yelling about something that happened that
day. I listened for a second to make sure he was yelling the
same thing he always did, then I checked my wristwatch, just
to confirm. Its big, golden face had three extra dials—date,
month, year. It was September 5th, 1932. Just after nine in
the morning.

Showtime.

By this point I'd whittled away all my most naive
selves—all the idiots so damned excited by their new life that
they let their guard down. It was hard for me—not so much
the killing, but the idea that any version of myself, past or
present, would be so stupid as to not watch his own back.
The first one I killed was reading the paper by himself with
his back to an alley—an *alley*, for God's sake! I garroted the
dumbass. I saw my face—my eyes—full of panic, bugging
out, choking out that death rattle. I admit it was pretty tough
for a minute there. Then I found the ten million dollars in
bearer bonds stuffed in his jacket pocket and I felt better. I

88

threw the body over my shoulder, gave my watch a twist, and ditched it in the fourteenth century for some Manhattan Indian to find and puzzle over.

It went like that for a little while. Like shooting fish in a barrel, you know? Musta knocked off thirty or forty of myself by that point. At last count, I now had about eight-hundred and ninety five million bucks in a safe deposit box off in 1993. I was almost there.

This guy, though, was different. This was a self more like myself, if you follow my meaning. Cagey, eyes in the back of his head, packing a switchblade he knew how to use. He clipped me the last time I tried. Had to twist off to 2024 and get patched up for a few days before heading back for another go. This time I was ready.

This version of myself had a rented room, just like me, but his was a block down from Hennessey's and not across the street. At nine AM sharp, the guy came out of the apartment and drifted with the big crowd of guys with hats, blending in from above, making him hard to spot from the street. Hell, it was hard to tell just how many of me there were in that crowd, honestly—even if I did find him, it might not be the right him, you know? I did that a couple times, too. I mean, no big loss, right? One more dead me was one more sack of loot for me to stash—nabbed myself a Fabergé Egg that way. This guy, though, was the main prize. I knew it. He probably knew it too. That's the advantage *and* disadvantage of stalking yourself—you know exactly how you think.

The only way I was going to catch him was at the entrance of Hennessey's itself—right as he was about to trot down those stairs and knock on the door. I could catch him from behind if I timed it just right. He knew this, of course, and he was on guard. If the timing wasn't perfect, he'd get away or, worse, kill me and the whole deal would be off. So I bided my time. The good thing about having a time machine is you can afford to be patient.

I slid into the crowd, dressed in an overcoat and a black hat, blending into the scenery. I spotted myself drinking coffee at a lunch counter and kept my hat low. That me was scoping out the scene, too, waiting for his moment. I made a mental note of his location and time and resolved to deal with him later. As far as I could tell, he didn't see me.

Crossing 3rd Avenue had to be perfectly timed. Been hit by a car at least twice, but now I had it down. At exactly 9:09 and thirty-seven seconds I went, waltzing through the engine noise and exhaust fumes like Fred Astaire through a Broadway show-stopper. Two minutes later and bam—I was across the street, hidden in the doorway of a tax attorney's office, waiting for Mr. Switchblade to come down the sidewalk like he always does—at 9:11 and forty-five seconds. I even had sixteen seconds to spare.

I got out the little blowgun and worked the cork off the tip of my little bamboo dart. Got the idea for these babies when I saw an otherself stick himself with one by accident. He croaked in five seconds flat. That guy's screw-up also got me a safe-deposit box with an original VanGogh which I then sold at auction in 2018 for a cool 42 million. That was a good day.

I put the dart in the blowgun and held it just below my lips, watching the shifting crowd for any sign of my face, my gait, my familiar coat and hat. Five seconds left. Four. I brought the blowgun to my lips. Three. Two. One.

Nothing. He ain't there. Something's wrong.

Click.

I heard the safety of a .45 caliber automatic flip off and felt its blunt muzzle being pressed to the back of my skull. I heard my own voice say, very slowly, "Take it easy, champ. You and me, we gotta talk."

He's got me. I can't even reach for the watch—he'll know that trick. I put my hands up and let the blowgun drop. "Okay. Let's talk."

When you're a time traveler, it gets really hard to say exactly how long ago things happened for you, subjectively, but let's just say this: I got my gold time-watch on December 8th, 1977. I was drifting across Nevada at the time, catching poker games where the action looked good and dropping money on slots and booze where it wasn't. My criminal career, such as it was, had just ended with a guy named Gino the Razor telling me if I ever "showed my fat nose in Vegas again, I'd wind up in a hole." Say what you like about that Italian fuck, but Gino always gave good career advice.

I hadn't so much lived a life of ambition, understand? For a big guy with flexible morals like me, organized crime was a pretty easy gig. With that gone, well, you might say I was at a personal crossroads. The idea, loosely, was to find my sister in Sedona and beg her husband to give me a job. I wasn't looking forward to that. He'd have me digging holes or some shit. I wasn't headed there in a hurry.

Somehow I wound up in the back room of some shitty little slot parlor outside of Reno. Somebody had passed around my picture with my name and a warning scribbled in magic marker in the corner: CHEATER.

So, there I was, sitting in this smoky room with fake wood paneling and a picture of Elvis on the wall. Across a steel desk is this gorilla. No, I'm not shitting you—an actual gorilla in a tux wearing glasses. Thought it was some kinda joke for a minute—somebody got himself a *Planet of the Apes* mask or something—but then this gorilla started talking to me and I saw them teeth. Then shit got weird.

"Coffee?" He asked. No accent. I mean, I dunno what

kinda accent I was expecting, but a little 'ook-ook' woulda calmed me a bit.

"No. Thanks."

"You seem to get in a lot of trouble, Mr. Grayne," said the gorilla. He slapped that picture of me on the table.

I looked. I tried to play it cool, you know? Yeah, so what if there's a big gorilla here, talking to me and wearing a tux and glasses. I'm Ollie Grayne, and I been in thicker shit than this, right? "Look, Bobo, I just got here. Your boys nabbed me coming in through the door. I ain't robbed you outta a dime."

The gorilla raised one thick finger and waggled it at me like I was a naughty boy. "You haven't robbed me *yet*, you mean. You meant to."

I rolled my head from side-to-side, working out the kinks from a long drive south from Vegas. "So, we gonna discuss the fact that you're a talking gorilla, or is that off the table?"

"Mr. Grayne, this is the end of the line for you." The gorilla took off his spectacles and looked me dead in the eyes. I confess this scared the shit outta me. I'm a big man and I know my way in a scrap, but we both knew he could break me in half like cheap baguette whenever he damned well pleased. "You will have stolen a handy sum of money from me, which means you will have robbed my organization, and my organization has a very limited sense of humor about such things."

I unbuttoned my collar, loosened my tie, and stood up. "That's how it's gotta be, huh?"

Bobo motioned for me to sit. "Please, Mr. Grayne—if I intended to kill you, I wouldn't have asked if you wanted any coffee. No, my organization has instead decided to give you the opportunity to make amends."

I sat down. Slowly. "Yeah, how's that, considering I ain't done nothing?"

The gorilla opened a drawer and pulled out a big, fat, solid gold wristwatch—the kind that weighs three pounds and leaves bruises on the back of your hand if you don't get the band fitted right. He laid it on the desk in front of me, right on top of that picture of me. "You see the time?"

I shrugged. "So what if I do?"

"This watch is not a watch—it is a timepiece. By that, I mean whatever time it reads right here," he tapped the face with a big finger, "is the time it is out there." He pointed to the door and the world outside the office. "Reset this watch while wearing it, and you are a time traveler."

"Seriously?" I stared at it. I picked it up and slipped it on.

"This office is outside the conventional flow of time." The gorilla warned. "You can't move back and forth in here—only sideways."

"Sideways?" I blinked.

The gorilla rolled his gorilla eyes. "Don't worry about it."

A time machine. Even then, dumb as I was, I knew what that meant. Jesus, I'd never lose at the track again, at the very least. It was something—beat the hell outta digging holes for my fucking brother-in-law. I messed with the control pin, watching the dials spin. "Assuming you ain't bullshitting me—and I assume you ain't, cause why would a gorilla in a tux lie—what's the catch?"

"Keep the watch and you work for us. Paying off your debt."

I smirked. "How much do I owe you?"

"You will pay us a value of one billion United States dollars, payable in its entirety at Hennessey's on 3rd Avenue in midtown Manhattan, New York on September 5th, 1932."

"One billion! Jesus!"

The gorilla stood up and gave me a good look at the size of his arms. They looked like furry tree trunks. "Or we can get physical. Your call."

I'm not an idiot. Sure, a billion is a lotta scratch, but I had *all of time* to get it. Plus Bobo told me once I paid off the debt, I could keep the time watch. It seemed like a really sweet deal, especially when compared to being rendered two-dimensional by a seven-hundred pound silverback in formal wear.

Once I got the watch, I went on, let's say, an *extended* vacation. All the best spots, understand? Second Century Rome (caught a melee at the Coliseum—worth the visit if you've got the stomach for it), 17th Century Versailles, the courts of the Abbasid Caliphate in 12th Century Baghdad, 22nd Century Luna—you name it. If things got hairy, all I had to do is reset the watch and *whammo*—I was sometime else.

After a while, though, I got to thinking about my debt. Bobo had made it very clear that they expected it to be paid in full on that precise day (why that exact date and place? "A convergence in space/time," he had said). After a stint in the Mob, I know firsthand how seriously some guys take debt collection. I got the feeling I was being followed—noticed it first in a whorehouse in Port Royal, Jamaica, 1665—a face I vaguely recognized in a crowd, the sense that there was somebody behind me at all times. I started jumping from time to time with one eye over my shoulder. Got so I could scarcely sleep at night, in case some time-traveling killer would pop into my bedroom and put an icepick through my eye.

Okay, I told myself, *I'll pay it off.*

A billion dollars ain't easy to come by. I figured it would take me several trips, since the most I could time-travel with was whatever I could hold on my person. I started going back to my smash-and-grab roots. I ripped off Cleopatra's crown, started stealing artwork (those "lost masterpieces" you hear about showing up in people's attics? Yeah—all me), and shit like that. You'd be amazed how much easier a robbery is when you can travel in time. Nabbed the Hope Diamond once and sold it back to the Smithsonian for a cool 235 million in 2025. That was my biggest single score.

Thing is it was hard freaking work. I was schlepping back and forth to Hennessey's all the goddamned time, risking life and limb on smash-and-grabs, all to pay off a debt I hadn't technically incurred. Bullshit.

So there I was one time, just after dropping off another score to Bobo (Czar Nicholas II's engagement ring—worth a piddling million bucks, if you'll believe it), sitting at this lunch counter across from that shitty speakeasy, sipping my coffee and watching the crowds go by (oh hey—that was *me*-me, how about that?), and I noticed something. I noticed myself going into Hennessey's. Over and over and over again. All day long. Like a goddamned chump.

That's when I realized it. That's when I figured out that time ain't linear.

My otherself backed me into the tax attorney's office and told me to turn around slowly. I did. There was no sense in trying to fake myself out at this range—I knew myself too well. Hell, this guy could even be a later me along the same timeline as myself, and so he'd *know* exactly what I had in my pockets—poison darts, acid capsules, a garrote wire—the whole she-bang. Of course, then I'd have to wonder if he'd shoot me or not. I'd been careful, this far at least, not to test how far this non-linear thing went.

The office was the usual—blocks of file cabinets and aluminum desks with ink-blotters and nameplates. The me with the gun sat on one side of the desk; I sat on the other.

Like I was literally gonna do my own taxes.

"Can I put my hands down?"

My otherself snorted. "This is me you're talkin' to."

I shrugged, hands still raised. "Well? What's the play, Ollie?"

"Don't call me Ollie, you shit. Don't say a goddamned word."

"So this is gonna be one of those one-way talks, then?"

My otherself looked pissed, so I shut up and let him stew. He finally figured out what he wanted to say. "How many of us you killed?"

"Kinda lost count."

"Are you nuts?"

"I've made four-hundred million in the past two weeks subjective. You tell me who's nuts."

"You sick fuck!"

"Oh come on!" I shook my head. "You wanna tell me you didn't consider it? You know how many others of us are trying the exact same damned thing? Shit, I saw one of us kill another one of us with a blackjack to the back of the skull no more than an hour ago."

"What happened to the killer?"

"Did him with the blowgun. Rated me a handful of emeralds—shitty haul, to be honest. That guy musta come from a desperate timeline."

My otherself grunted. "Or he was just stupid."

We shared a chuckle. It's pretty weird, laughing along with yourself. It sounded like an echo. "So, what are we doing here? You gonna shake me down?"

My otherself shook his head. "What, and have you twist the watch so you can shoot me from behind right before I catch you? I'm not a sucker, Ollie."

"Well then you gotta kill me." I said, surprised at how straight forward I sounded. "Or I gotta kill you. Honestly, it would be better for us if you was the one who died, right? I've got almost nine-hundred million saved up."

"What are you kidding? I'm the one with the gun here, pal."

I rolled my eyes. "What difference does it make? We're both Ollie Grayne, right? One of us has gotta pull this off, and then we get to go on living without looking over our shoulder. We'll never know the difference!"

"Yeah, but *I* don't wanna die."

I groaned. I've had this argument with myself before. Right around when I figured out that there were multiple versions of myself—Ollie Graynes from multiple, parallel timelines—showing up to make deliveries at this exact spot at this exact time. My first thought was to get myselves to work together—to pool our collective loot and pay the whole damned debt off in one swoop. Didn't work, though. Turns out I'm not the sharing type. Shoulda known.

Besides, my debt, it turned out, is multidirectional as well. *All* Ollie Graynes owe Mr. Gorilla and his organization a billion clams. Even if we pooled funds, the vast majority of myselves would be left out in the cold, all their effort for nothing. Only one of me would get to clear his debt.

That's when I started bumping myself off. The whole thing was easier that way. I hated talking to myself. Turns out I'm an asshole.

"You ain't thought this through," my otherself said finally, shaking his head. "You're rubbing out the wrong guys."

"What, and you're planning to take out Mr. Gorilla?" I laughed. "You're nuts. Only one of us gets in that room at a time, you can't break down the door from outside, and the time watch don't work in his office."

"To do this, I need partners." My otherself looked me in the eye—which both of us hated, I'm sure—and put on his best sneer. "Are you Ollie Grayne, or are you just some chicken-shit grifter?"

I scowled and looked away. According the gold watch—which *can't* be wrong—it was almost 9:30. There'd be at least five of me in Hennessey's right now tied up in three different timelines. None of them were chumps, either. I'd been after those guys for days (subjectively speaking), and I ain't even come close. I don't even know how they got in yet.

"You can't keep this up forever, Ollie," my otherself said. "I   should   know."
I gotta admit I had a point there. Like I said, killing myself was getting harder and harder. The cattle Ollies were all out of the way. I was starting to face down other predators—other versions of myself who'd had the same idea I had—and so far I'd been lucky. The next Ollie Grayne that caught me with my pants down probably wouldn't want to talk. Like I said, I hated talking to myself.

I stuck out a hand. "Fine. You got yourself a deal."

Switching his pistol to the other hand, my otherself reached forward and shook my hand like I might bite. I don't blame him. If he'd given me an opening, I would have.

Until I was sitting at that lunch counter, sipping coffee, I used to think time was a straight line. There was the future—that was ahead of you—and there was the past—that was behind you—and there you were in the present, smack dab in-between. It don't work that way. Not at all.

Say you got yourself a burger. What are the odds you get cheese on it? Like, maybe some days you feel like some cheddar and maybe some days you feel like American and other days you just want that sucker *au naturel.* Now, if time is a fixed line, what you're gonna get on your burger—what you're gonna get on *every* burger from now until the day you die—is fixed in place. Can't change it, cause you're just a guy walking a line that started when you were born and ends when you croak.

But the thing is, you can change your mind, right? Like maybe you were planning on cheddar and then, all of a sudden, you say "no cheese." Now, there are eggheads out there that say this is just an illusion of choice—don't matter what you intend, it only matters what *happens*—but there are *other* eggheads out there that say you just created an *alternate* future. In one of those timelines you got cheddar and in the other you didn't, and so the world splits. That other timeline—the one where you went with the cheese—still exists, and there's an alternate you living its gooey, cheddar-y goodness. This happens all the time, every day, at almost every possible moment of your life—endlessly splintering timelines, threading off into eternity.

Bear with me here, because it gets weirder. The *past* isn't fixed, either. You are not the unique product of a unique and special past series of events that led to a unique and special you—oh no. There are a million billion possible ways any given past series of events could lead to a present you. This means that, across all those infinite splintering timelines, there are an equally infinite splintering series of pasts that created all them Ollie Graynes and his time-traveling gold watch. That's why there's a couple versions of me doing things I'd never do—like eating a veggie burger or learning to use fucking nunchucks (that guy was *such* a pain in the ass, by the way. Fed his body to a fucking Tyrannosaurus, the miserable fuck).

Now, what this should mean, conventionally, is that all Ollie Graynes owed their own timeline's version of Bobo a single billion. There would be only one me here, right? But his office—this street, this place, this time—was somehow set up like a funnel. All Ollie Graynes were getting funneled into one, single timeline that ended and began in that back room behind Hennessey's, where all of them would be paying the *same* gorilla. I couldn't help but think the watch had something to do with it.

What all this boiled down to was that Mr. Gorilla and his buddies were ripping me off. Were ripping *all* of me off, actually. Ollie Grayne entered this deal thinking he owed this jerk's gang a billion dollars. What he actually owed them was an *infinite* quantity of dollars. And what did I owe it to them for? For a crime I obviously might have committed, but also might not. In fact, there had to be at least as many timelines where I *didn't* rob Bobo's stupid slot parlor as there were where I did. And here I am busting my ass to pay those shit-heads? You can imagine my disillusionment.

I figured out pretty quickly then that I could kill almost any version of myself and not suffer any consequences—the odds of me bumping my actual self off from this same timeline were nearly zero. It seemed the simplest possible solution to this bullshit problem: kill a bunch of my other selves, pay off my personal debt, and screw over Bobo and his employers. The idea of coming after Bobo himself *had* occurred to me, but it seemed a lot riskier. The back room in Hennessey's—Bobo's office, where I dropped off the loot— wasn't an easy hit. I didn't feel up to taking the risk.

Well, at least not alone.

Hennessey's was one of those places built into the basement—a speakeasy. No sign, no welcome mat—just a thick black door with an eye-slot at the bottom of some slick cement stairs.

My otherself marched me down the stairs to the door at gunpoint. I knocked. The guy at the slot didn't seem surprised at all that the same guy was knocking on his door all the time. He let us in.

Inside was barely lit—a couple bare electric bulbs over the bar, the splintered sunlight creeping in from tiny, street level windows, and that was it. The bartender was a robot—a spindly thing made of white plastic stained yellow with age and cigarette smoke. It made perfect cocktails that tasted exactly the same every time you ordered and me, being me, always drank on the house. The bot was my favorite guy in here.

Besides the bot and the bouncer, the other five guys were all different versions of myself. Two were at opposite ends of the bar—one was disassembling a 21st century autopistol on a little towel and cleaning it with a little brush, the other was drinking an Old Fashioned (my drink of choice across time and space, apparently) and pressing a raw steak to a black eye. Another me was smoking a cigarette in the corner, leaning against the wall. He wore a samurai sword, though whether he knew how to use it or whether it was loot he was here to drop off wasn't clear. Ollies four and five were playing cards against each other. I knew exactly their angle—they were seeking out each other's (and therefore their own) tells.

The me with the pistol nudged me forward. "Back table. Go."

I went, hands raised. My five otherselves watched us go. Nobody said anything. We sat down and my otherself held the gun on top of the table, clearly in the open. Because why not.

I called to the bot for an Old Fashioned. "So, you got a plan, or..."

My otherself nodded hello to Mr. Samurai-sword. "Hey, we gotta talk."

Samurai blew smoke through his nose. "Eat shit and die."

My otherself waggled the pistol. "You want me to get persuasive?"

I grunted. "Goddamn you're charming."

"Shut the fuck up!"

"Hey!" One of the Ollie Grayne's playing cards glared at us. "You wanna keep it down? We're concentrating!"

I rolled my eyes—I couldn't let that one pass. "Oh fuck you and your concentration! We got a fucking time machine, shit-heads—we don't need to worry about fucking tells anymore. You just gotta twist back a half hour and replay the same fucking game again. You don't need to cheat—you know where all the goddamned cards are!"

Samurai Ollie snorted a laugh. "Yeah, if time were linear."

"Just cause it ain't linear don't mean you can't play it in a line, dumbass. The order of cards isn't determined by human free will—just dumb chance."

"And dumb chance can change across timelines. Shit, ain't you ever been a place twice at the same time and the weather's been different? Whaddya think Bobo meant by 'sideways time,' huh?"

The otherself with the pistol waved it in the air. "Hey! HEY! Shut the fuck up! We ain't here to talk about time travel shit! We're here 'cause I got an idea!"

The me cleaning the autopistol looked over at myself. "What's he talking about?"

"Hell if I know. He's got some plan to take out Bobo."

"Not some plan—*the* plan." Mr. Pistol scowled. "You think I'm making this shit up as I go? I've tried this fucking plan ten times already. I've got all the bugs worked out, understand? None of this," he motioned to the bar, "is by chance."

We all got quiet then. We all knew what he meant. The seven of us in that bar—we were all the ones who'd made it through the murderfest outside. We'd done a bunch of the killing ourselves. Hell, we probably had tons of cash socked away. We were all *almost* there, but we also knew it was all a con. If we paid up in full, what then? We'd fund Mr. Gorilla's organization forever for no reason, and that was a bullshit deal. Ollie Grayne hates bullshit deals.

The way I saw it—the way all of us probably saw it at exactly that moment—the relevant timelines this close to Bobo's office had been narrowed down to just a few. We were it. We were the survivors—the Alpha Ollies.

The guy with the pistol nodded at the guy with the black eye. "You—you're my timeline. You got socked in the face by one of our otherselves who was trying to rip you off but didn't have the stones to do you in. Shanked him good with the switchblade in your pocket, right? That was about a year ago subjective."

I whistled. "Shit. A year?"

Black-eye Ollie looked long and hard at pistol boy. "So, it'll work."

Pistol boy shrugged. "So far."

Black-eye downed his drink in one and left. We all watched him go. Samurai Ollie put out his cigarette. "What will work?"

The bot brought over my Old Fashioned. Before I could get to it, Pistol Ollie grabbed it and took a sip. "We—us six— are the only Ollies left who matter. All those other guys out there are either dead, gonna be dead, or are such chumps that they won't figure out how bad they're getting the shaft." He shrugged. "Or maybe a bunch of them turn into us. Doesn't matter—we're the guys who are going to see this through to the end."

Autopistol Ollie was re-assembling his weapon now. "You know, *one* of the ways this ends is me gunning all your fools down and taking your loot."

My two card-playing otherselves laughed. "Joke's on you, shit-head—we ain't packing any loot."

Samurai Ollie nodded. "The whole reason I'm here is because I was planning to nab one of you slippery bastards as he left." He looked around. "Which one of you fucks around with them poison needles."

I didn't raise my hand. Poison needles? What poison needles?

Pistol Ollie got the conversation back on track. "We all know this can't go on forever. We've been cagey, sure, but we've also been lucky, right? When does our luck run out? Like Mr. Samurai here says, even *luck* can shift. I've been running this day over and over so many times, I can't even explain how many different ways I've seen other versions of us die." He let the idea of that sink in. Jaded as I was to my own demise, I had to admit that was a pretty grisly proposition.

He shook his head. "There's no goddamned good reason we should have to put up with this shit." He pointed to the back door—a heavy steel thing with an anachronous electronic keypad lock. "Behind that door is a big fucking hairy gorilla with our balls in a sling. Out here are six different Ollie Graynes—mean sons of bitches, too—who are sick of being that guy's gopher."

I smiled. "And all we gotta do is trust each other, right?"

Samurai snorted a laugh. "Yeah, so if we're going in there, guns blazing, who goes first, huh? And you wanna convince me Bobo ain't behind that door listening to this whole conversation?" He pulled out another cigarette and let it hang from his lower lip. "Sure."

Pistol Ollie pointed at the door again. "Time doesn't pass in that room—we've all tried it at least once, right? It's the same fucking room as the one in back of that shithole in Reno, same fucking gorilla. He can try to listen in on this conversation, but you got any idea how many different versions of this conversation there are? We are a statistical anomaly in an inherently anomalous pattern."

One of the card-shark Ollies shook his head. "What the fuck does that mean?"

The other card-shark Ollie shrugged apologetically at the rest of us. "Don't worry about him—he's an earlier me. He doesn't know what the fuck he's doing yet."

Pistol Ollie laid out his plan. I could see the flaws as clear as any of me. It all relied on trust, see? Trust ain't my thing. It's always been Ollie against the Universe, ever since I was a kid. It got me through my drunk old man's rages, got me through Vietnam, got me through my stint contracting for the Mob—everything. You trust somebody, you make yourself vulnerable. That went double when the somebody I was thinking to trust was myself. Always stay limber, don't get tied down, keep floating—that's my thing.

Pistol Ollie raised a good point, though. "Besides, how do we even know the billion will get us off the hook? What's to stop Bobo from knocking our faces in and taking back the watch as soon as we pay up?"

That played well with all of me. We all agreed to the plan. First guy in would be me—I'd plant my acid capsule on the door's deadbolt on the way in. Then, when the acid ate its way through the steel, the rest would bust through. Autopistol guy would go first and spray the room. Samurai Ollie would cut in next and clean up. The other three of us would be back-up in case the initial attack went sour. Who knew what Bobo the Time Gorilla was packing under that desk, you know? After that, we'd split the loot and go our separate ways. Just another smash and grab, but this time with six times the muscle. I gotta say, the plan looked good. Only so many ways you can screw up "kick in the door and kill 'em."

Autopistol guy had his weapon loaded and ready. "Okay, but let's twist back a few minutes, just in case the gorilla is listening."

"I'm telling you, it ain't needed," Pistol Ollie said.

Autopistol Ollie shrugged. "Humor me." He looked around. "We agree?"

Everybody nodded. "How far?"

"Ten minutes exactly." Autopistol pulled the control pin out on his watch and began to wind it back a few twists. We all did the same. He looked up at all of us. "Ready?"

We nodded, hands ready to press the pin and send us back. "Three. Two. One. Go!"

I hit the pin. The world shuddered and bounced, like a goldfish bowl hit from the side. I shoulda found myself standing in a little circle at the center of the bar with all my otherselves. Instead I found myself alone.

We'd all lied. We'd all jumped back to slightly different times. I was the only guy who did what he said he would—how 'bout that?

There were twelve of us in the room now—two of each of us, four of the card-playing guy, assuming you counted all of him as one version of me. Pistol Ollie was just telling the past version of myself to shut the fuck up. That's when Current Samurai Ollie dropped his katana on Old Pistol Ollie's wrist, severing his gun hand. Of course, that would mean *Current* Pistol Ollie should have lost a hand, right? Well, wrong. Time ain't linear like that, either, I guess. Current Pistol Ollie shot Current Samurai Ollie in the forehead from across the room. He dropped across the table from Old Me. That's when Current Autopistol Ollie started spraying the room with bullets. Then Old Me grabbed the samurai sword.

Then shit got confusing.

As for *Me*-me, I jumped behind the bar with the robot, which apparently had a "gunfight in saloon" program—it was folded up into a little box and hiding under a keg of whiskey. The autopistol in the bar was a pretty brutal weapon and really fucking loud—I had no idea who was winning or losing, but a lot of me were dying, that was for sure. So much for the fucking plan.

The samurai sword—well, one of them—dropped over the bar along with the arm of one of my otherselves. Maybe even myself from the recent past. I was safe now, though—we were in a different timeline, splintered at the moment where one version of me lost an arm and the other didn't.

Silence. There was the smell of something burning—maybe the acid capsule in the old me's pocket. Instinctually I checked to see if it was still there in my current pocket—it was. So was a poison bamboo needle.

I poked my head above the bar. All of me were dead except for Autopistol me. He took a bead on me, but he was out. "Fuck," he said.

"What the hell, asshole," I yelled, ears still ringing. "Why did you *do* that?"

He scowled, backing away from me and fishing in his pockets for another clip. "You stupid bastard! Who do you think is in charge of Bobo's operation, huh? Aliens or some shit? It's *us*, you fucking tool!"

I grabbed a plastic straw from under the bar—an attempt to hide the anachronous elements of Hennessey's, I guess, as though the robot wouldn't have given it away. "What do you mean *us?*"

He found a clip and slapped it in. "Ollie Grayne, dumbass! Me! Us!"

I raised the straw to my lips and blew. The bamboo needle shot across the room—beaut of a shot. Got the guy right in the eyeball. Did for him.

The office was just the same as it always was. Fake wood-paneling, velvet Elvis, big desk, and a gorilla in a tux. It was the same every time—always would be the same. A room somehow kept out of time's flow. I tried to keep a straight face looking at Bobo.

"Coffee?" He asked.

"Nope."

"Do you even like coffee?"

"Sure I do, just not from you." I smiled.

Bobo frowned at me. "You're covered in blood. Not yours, I hope."

"It's exclusively mine, actually." I couldn't stop smiling.

"What's so funny," Bobo asked.

"I think I figured out how you're a talking gorilla. Sideways time, right? You come from a timeline that splintered so far back that you're from—"

Bobo sighed, "From a time where gorillas rule. For the last time—no. I'm genetically engineered from the year 2085. Now, what are you here to drop off?" The gorilla pulled out a fat ledger from a desk drawer.

"Nothing." I said.

The gorilla peered at me over his spectacles. "Nothing?"

"I'm not one of those Ollie Graynes. I'm *the* Ollie Grayne." I motioned to the office. "I want you to pack up. Close it down. Go back to the zoo."

"I'm sorry sir, but you explicitly informed me never to do that, even if you asked me to." The gorilla stood. "In fact, it seems to me your asking indicates you are *not* one of those Ollie Graynes who run the organization."

I stood up, too. I backed away. "What is this? Did I hire you to keep the rest of me busting their asses so I could live on a beach somewhere?"

Bobo moved the desk aside with an ease that made my balls shrink up. "Exactly. You, Mr. Grayne, are not particularly good at motivating yourself." He lumbered closer, knuckles brushing the carpet. "You felt this was the easiest way to make a fortune and live the life of leisure you felt you deserved. With that now said..." He extended a big, monkey hand to shake, "I'm authorized to let you in on the deal."

My mouth fell open. This was *not* how I intended for things to go. "Wait...what did you say?"

Too late. The door burst in, the acid capsule I'd just placed having burned through the bolt. Samurai Ollie skipped over the threshold and brought his sword down on Bobo. The big ape blocked with one arm, but the katana's blade was sharp enough to shear off the big guy's hand and embed itself in his torso. A gorilla, though, doesn't go down that easy. He grabbed Samurai Ollie by the face and threw him against the wall so hard it made a wet spot.

Behind him, though, was Pistol Ollie. He emptied the clip of his .45 into the gorilla's chest, and that did it. Bobo slumped back against the wall. We'd won.

"Shit!" I yelled, grabbing the gorilla by his big lapels. "The deal! Tell me about the deal!"

No dice. The big fella was gone—long gone.

Pistol Ollie checked Samurai Ollie's pulse for a second, then dropped his wrist with a shrug. "Eh. No big loss."

"You dumbass!" I stood up. "I coulda been in on it! Shit, it coulda been me sitting on that beach, soaking up the dough forever and ever! You fucked it all up!"

Pistol Ollie snorted. "Big fucking deal, Ollie." He shook his head. "How long's it gonna take you to get it through your fat head, anyway? We suck, man. We are pretty much the worst fucking person ever to walk the planet."

I blinked. "What?"

Pistol Ollie sat down in the gorilla's chair, pistol on his knee. "Yeah, you want to blame it on your old man, or on Vietnam, or all the bad shit that ever happened to you, but it's all bullshit, Ollie. We're just a bunch of selfish, miserable assholes."

I blinked. His words—my words—were hard to hear. Something about them hit me in just the wrong spot. "Shut up, man!"

"No, *you* shut up!" He pointed at the dead version of myself with the samurai sword and the caved-in skull. "You want to tell me you're okay sitting on a beach while you murder yourself over and over again for eternity? Huh? That's a pretty special kind of self-loathing. Christ, I can't believe I did it for as long as I did. I spent six months subjective stealing my billion before I figured out what a tool I was being. What a chicken-shit."

I shook my head. "Look, we can do it again—walk out into the bar, twist the watch, give it another try. This time maybe both of us can get the deal, right?"

"Nope." Pistol-me smiled. "This is it, man—this is the end of the deal and all other deals. The watch can't take you sideways, remember? This is a fixed point, and we just blew it all away. No more us sitting on a beach while a billion of our otherselves suffer. No more floating on the breeze."

"Then what am I supposed to do, then?" I yelled, getting in his face. "What, you want me to go to Sedona and dig fucking holes for James? Huh?"

He pressed the gun under my chin and pulled the watch off my wrist. He threw it on the ground and stomped. It broke apart in very watch-like pieces. "I don't give a shit what you do. Just don't drag the rest of us down with you."

I knelt over the parts of my broken time machine. "You...you fucking idiot! Why did you do that?"

He scowled. "Because some versions of yourself deserve better than *you*, Ollie Grayne. And I just gave it to them." And then he left. Left without so much as a goodbye.

I crouched there in that office for a good long while, trying to figure out how to put back together the watch. Didn't take. Numb, I eventually stumbled out the door, only to find myself back in the slot parlor in Reno in 1977. My car was still in the lot. I got in and I drove towards Sedona, bitching to myself the whole way.

Told you I was an asshole.

Auston Habershaw is a winner of the Writers of the Future Contest (Volume 31) and has been published in Analog, Galaxy's Edge, Escape Pod, and a bunch of other places. His fantasy series, The Saga of the Redeemed (starting with The Oldest Trick), is available through Harper Voyager Impulse. By day, he is a college English professor who lives and works in Boston, Massachusetts. You can find him at www.aahabershaw.com or stalk him on Twitter at @AustonHab.

A Murder of Crows
by Brenda Anderson

I pushed the sheet of paper across the table. "That date, time, place. I want to buy ten minutes with my father, alone."

The Time Salesman examined the paper and looked up. "My fee, Miss, uh ..."

"I've paid."

"Excellent." He smiled. "Now, the distracting feature."

"I didn't get that. Could you explain it again?"

"Let's see." He looked at the ceiling. "You want to go back and spend ten minutes in your eight year old body, in the company of your father. Here's the deal. With parents, I have to be extra careful, whatever their relationship with the child." He glanced at me. I said nothing. "After all you, aged twenty eight, will take temporary residence in the young child's mind. The parent could spot the difference. My job is to prevent this. Do you follow?"

"Yes, but what about my eight-year-old self? What happens to her mind, while I'm in 'residence', as you said?"

"That's easy. The young child experiences unusual heightening of the senses, purely temporary, of course. She doesn't cease to be your younger self, but she sees, hears, feels with greater intensity, accuracy, if you like. Is that understood?"

I nodded.

"All Time Salesmen introduce a distracting feature into a meeting of this kind, to deflect the parent's attention from their subtly-different child. That way we ensure that the parent doesn't spot the difference and react. Nothing must change. Now, tell me what I can introduce. Something that your father won't notice. Think, now. I don't want to lose my time-share licence. I intend to continue in this business."

I thought hard. "There were always crows. My father kept a shotgun, always loaded. I think crows would work."

"A murder of crows," he said with relish, as if savouring a rare, illicit treat. "Now, I must also remind you to act as a normal eight year old would, even if you've forgotten how."

But I hadn't forgotten. That day was so important. Ten minutes was all I needed.

"Remember, no sudden moves. Act naturally. You will not change history at all by this short trip. You are simply dropping in, so to speak."

He began his sales pitch but I cut him off. "I'm ready. You'll bring me back here, to this room, in ten minutes' time?"

He nodded. "Close your eyes. Count to three. Open them."

I stood in my old bedroom. Everything was exactly as I remembered it: yellowing wallpaper, thin mesh curtains, unmade bed, houndstooth rug on the floor that always felt knobbly against my bare feet. I waited for several minutes. Outside, a spectacular sunset cast weird red shadows onto the curtains, and there was a smell of dust in the air. It would rain the following day.

At the sound of movement I turned round. My father had just climbed in the window, his broad face sweaty from a day's work.

"Hey, Lucy," he said with the biggest grin. His voice. I remembered now. So deep, rich. I hadn't heard it in so many years, tears sprang to my eyes.

"Don't tell your mother I've been here," he said, walking forward.

I nodded. Of course I wouldn't betray him. They'd argued, fought, yelled and screamed, then he'd found somewhere else to live. But he'd come back today, to see me.

"Lucy!" My mother's voice, so shrill, and her footsteps, so loud on the board floors outside.

"Happy birthday." My father gave me a quick hug. "I love you, baby. Remember that."

He rushed back to the window, climbed out and was off. I didn't even hear him hit the ground. Perhaps he was already half way across the yard. I swung round to face the door.

My mother entered the room and looked around with suspicion.

"I thought I heard voices," she said.

"No." The lie came easily. As a child, I'd been a great survivor.

She sniffed the air. "Someone's been here," she said. "A man."

I shook my head.

"You're a liar," she said. "Who was it? One of the workers?"

"Mum, it's my birthday today." I couldn't think of anything better to say. "Remember?"

A sudden squawking sounded outside. My mother turned to the window.

"Crows," she said. "Damn crows. "I gotta protect the lambs. I'll get the gun."

She disappeared. In the distance, I heard the dull boom of the scare gun we'd set up to frighten ducks from the rice paddocks. Farms had so many pests, but crows ate the eyes of the lambs, which then had to be destroyed. This always made my mother angry. She used to nail the dead crows to the chicken shed, as a warning, she said.

I listened hard. One, two, three shots, very loud and very close: the unmistakable sound of my mother firing the shotgun. I had not forgotten. The sound was quite different from the dull noise of the scare gun that went off through the night.

I returned to the Time Salesman's room.

"Satisfied?" he said.

"Yes."

"The crows worked out?" he said.

"Yes. My father loved me. He said so. It was wonderful, worth everything."

He studied me. "You dropped in. You didn't rewrite history, you know."

I nodded. "I know." My father disappeared that day. My mother sent our farm hands packing the next day and hired new ones who hung round and leered at me. She spent her time fighting with farm hands, complaining about them and then working them so hard they quit. My mother had always said she'd string my father up, like the crows. I believed her. She was a good shot. Mercifully, dead these many years.

Now I knew what happened on my eighth birthday. As the Time Salesman said, it's history.

All that matters is that my father loved me. He hugged me before he ran away, before the crows distracted my mother and she fired the gun that killed him. The Time Salesman introduced the distracting feature, the noise of the crows. Nothing to do with me.

My father loved me. He came back to see me.

That is what I'll remember. Not the sound of the crows, or the shotgun.

Brenda Anderson's fiction has appeared or is forthcoming in Andromeda Spaceways Inflight Magazine, Abstract Jam, 50-Word Stories and Flash Fiction Online. She lives a few minutes from the sea in Adelaide, South Australia and tweets irregularly @CinnamonShops. She loves, and sometimes grows, sunflowers.

The Documentarian
by SL Huang

"When time travel was invented, they said it was impossible to rewrite history," Swati Trivedi wrote in her memoir. "They didn't acknowledge it had already been done."

"You're a documentarian," I began, sitting carefully in Dr. Trivedi's sharp, modern living room. "Some would say *the* documentarian."

"I should get my own television program," she said. *"'Who are you? I'm The Documentarian!'* And the masses tremble."

I hadn't expected her to have such a sense of humor about it.

"Would you like some tea?" she asked, already busy with the kettle. "It warms these old bones. I can travel anywhere in time but back to my youth."

I laughed politely and said yes. She brought the large ceramic mugs out one in each hand, stepping carefully, as if she did not dare move with speed anymore. The bones in her hands stood out like talons.

"Now," she said, settling in across from me under a blanket, "you said you're doing an interview. What about?"

"You," I answered. The tea was so hot it burned my tongue. "You've used time travel to rewrite history. You changed the present."

"I suppose I did," she answered. "Although it sounds so dramatic, when you put it like that."

It is dramatic, I thought. Her levity was disconcerting.

I gathered myself. "Let's start at the beginning, if you

don't mind. You were a film editor, correct? Before you became a traveler."

"Indeed. Do you know what a film editor does?"

"Uh. Vaguely."

"The answer is that it depends on the director," she said. "If the writer and director know what they are about, the editor does what you probably believe. If they do not... well, then the editor is the one who creates the movie. Herself."

"How so?" I asked.

"Before this, I worked for some very famous directors making movies," Dr. Trivedi answered. "You would recognize their names. But in reality, they have no technique, no vision. They simply film every shot possible, hundreds and hundreds of angles and takes. And they would send them all to me, because they knew I was very good. I took the whole of reality they thrust at me, and from that, I built the movies they are credited with."

"Is this on the record?" I blurted.

"Why not? I've rewritten history, as you say. Why stop with my lifetime?"

She sipped her tea.

"What gave you the idea," I said, "to start doing the documentaries?"

"Oh, the usual piffle," she said. "Some uppity network executive was going on about historical accuracy. I said to him, 'well, I don't think you're right about that, and what's more, we can check.' That evening I bought a machine and a natural language translator. I went into work the next day seven years older, with the first documentary."

"The series about medieval times," I said.

"Yes. The same network executive claimed it was one-sided. Biased. He refused to buy it, so I took it elsewhere."

"Did you expect the response you received?"

"To be honest? No. Not even a little. Public

consciousness swung so fast it dizzied me. What 'everybody knew' about the middle ages... I saw it metamorphosize overnight."

"It's a credit to your style," I said. "Your documentaries are more like films. People don't watch them for education; they watch them to enjoy. They care about your... characters, for lack of a better word."

"It's a bit voyeuristic, isn't it?" she said. She smiled, but it looked like pain. "When people die in the documentaries, they died for real. I suspect it makes my films more popular."

In my mind's eye rose the witty Agnes in the first film of the series, and how I'd screamed aloud when her story ended. Then Salim and Nafisa in the second, shouting with joy as they unlocked the secrets of the triangle—before Salim's hands blackened and shook and Nafisa pleaded for just one more day. The saviors at Gijón and their stunning heroism, and the screams as those they couldn't reach were swallowed beneath the black waves. Katarina's bloodied corpse on the battlefield, flies buzzing against her matted hair.

I shuddered.

I steered the conversation with Dr. Trivedi back toward safer topics. Back toward her. "What was it like?" I asked. "To come back, after seven years skipping through time?"

"I left some notes for myself," she answered. "But I should have left more. It's amazing what you forget in seven years. My old life had become so alien. Do you know, when I came back I stood in front of a washing machine for ten minutes? I couldn't recall the order of the steps for using it."

"Did it feel like seven years, then? Or more like hundreds?"

"Truthfully... I don't know. I was a rock skimming across water, a woman fast-forwarding through life. It felt like a day, and seven years, and hundreds of years. Everyone I knew grew old and died, and everyone I knew stayed the same age while I lived on."

Intellectually, I knew why she'd done the documentary all at once. The error margins on the machines were exponentially higher the longer a jump one traveled, so it took subjective weeks to get close to a specific time and place but only minutes to travel a handful of years forward or back once there. Commuting to and from the same era from the present would have taken her more than a lifetime for the same footage.

Her solution was not something most people would have pursued on a whim to win an argument.

"I can't imagine," I said politely, because I couldn't.

"I would have been nothing," Dr. Trivedi went on, "without the others. No one was more shocked than I when this became a movement. And one that grew so fast, thanks to the nature of time travel. Within a week our library had hundreds of films; within two weeks, thousands. Plus reams upon reams of primary source documents, photographed and brought forward—more than academic historians have gathered since travel was invented. Decades of effort appeared in the space of less than a month."

"There are people who oppose you," I said. I was edging toward what I most wanted to hear her answers on, and my heart thudded. "They're trying to film their own versions, ones that contest yours. Most of them have not seen great success so far. To what do you attribute that?"

Her face slackened in surprise. "There are many films in the library that contest each other. We file them to be viewed together, for more complete context. Ah! You are talking of the people who wished to prove the past was as they thought. The ones who set out to show our history books were correct."

"Yes," I said. "They haven't yet gained the traction you have. Why not? Can't one tell a story from the perspective of the victors as easily as from the eyes of those who were forgotten?"

Dr. Trivedi gazed off into the distance for a moment. "I think," she said, "that it is not so much whom they choose to focus on, but that they desire to find... something that was not reality. It is difficult to film what does not exist."

Her kind eyes turned sharp, glinting like black stone. The thought crossed my mind that I would not like to oppose her in an argument, and my pulse quickened further.

Something must have shown in my expression, because Dr. Trivedi said, "Yes? You disagree?"

"It's only, you said..." The words died on my tongue, my mouth too dry. I tried again. "You're an editor. You said yourself a filmmaker can create any movie they like, highlighting whatever subject they like, no matter how sparse the material. Why don't we yet have primary sources detailing the type of history we learned in school?" *The history you're trying to destroy,* I didn't say. "Not to replace your library's work, of course—but to exist together. Wouldn't that tell the more complete story?"

She considered me for a long moment. "The people who want to see such a history are its own descendents, and are used to the unquestioned dominance of their ancestors," she said. "What we do... it is a difficult task. Such dedication rarely exists unless it is fueled by a passion for justice. Or truth. Perhaps the people you speak of have never had the need to be heard. And if they have not... then I cannot say I lose sleep over the wilting of their pasts."

"Then you're saying you don't even think those stories deserve to be heard equally." I'd clenched my hands against the couch cushions, physically bracing myself. "You speak of justice. But the Erratists grow out of your movement, don't they?"

"Yes."

"And you approve of what they are doing."

"I cannot say it does not seem in order."

"You're in favor of the lawsuits?" My voice climbed slightly; I forced it back to journalistic steadiness. "Forcing the withdrawal of every single sourcebook in existence, for inaccuracies? Picking specific tiny events to drag up contradictions and get whole texts removed?"

Her thin shoulders raised and then lowered. "Those texts were, as you say, inaccurate."

"All of them? All the hard work of historians throughout the centuries—it's all wrong enough to be censored, pulped, deleted? Not even worthy to have a space on the shelf next to your versions?"

"We have many times more primary sources now," she said. "Encyclopedias are being rewritten to reference them."

"But how can you say your primary sources are the whole story?" I exclaimed. "If there's one thing you've taught us, isn't it that history is so much more complicated than we can conceive? Why take away from our knowledge of it? Why set out to destroy what you don't like?"

"Sometimes a city must be gutted in order to be rebuilt." She flicked at her blanket, as if spurning me for asking such ignorant questions. "Of course our films are not the whole story—but they are *true* stories. When our knowledge of the past is based on lies, we must burn them out before growing a new understanding."

"But aren't your own—you can't be angry I'm asking this, because haven't you already admitted you can edit a story to make it say whatever you would like? So what makes your films 'truth,' then?" I fought to keep my tone reasonable, did not quite manage. "Your primary sources are still filtered through the footage you choose, through every decision you make while you're filming. And through the subjects you pick—in the year since you started this, you've made twelve more documentaries yourself, and isn't even the times and people you've chosen a type of bias?"

"Yes," she said. Calmly. "To all those questions, yes."

"Then why encourage the Erratists? Why push for the deletion of the old historical accounts? If your aim is to leave people in a muddle of contradictory sources, doesn't having other narratives around only help that cause?"

She finished her tea and placed the mug on the table next to her. "There is no need for bad history. If someone wants to see how our textbooks used to be, they can simply go back in time."

"They won't," I said.

"I know," she answered.

People didn't go back in time to study. Nobody except academic historians and people like... people like her. The average traveler went back in time to carouse for a few hours or days, as a fun jaunt, not to distill a span of centuries.

She was right. They didn't care enough.

I swallowed. "By deleting the traditional historical accounts, you're substituting your own work as the dominant narrative."

She did not shrink from the accusation. "You seem to think there are two sides to this. There are not. Over a hundred billion people have lived on this planet since humanity began—thus there are over a hundred billion sides to history. And before this movement, we have had only one. If that one is seen as weighing more heavily than the swell of the hundred billion others together, then it deserves to be diminished into the same speck as any other strand. And if it dwindles away in the shadow of other voices... so be it."

"I don't know if I agree with you," I said.

"Then make your own primary sources. I will not stop you."

I studied the infinite web of wrinkles cracking the

sagging skin of her face, the brittle, thinning hair that barely covered her liver-spotted scalp. I thought about my girlfriend and my daughter, about going on pub crawls with my buddies at the magazine, about my sex life, about my weekends skiing and weightlifting and rock climbing. About planes and cars and telephones and the Internet, about comfortable beds and adequate food. I thought about the number of documentarians in Dr. Trivedi's movement who'd simply never come back, whom no one else had ever been able to find even after combing through the past.

I thought about the pictures I'd seen of Dr. Trivedi from a year ago, when she was a thirty-three-year-old film editor.

She seemed to read my mind. "History is no longer written by those lucky enough to become victors," she said. "It is now written by those who choose to become sacrifices. Does that disturb you?"

"Yes," I answered honestly, my journalistic mien forgotten. "Yes, it does. It... frightens me."

"Then all is as it should be," said The Documentarian.

SL Huang has a degree in mathematics from MIT, which she now uses to write an eccentric novel series about a superpowered mercenary mathematician. The series started with her debut novel, Zero Sum Game, and the fourth book was published this year with the fifth upcoming. Her short fiction can be found at Strange Horizons, The Book Smugglers, and Daily Science Fiction, among others, as well as in The Best American Science Fiction and Fantasy 2016. She currently lives in Tokyo, where she's on the lookout for a place to race motorcycles.

Dragon Father's Wounds
by Tony Pi

In the days of the Three Kingdoms, I was fosterling to the Dragon King of the South Sea. I had led his finned armies victorious against the Pearl Empress, but her dying curse had trapped me in my true time, twenty-first century Hong Kong. I ached to return to the ancient past, and now a mournful song gave me hope, rising faint from the depths with the voice of Minister Whale.

In the shape of a swordfish I swam deeper into murk, where I felt the pull of an otherworldly current. I gulped its magic as I swam across the centuries, night and day in strobe above. It troubled me that my travel through time took little effort, and that trash–like plastic bags, bottle tops, and torn shirts–followed in my wake.

The current spat me out of the Coral Trigram Gate, where the Pearl Empress had made her last stand. Minister Whale swam before me, the grandest of the blues in the Dragon King's service. I was overjoyed to see the master of elocution and music. He blew a bubble ring that girded me, and greeted me in his booming mind-voice. "Thank the Seas you've returned, my Swordfish Prince!"

"My sentiments exactly, Minister," I replied. I was glad to be home, but something felt wrong. The waters reeked of poison and grease, when they should have tasted clean. "How long have I been gone?"

"Eight spring tides, my prince. I fear dark tidings welcome you home. The Dragon King lies dying. You must–"

I turned and bolted for the palace before Whale could finish his thought. *What ills under heaven could befall even Dragon*

Father?

As a swordfish I could swim fast, but swifter still was the sailfish. I slimmed my shape with the power of the Eighteen Transformations, grew my fin tall and knifed through the waves. I had lost one father; I would not lose another.

Seven years ago, my real father Hui Po-Fong was taking my friend Eel and me to the Macau Zoo when an unearthly storm capsized our ferry. Eel and I were swept almost two thousand years into the past and would have drowned, had Dragon Father not found us and changed us into fish. I owed my foster father my life.

Within a thousand *li* of Tortoiseshell Palace, I flinched from the force of Dragon Father's mind-howl. How great was the king's suffering, that his cry would reach this far?

The stingray guards heard my coming and chased away shoals of worried fish, leaving me clear water. Coursing between fishbone pagodas and curtains of living seahorse, I followed the pain to their source: the Hall of Brimming Rejuvenation.

There, the royal leviathan lay coiled upon a bed of kelp, his once scintillating scales now waxen. At the bidding of Imperial Physician Watermother, blooms of luminous jellyfish daubed at the Dragon King's wounds. The waters bore the fiery-mustard tang of dragonblood.

I swam before his grand right eye, milky when it ought be jade. "Dragon Father, forgive this worthless son for his desertion!"

A lone whisker rose, sluggish. "Sword, my son. Welcome home. Is Eel with you?"

"No. He walks human again in the future, with his family."

"Safe, is he? Good. And you, Sword? Did you see your father?"

Memories of my human father came to the fore. *The*

widower who raised me strong. The high school teacher who taught me about science, chemistry, physics, biology and the world. I should have been there to save him from himself.

"The poisons cloud my vision, but not my mind's eye. You grieve for him and fear for me."

"Wise is the King," I said. "I returned too late. After the ferry sank, he blamed himself for losing us. He took his own life."

Dragon Father's eye grew whiter. "Forgive me, I should never have prayed to the sea for sons of my own."

"You mustn't think that. You made us who we–"

"I robbed you of your futures. I stole a man's will to live. My time has come."

"Nonsense, Father. You're as timeless as the moon."

Timeless, he agreed.

"You'll live to witness the mountains rise and fall."

Fall, he repeated.

"Soar beside airmen flying fighter jets."

Airmen? he murmured.

"And sing like thunder at my wedding."

His thoughts ebbed.

Watermother swam to me. "He must rest, good prince."

"What poisons does he mean?" I asked.

She guided me to a gaping wound, one of countless along his length. A shard of dark metal rose like the fin of a shark from a sea of scales.

"Dragon Father's master of the Seventy-Two Transformations," I said. "I've seen him take many guises, even change into sand, ice, or mist. Why not shed these shards like stones through air?"

"See what I see." She stung me with a tentacle. Envenomed with her magic, my eyes tingled with their newfound power. I saw ghostly, iridescent threads latched onto each shard of metal, their other ends leading distant south. "After your battle against the Pearl, His Radiance refused to count you dead. We scoured the reef for you, but foul things spewed forth from the Trigram Gate. Among them, iron pufferfish fat with the rage of storms. When they began to burst, their shards would have killed us all...but for the king shielding us with his own body. He saved us but at the cost of his own health."

The Pearl Empress had oyster demons and nautilus ghosts under her service, but iron fish? "Can you remove the metal?"

"We've tried, but the phantom threads prevent us. We know their source, however. A pod of dolphins traced the threads and unearthed an eerie shellfish that feeds the spell. If it is destroyed, the Dragon King should mend, but none of our magicians could pierce the monster's protections. Nor could our soldiers break its shell."

Uneasy, I swam a tighter and tighter spiral. "Where's this creature now?"

"In the trench called Thousand-Miles Eye. Minister Whale had hoped that the forces in the depths would crush the creature, but to no avail."

The trench was far to the south. Was my duty now to seek out a cure, or remain by Dragon Father's side in his hour of need?

I caught sight of my own tail. It shimmered with a similar iridescent aura, though no thread was tied to me. Suddenly it all made sense. Things out of time could overcome this era's magic. That was why the Pearl Empress had feared me. Why I could slay her. Those iron pufferfish...could they have been naval mines?

The future had poisoned the Dragon Father's wounds. I had lost my first father to the whims of time. I would not let time kill another father of mine.

"Why didn't you tell me, Watermother?"

"He forbade me to speak of it, in the event that you returned. His Radiance hoped to see you one last time before the end, and feared you might stay away if you knew the cause."

"I'm not tethered to this curse, and I *will* undo it," I promised.

"Before you go. The king entrusted me with a measure of his *qi*, to give to you should you return." She stung me and bestowed the spark into my care. "Know that he lives by its light."

Emerald beams shone from my eyes, beating in time with Dragon Father's heart.

"Thank you, Watermother. Do not let him die."

I sped south from the palace, my thoughts haunted by my two fathers. I looked up to both and loved them, though each was flawed in their own way.

My true father, Hui Po-Fong, had been my only family for as long as I could remember. My mother had passed away when I was very young, and Dad had been an orphan so we had no relatives to rely on. He led a life of hardships but gave me all that I needed. He had bouts of depression and tried to hide that from me, but I knew. Only three things were sure to cheer him: dim sum, baroque music, and science, teaching me how beautiful science was through equations like the Pythagorean Theorem or $E=mc^2$, and me. Every Sunday morning we'd go for *har gow* and *siu mai*, and he'd sketch out on a napkin more fun facts, illustrations about physics, like how the Doppler effect works or how time dilation creates the twin paradox. He had a knack for rendering these difficult concepts into toons easy for a kid to remember, like when he showed me how mass bends spacetime.

After the ferry sank, Eel's family had blamed Dad for their son's drowning as well. He couldn't cope with the guilt, and it drove him to suicide. I should have tried harder to find a way to return to the modern day, to let him know I hadn't died. Maybe things would have been different then.

In this era, the Dragon King of the South Sea had taken us in. He taught us the art of war, and skill with the Eighteen Transformations. But the Pearl Empress coveted the seas he ruled. She sent demons to plague us, and planted traitors to strike from within. Far too trusting by nature, Dragon Father almost fell to treachery many times, had Eel and I not uncovered the plots.

He was the only family I had left.

Minister Whale and his attendants were already at the Thousand-Miles Eye, swimming the dark waters above the trench. The only light here came from my eyes, pulsing dimmer and dimmer.

"Report, Minister."

"My Swordfish Prince, the Coral Trigram Gate continues to spew forth dangerous things, and some denizens have died after mistaking the odd flotsam for food. All our woes seem to be tied to this iron creature we found. If only we can kill it."

"Aside from the trench, what else have you tried?" I asked.

"The monster resists our deepest spells. Our cleverest octopi could not decipher its puzzling shell. Our whales have rammed it against the rocks and it would not even scratch! We tried to speak to the woman inside–"

"Woman?"

"We debated who she might be," Whale said. "The Empress's daughter? Or the grain of sand in the oyster that would make a new pearl?"

I understood. Our spies had uncovered the Empress's plan to reincarnate herself, though we never learned how. This woman could be the key to that scheme. "Bring the creature here."

Whale sang a song of summons, while I rested to regain my strength.

At last, a great glow arose from the chasm. A hundred-thousand anglerfish swam in a vast sphere around the creature, buoying it upward within a cage of sorcerous light.

What Whale mistook for a mollusk, I recognized immediately as a deep-sea exploration vessel called a bathyscaphe. Half the size of my whale friend, it resembled a small submarine with an observation sphere locked to its underside. The craft from the nineteen-sixties would seem like one of the Empress's monsters.

Under my mystic sight, the ship's surface shimmered like mother-of-pearl, save where hundreds of trigrams lay dark upon the steel. The phantom strands converged within the cabin. I swam closer to the sphere and looked through the Plexiglas iris. A woman, illuminated by the jade light from my eyes, huddled in a wrap of crimson cloth. Her skin gleamed with pearly sheen, like the ghost threads that became her hair.

I tapped on the window with my bill, and she seemed to hear that, but didn't reply to my mind-call. Her emotions bled through, however: fear, anguish, but also defiance. But was she an innocent pawn or a consummate liar?

"If there's no way to break the shell from the outside, Minister, we'll have to try from inside."

Whale moaned. "But nothing can get in or out."

I thought back to a physics lesson Dad taught me. "Not entirely true. Light passes through that glass, both ways. If I can turn myself into light, I can enter that ship."

"My prince, you may be a fast learner, but you know only the Eighteen Transformations. Changing into a creature of light is an order of transformation beyond—"

"Minister, this is a lesson I cannot fail. Teach me before the Dragon King runs out of time."

"You're the heir! We cannot risk it. Let me go instead,"

he insisted.

"Only *I* know what this vessel is, what it's capable of. It has to be me."

After much argument, the minister relented. "To the surface, then. There *is* a trick to it, but you must master the skill."

Dolphins accompanied us up to the sunlit waters. "What's the key, Minister?" I asked.

"The border between water and air has a magic of its own," Whale said. "Take advantage of it as you transform. Cast off your old self as you breach from the water. Watch."

He propelled himself directly upward, while I followed in sailfish form. Whereas I merely cleared the water in my leap, when Minister Whale broke the surface he became black smoke laced with white, spiraling above the waves.

"Bind yourself together through sheer will. But even I have not the fortitude to keep an elemental shape long." The sea winds flensed wisps of smoke from his bulk. He twisted eightfold in the breeze before losing his airy form, and belly-flopped back into the water with an epic splash. "*Aiya. That. Hurt.*"

"I'd only need to become light for the blink of an eye. Let's try smoke first." I swam below the surface at my fastest speed. As I angled upward and breached the water, I imagined myself sculpted from cloud. I did feel a hit of magic as I broke the surface, but it was so fleeting that I missed my chance.

Second, third, and fourth tries, I familiarized myself with the feel of the boost. It was akin to spray from a breaking wave, or a bubble bursting free. I turned back for another chain of leaps, then another. Sometimes I felt my weight change, other times nothing at all. Whale sang songs of encouragement as I struggled. My swims were exhausting me, but I thought of my fathers, one dead and the other dying, and pushed through the pain.

The minister swam beside me. "The sun's setting, sire. You ought to rest."

What would my fathers say? Dragon Father would tell me that I should place more trust in my abilities. Dad would tell me to consider the problem from a different angle. They were both right.

I mulled over the problem of changing into light. Might it be, I'd fare better trying what my body knows already? Humans were more than half water, Dad once said. Perhaps smoke was the wrong thing to start with!

I gave it another try. This time, I imagined myself to be a great fish made from saltwater, and as I breached the surface I cast off all that was not brine.

Sailfish shape, liquid body, almost breaking into foam, but I was *elemental*.

When I fell back into water, I took flesh again in the nick of time, or else I might have merged with the sea forever. Every cell of my body seemed to burn from within and without, but I didn't care. I had done it.

The praises of Minister Whale gave me great satisfaction, but I had to keep focus. I dived for the submersible.

Through the window, in the jade light I cast, the woman sat in wait.

I had only just learned to transform into water. Could I turn into light when I couldn't turn into smoke? Unless—

Dragon Father's *qi* was light within me. An emerald strand even reached north, linking me to his life and power. If my body could learn the nature of that light, it might ease me into the right form.

I invoked the power of the Eighteen Transformations and became a small jellyfish. This shape allowed the light to suffuse my every cell, but as it did I felt the Dragon King's *qi* wane. Drawing on this spark of life would make the transformation easier, but if I took too much, I could weaken or even kill Dragon Father.

After my near-disaster with the water shape, keeping myself whole was critical. Dad's science lessons flooded my thoughts again. Though I'd only be light for a fraction of a second, would I lose parts of myself to reflection or refraction as I passed through?

I swam to the cabin and pressed my jelly body to the window. Water, Plexiglas, air: those were the borders I must now cross. Dad had said matter and energy were the same, and even taught me the formula. That would be my mantra now.

E equals m c squared.

E equals m c squared.

E equals m c squared.

I willed myself to become light.

One moment I was moon jelly plastered against the viewing lens. The next, I had beamed into the observation cabin before I even realized it. My own incompetence at the light form saved me from breaking into a million rays, for I turned back into my true shape as soon as I exited the Plexiglas: a naked young man with second-degree burns all over. I bit back a scream, but everyone must have heard my mind cry.

In the tight confines of the cabin, the young woman backed away as best she could. She was bathed in pulsing green light from my eyes. That meant Dragon Father still lived, and it heartened me. But I was well aware that I was naked, and covered myself in embarrassment.

She said something in a Chinese dialect I didn't recognize, but our minds touched and the words translated clear. "Who are you? What do you want?"

"It seems we have the same questions. I'm the Swordfish Prince. And you are?"

She wasn't surprised that we spoke through thought. "My name's Moniang. My family are fishermen from Fujian. It was my duty to stand on the shore, garbed in red so that they might find their way home." She pulled the cloth tighter around herself.

I nodded. "Tell me how you got here. Imagine it in your mind."

Moniang closed her eyes. "On the day of a terrible storm, I saw my father swept off his boat and into the sea. I leapt in to save him, but the waves were too strong. I thought I had drowned, but when I awakened, I found myself trapped here. The Pearl Empress laughed at me through the glass, and told me I was to be her new pearl, her teardrop should she die."

The memories she replayed in her mind seemed genuine. I was starting to believe her.

"I've been trapped here since she caught me," Moniang continued. "She took thirst, hunger, and sleep from me."

"And breathing too," I said. If Moniang had been using up the oxygen in the air, I'd be suffocating now. The Empress must have enchanted her to resist the passage of time. I could see the lustrous aura flake from the bathyscaphe walls, painting a new layer of magic upon Moniang. "The demoness is dead, but her spell continues to change you," I said, and told her about the aura she couldn't see.

"Then my life may be forfeit, soon."

I questioned Moniang, trying to place her time of origin. She thought the Three Kingdoms existed six or seven hundred years ago, which meant she was from the future, though not as distant as my time.

It seemed the Empress knew how to bring things from the future, which was troubling enough. If she could also inhabit a body from the future, she would be nigh unstoppable. But dare I trust Moniang? For all I knew, she *was* already the Pearl Empress, toying with me. If so, I should slay her now. But what if Moniang was telling the truth? I'd be slaying an innocent girl.

"We must escape before she claims your body as her own." I righted myself and scanned the confined space. Gauges, canisters, pipes, and a ladder leading up. "Where does that go?"

"A door that won't open."

I climbed up to test the hatch. Despite my best efforts, the locking wheel wouldn't budge.

I could try to escape without Moniang, but could I manage a light form again? I had already drawn on too much of Dragon Father's *qi* in that last transformation. Regardless, Moniang would still be trapped.

Kill her and leave, cried a part of me, but I refused to listen to it.

Moniang must have caught that thought, and gripped my hand. "My life isn't worth the suffering the Empress would bring, if she returned. If I must die to stop her, then so be it."

"I will try all else before that." I slid back down, flipped every switch, and turned every dial I could find.

"They don't do anything," she said.

I tore a gas canister from its bindings and struck the Plexiglas with it, but it did no damage. "There must be a way."

"Not to save us both."

"My fathers didn't raise me to kill innocents." I was meant to be here, to save one father with the teachings of the other. I was sure of it.

Outside, Minister Whale sang a song of hope.

Sound. Carried through from outside.

What did Dad teach me about sound? An opera singer could theoretically hit the right note and shatter glass. But the window was thick Plexiglas and designed to withstand the pressure in the ocean depths. Would it shatter at all?

I tapped the Plexiglas, listening to the sound to get a feel for it. "Are you a good swimmer?"

"Yes."

"Good." I cast a thought towards Whale. "Minister, can you hear me?"

"Yes, my prince."

"I need you to sing a scale of high notes. I'll let you know when to stop."

Whale was puzzled, but he obeyed. I studied the window carefully, watching for any vibration, listening for any resonance. When the Plexiglas gave the right tremor, I told him to pause. "Muster a chorus to sing that exact note in unison, as close to this window as possible. Hurry!"

The minister swam to gather his choir.

"Cover your ears," I told Moniang. I sang the note close to the Plexiglas, holding it steady the way Minister Whale had taught me in his music lessons.

Moniang didn't do as she was told, but instead took my hand and sang with me. Outside, a choir of whales added their voice to ours, while dolphin after dolphin swam to the window in succession and bombarded it with focused bursts of the same sound.

The Plexiglas vibrated to that frequency. Had it been glass it might have shattered already, but the plastic fought our one song. The eyes of my reflection barely glimmered green.

Despair welled within me as I realized that this was as much as I could do to save the Dragon King, that he would die wondering if I had tried enough, if he had failed to teach me enough.

Death would take my foster father, and I would never forgive myself.

We would fail the Dragon King.

I would let my foster father die.

But then I saw the thin fracture on our side of the Plexiglas.

I grabbed the canister and smashed it with all my rage against the flaw.

"Father will make mountains rise, and skyscrapers fall!" I cried, and struck the window again.

"He'll race planes across the sky!"

Slam.

"He'll dance when I marry, and thunder his pride!"

Crack!

Under our unified assault, the Plexiglas could no longer hold back the sea. It shattered.

Water rushed into the cabin. I helped Moniang fight against the onslaught, and when the seawater equalized she squeezed out of the opening. As soon as she escaped, the ghostly threads of magic snapped and the pearly aura around her began to fade. I changed into a dolphin outside the vessel and nudged her to hang on. I only hoped that the magic protecting her would last until we reached air.

Minister Whale and the others accompanied us upward. Below us, the anglerfish let the bathyscaphe fall into the chasm.

When we broke the surface, the last of the iridescent shimmer around Moniang had vanished. She whispered her thanks. In turn, I thanked Dad in silent prayer. *Without your beautiful maths on napkins science lessons, Dad, I could never have saved Dragon Father.*

A ball of emerald *qi* escaped from my right eye and tumbled upon the waves. We looked north, where it had raced. Stars seemed to geyser from the dark sea, swirling into the shape of a majestic dragon.

Father's eyes burned like jade suns against the night sky.

Originally from Taiwan, Dr. Tony Pi holds a degree in Linguistics and lives in Toronto, Canada. Winner of an Aurora Award for Best Poem/Song, his short fiction has also been multiply nominated for the Aurora Awards and the Parsec Awards, as well as being a former finalist for the John W. Campbell Award for Best New Writer. His fiction has appeared in Clarkesworld Magazine, Orson Scott Card's InterGalactic Medicine Show, and Fantasy Magazine, among many others. More information may be found on his website: tonypi.com.

Danta in Black
by Steve Simpson

He had a job usually, and Joana was his girlfriend more often than not. Certain events kept happening, and evenings in Joana's apartment on Avenida Paulista was one of them.

"You're like a big furry dog."

That was true—he didn't shave on weekends, and cheap dentistry couldn't afford to fix his protruding canines. But Joana didn't know he had a tail.

Adimir's tail was made of time, time that had already flowed by and become the past, and it wouldn't stop wagging.

Young Adimir had lived a different life—all the days had been warm and the same, and the nights, cozy and safe. But when he turned twelve, everything changed.

A child is never cautious, "Mum, our house is apple green now. Did someone paint it in the night?"

A child doesn't know illusion from reality, doesn't know when to keep quiet. A lot of adults don't either.

'Autism,' the white-coated specialists had said. Now he knew that was just a catch-all for when they didn't have a clue.

Through his teens, he learned to keep quiet about the day-to-day changes he saw, to say nothing.

Adimir is an enigma, his school reports said, he knows what isn't taught and doesn't know what is. When they asked him what he wanted to do when he left school, he said he wanted a steady job, any steady job.

After he graduated, he fell from position to position, and kept falling, mostly unskilled labor that never paid well, and in the evenings he studied—anything remotely relevant to his condition.

He'd met Joana in the State Library, a close encounter in the 529's aisle between the chronology books.

"What do you write in there? Anything about me?"

"A little."

"You're so secretive about that diary, Addie." She called him that. "The steel case, the lock. Do you think anyone cares about your schoolgirl diary?"

"You do. You just asked me."

For most of his twenty nine years, Adimir had drifted in a sea of contradictions. He knew that the world around him didn't change overnight, knew it was all in his mind, whatever 'it' was, but if Adimir didn't have faith in himself, in his memories, he'd soon enough find himself with free padded accommodation. So he went on believing that his memories were real, that they told him how the past had really been, and that it was the world around him that was schizophrenic, changing day by day.

To keep his secret, Adimir had to manage his life carefully, and that was where his diary came in. Every evening before bed and Joana, he wrote a succinct description of what his day had been like—his address, what he'd done, where he worked, a little about the people around him, and any newsworthy events. It was boring and repetitive, not like anyone else's diary—no revelations, secret hopes or dreams. They didn't matter, because he'd remember his inner life the next day.

Every morning he read it, in his own handwriting with his own signature, and every morning it was different to what he remembered. And it wasn't just the day before, all the pages rewrote themselves through the night, either a little or a lot, but they were always changed.

Joana thought it was another of his eccentricities. He'd told her he'd had a few emotional problems, that he read about yesterday's Adimir to keep himself stable, not to learn about the new day's world.

She didn't mind his peculiarities, they amused her. *Don't read your diary today Addie. Let's see how you behave when you're making yourself up.*

For the succession of empathic and well-paid psychiatrists that had studied him, the conflict between his memory and the diary would have proven that he was as mad as they'd told him he was. But for Adimir, the diary was part of the ever-changing world, a measure of the fluctuations in reality, and when he opened it the next day, despite himself, he hoped that the story it told would be the one he remembered, that he'd somehow reached a place where the past was solid and immutable, and he could finally have a normal life. But every day he was disappointed.

The diary served a practical purpose as well. When he read it, he knew how he fitted into his immediate world, and he could be Adimir, a little odd and absent-minded, but not someone who was completely lost.

"Put it down, Addie. You've written enough for today, time for bed. Why don't you put your eyeshades on? It might be fun."

"I'd have to feel my way."

"Let's see how it works out."

Joana and Adimir were infatuation and convenience, lust and utility, but sometimes after dark she asked him about love.

—*How much do you love me, Addie? Really. How much?*

He answered with vagueness, clouds and the endless

ocean, but he wondered what she meant, and whether sooner or later he'd have to quantify the immeasurable.

Joana's doctorate in Modern History was a fringe benefit of their relationship, and Adimir had lots of questions about recent historical events.

—*Why do you keep asking me that? I've told you already.*

For Joana, it was another of Adimir's oddities. But he asked because the answer wasn't always the same, and with his questioning he'd worked out that the past had started to drift when he was twelve, at the time his 'condition' had revealed itself. Anything before that time was fixed—the declaration of the Republic of Brazil happened on November 15, 1889 always. But after he turned twelve everything was in flux—the unification of the Central American states wandered, and on some days it had never happened at all.

He put on the eyeshades, "no peeking," he heard her footsteps leaving the bedroom, and when she came back, there were bursts of laughter—Joana never giggled—and he felt brushes of wetness.

He tasted a sweet Joana, definitely chocolate topping, patches of marmalade maybe, and other mysteries. He had no idea what was in the kitchen cupboards, that information didn't go into his diary.

"I'm taking the eyeshades off now."

Red-haired Joana was an abstract painting of herself, a reclining nude. She sighed. "Too many sweets. I'll have to go to the gym tomorrow."

Adimir was curious, he'd tasted lemon, and the sticky white smears looked like ice cream. He ran the tip of his finger along the scar below his ribs where it had collected, and tried again—too sweet, but everything cold sweetened when it warmed up.

"Lemon sorbet?"

"Yes, but there's none left now, piggy." She sampled his scar as well. "You were lucky weren't you?"

Joana was talking about his accident. It had happened when he was working in a car plant—a welding robot had started moving without warning and sliced him open.

"An inch deeper and I wouldn't be here for dessert."

It was true, but not the whole truth. Afterwards, when he'd woken up in hospital, his workmates had told him to start going to confession, because it was holy miracle that he hadn't been killed.

But he remembered his own version of the day before, when the robotic arm had smashed his ribs and torn into his body. He remembered lying on the floor with blood pumping from his chest. And he remembered dying.

He was curious about it, coming back after death was part of humanity's mythos, but he hadn't really died, had he? And he had absolutely no interest in experimenting, in experiencing that temporary finality again.

After showers and fresh sheets, it was time for bed, and another of his 'eccentric' rituals—shut the bedroom door, draw the blinds tightly closed, put the earplugs in and the eyeshades on.

Adimir rarely got out of bed at night, and he never looked out the window. Outside the horrors of the night grew like weeds in the moonlight, and all the world changed. With Joana snoring peacefully, he pulled the cover over himself like a wave and hid beneath it, kept himself sane.

Years before, when he'd lived in a house on Avenida Rebouças, he'd tested the darkness, set the alarm for three o'clock, the belly of the night, and watched it through the windows.

He'd seen strange shapes flitting across the sky, and the largest ones hovered above suburban streets blotting out the stars. They were bivalves—two enormous saucers joined together—and they discharged gushes of caustic fluid that dribbled down the apartment buildings and dissolved them as if a witch had made them out of icing sugar. He'd heard screaming, and watched his neighbors jump to their deaths from upper floor windows.

In the daylight, there was never any sign of the bivalves, and Adimir decided that the high night was a time when reality strayed on its leash, when it went much further afield. No-one else knew, and when concerned colleagues at work asked him why his hands were shaking or why he was staring at the empty sky, he told them that nightmares had disturbed his sleep.

He watched for three nights, telling himself there was nothing to fear, thinking he would grow accustomed, be able to withstand the nocturnal terrors.

But on the third night, he saw a grimy version of himself staring back in through the window. His reflection held out its hands in supplication, with its fingers dangling down at impossible angles like moon worms. It looked upward, and its eyes opened wide. It mouthed something inaudible and fled into the shadows.

After that, Adimir never challenged the night.

He remembered Joana setting the alarm for seven, but it didn't go off because she hadn't set it in today's version of yesterday's world, and Adimir woke up alone with daylight streaming through the bedroom window.

According to his diary, he'd been retrenched from a job he didn't know he had, Joana was visiting her mother in Rio, and São José was in the news. Scientists working at a company called Emit Metrics had extended quantum tunneling from the microscopic to the macroscopic world.

Everything strange interested Adimir, anything that might give him a clue to his own strangeness, and quantum tunneling fitted the description—it allowed subatomic particles to pass right through impossibly high energy barriers as if they weren't there.

Today he was unemployed, but tomorrow who knew? He'd saved up a little cash, the amount fluctuated, but there always something in the case with his diary, and São José was two hours by coach from São Paulo. It was time for a busman's holiday.

The Emit Metrics staff were friendly enough. He'd told them he was a reporter, that he was doing a story for the Guarulhos Star—he'd worked there for a month as an office gopher—and he was shown to the Quantum Tunneling Lab.

His guide called out through the laboratory door. "Ernesto, another reporter here to see you, Adimir from the Guarulhos Star."

Ernesto had the air of someone in a hurry, being distracted from an important task. He waved a socket wrench at a confused interconnection of stainless steel plumbing fittings.

"We've achieved reverse transmission of quantum coded bytes with a dual positron beam quadrupole."

"Amazing."

"Yes, it is."

"I'll need it in simple Portuguese for our readers."

"Oh." Apparently it wasn't obvious to Ernesto that not everyone understood technobabble. "Just a moment and I'll finish up here. The torque has to be exactly right or the vibrations from the turbo pump will misalign the rods in quadrupole."

He crouched down and began tightening a circle of nuts that bolted a humming cylinder to a rubber mount on the floor. As he did each one, he peered at glowing numbers on the wrench.

"All done. Now where were we?" He put his wrench down and went into lecture mode. "In the microscopic world, quantum signals already travel backwards in time. We think we can do it on a larger scale, send a micromessage from the future to the past. About five minutes into the past."

"What will the message say?"

"Nothing about winning lotto numbers."

Ernesto grinned and Adimir realized he was trying to be funny. "Right."

"It'll just be random binary bits, not useful for anything. My boss has insisted on that. We won't even look at the messages, the equipment will just register that they've arrived."

"Why's that?" Adimir had read stories where time travelers interfered with the past right, left, and center.

"She thinks there might be problems."

"What sort of problems?"

Ernesto shrugged. "Look, it's all nonsense anyway. I don't want you putting it in your story."

Adimir put his notepad away, as if it mattered. "I won't. It's just personal curiosity."

"It's the old idea of creating a paradox in time. It's like a feedback loop. You change something in the past and it affects the future, then that change means you have to time travel to the past in your DeLorean again and fix it, and so on."

Adimir laughed on cue.

The following morning, he was still in the same cheap hotel near the São José bus terminus, on the same floor, in the same room, and that was surprising. More than that, the diary page describing what he'd done the day before, his meeting with Ernesto, was similar as well.

He thought about it on the bus trip back to São Paulo, and decided it didn't mean anything. Randomness could masquerade as consistency in Adimir's world.

The alarm went off, an old fashioned beeping sound, and Adimir rolled over and slammed his elbow into a wall on the wrong side of the bed. He knew where he was, and it wasn't Joana's apartment in São Paulo. It was the hotel in São José.

There was something special about São José, and now it had called him back. His diary told him he was a lab assistant who started work at seven, and he worked at Emit Metrics. He flicked back a few pages and discovered he'd been working there for a while.

The pages gave him the names of some of his colleagues—he worked for someone called Doctor Danta, but there was no mention of Ernesto. All he had to do was follow instructions, cart equipment around, make coffee, and whatever.

He didn't have time to read it all, he had to go to work.

"You'll need the stepladder, Adimir."

He was trying to reach something called a coherency stabilizer on an upper shelf, and his boss seemed to be amused. Apart from natural changes, his body was usually stable, but he had the impression he was a little shorter today.

Danta saw the blank look on his face and pointed. "In the supply room."

Adimir was the only one who remembered a past that drifted day-by-day in unpredictable ways. Danta's memories of him had to be consistent. She would see him as a little eccentric and absent-minded, but hopefully nothing too extreme.

She tasted the coffee he'd prepared for her. "Three sugars, Adimir. I don't know what's wrong with you today."

"I thought ... you said something about dieting, doctor."

Adimir had a lot of practice at misdirection, it was one thing he was an expert in. Almost everyone said something about dieting at some point.

"Do you think I need to diet, Adimir?"

Danta wore horn-rim glasses, her brown hair was pulled back in a bun, and her lab coat fitted nicely.

"No. Of course not. I must have misunderstood."

"Are we still on for this evening?"

She wasn't his type, but maybe the other Adimir liked her, the Adimir who'd been working at Emit Metrics for longer than half a day.

"Of course. What time?"

"We said seven."

He had no idea what he was doing with Danta or where he was doing it. But it had to be in his diary back at the hotel, and he would have time to check.

"You know, Adimir, you're not a fool, but you're still just a drone at Emit Metrics. I know, I know—your disability. But I don't see why you couldn't study and get some sort of qualification."

Adimir had found the Cantina Restaurant in his diary and dashed out of his hotel room, but he should have read more, a lot further back, and now he panicked. What did Danta mean by 'disability'? That was what his last psychoanalyst, long lost in another reality, had called it.

He must have invented some sort of story about his oddities. After all, there was no need to tell anyone the truth, and who would believe him?

He shrugged and lied. "I never really had much interest. I was always looking for something new, something different." Adimir would give anything to live in a world that wasn't always new and different.

"Anyway, I found something out. What we spoke about."

She straightened her glasses and leaned across the table conspiratorially.

He leaned in as well and they bumped noses. "Sorry," they both whispered.

This was new, and a little frightening. "About ... timelines?"

She nodded.

This wasn't a date at all, and part of him was disappointed. He wondered what he'd shared with Danta, how far he'd gone.

Danta filled him in on what she found out. Emit Metrics had secrets—no-one knew how the founder, Benita Silverwood, had managed to build the company up almost overnight, and Danta had discovered nothing about the high-security laboratories on the tenth floor despite her discrete inquiries.

He said something noncommittal, without revealing anything about his real problem. She was still close to him, whispering nasally.

"I can't see how any of this is going to help you with your reality shifts. I don't think anything at Emit Metrics is useful for you."

Adimir felt his heart thump against his ribcage. The other Adimir had told Danta his most intimate secret. He was shocked, but he didn't let it show. Hiding his astonishment was another one of his specialties—the world was always throwing surprises at him, strangeness that was familiar to everyone around him.

"Well, I'm grateful that you tried, Danta."

"I can't imagine how hard your life must be." She sipped her wine. "But you know how curious I am. You've seen things that no-one else has."

The candlelight gleamed in her glasses. "You have stories of fantastic worlds—it's so romantic. Tell me about one of them, darling."

He couldn't see a reason why not. The other Adimir must have known what he was doing. "Well ... have I told you about the flights of the aerial trains in Alfaville?"

"Why don't you take off your glasses?"

"I'm blind as a lettuce without them."

"I feel like I'm one of your experiments."

Danta was sitting on top of him, concentrating on a personal experiment. "You are ... you are ... a special case, Adimir."

Adimir was suddenly jealous of himself—the other Adimir who'd known Danta a lot longer.

The next morning Adimir was still in Danta's apartment. He was alone, and she'd left a note saying he'd been snoring and he was going to be late for work. There was a row of uneven crosses at the bottom, with the last couple larger.

He didn't have his diary, and the rule of consistent reality meant he almost certainly hadn't filled it in the night before. In any case he'd check, go back to his hotel before he went to Emit Metrics, and read it through.

The diary confirmed what Adimir had thought. It was the same old, same old, with no entry for yesterday. He didn't notice any revisions of the earlier pages that he'd looked at, and he was still in the same hotel room.

It had happened to him before, but never like this. He knew he had to be patient, to wait, not even dare to dream that this version of São José was it, that reality had finally washed him up on the stable shore he'd been searching for.

But his heart was filled with helium. He floated down the stairs, discussed the weather with the concierge, and because he was in no hurry to go to work, joined a crowd of hotel guests gathered around a television in the lobby.

Something was happening. Maybe it was the Copa América, Brazil in the semi-finals.

"You see this, Adimir." Danta was pointing at an electron microscope scan. "Their shells are metallic glasses in a silicate matrix. The internal organs, if that's what they are, are exactly the same. It's as if the isomorphs aren't even alive. They're like minerals, like crystals."

Three weeks before, Adimir had seen his first isomorph on the screen in the hotel lobby. It was hard to make out, blurred footage shot with a shaking mobile, but when the news first broke they'd run it over and over. Something that looked like a child's drawing of a flying saucer hovered over an unimportant building in downtown São Paulo. There was a loud hissing sound, the flying saucer emitted a stream of vapor, and the building melted like concrete ice cream left out in the sun.

Everyone called them isomorphs, but Adimir knew what they really were. He'd seen them years before, when he'd dared to face the nightmares after midnight.

They were the bivalves, and now he didn't have to rouse himself in the early hours to know the horrors that only he could see. They were in Brazil in broad daylight, solid and deadly real.

At Emit Metrics, it was all hands on deck. Everyone was studying the bivalves, trying to understand what they were, and trying to find a way to destroy them. The military had blasted them with missiles, with mortar fire, and from their remains, smaller bivalves had risen like phoenixes. They grew without changing shape—isomorphs—and their numbers kept on increasing.

So far São José had been spared, but the bivalves had crisscrossed Brazil like a biblical plague, and yesterday they'd reached the outskirts of Rio de Janeiro. While believers prayed to the gods of their choice and non-believers considered their positions, Brazil was dissolving into an uncertain hell.

"You're saying the bivalves—sorry, the isomorphs—are basically rocks?"

"Sort of, but they can propagate like crystals, and they feed on the concrete."

"If they're like minerals, do you think they might have come out of that volcano in Chile?"

Suggestive news footage had shown dark shapes emerging from an eruption of the Osorno volcano.

"Who knows? With all that smoke and ash, those blobs could have been anything. Canals on Mars." Danta shrugged. "We need to do another spectroscopic analysis of the isomorph's emissions."

At work, Danta was Doctor Danta, and there was never a warm moment between them. Not that there could be any real distractions—they both wore chrome-yellow biohazard suits in the laboratory.

Adimir inserted a glass tube filled with the bivalve's

poison into a vacuum chamber where it would be broken remotely.

It wasn't just the collapse of city structures—everything about the bivalves was toxic to life. Their emissions coated the lungs and caused a kind of silicosis. In the big cities, people wore facemasks if they could afford them and dirty handkerchiefs if they couldn't.

If they survived at all, victims exposed to high concentrations of the venom were blinded, and lost limbs as their bones dissolved. Footage shot by media helicopters showed tent hospitals on the outskirts of São Paulo, and endless rivers of refugees, going anywhere that was far away.

For three weeks, Adimir had tried to accept the horror all around him. São José was the refuge he'd been looking for since his twelfth birthday, his island in the sea of time. Before São José, he'd been a castaway drifting through his life, and now his reality was so stable that his diary was just a formality.

But in his heart, he knew that this Brazil was an aberration in a world gone wrong, a world that shouldn't exist at all.

"Adimir. Come on."

He was staring at nothing through the visor of his suit.

"I know what you're thinking."

She always did.

"You want to leave São José. You don't like this reality, you want to try another one. Well I've got news for you. No-one likes what's happened to Brazil, but we have work to do, and I'm not going to do it alone."

They'd had the conversation more than once. "It's not like that, Danta. Everything would change. You'd be a different Danta in a better world, a Brazil without the isomorphs. I'd find you again."

"You're talking as if you have some kind of control, but

that can't be right. You're an observer, just an onlooker. And even if reality changes for you, you don't know whether the isomorphs will disappear. Your new world might be even worse."

He sighed. The discussion always finished the same way. "I suppose you're right. I'll stay."

And it wasn't because São José was his rock, where reality never drifted through the night, or because Danta and Adimir were going to save the world from the bivalves, that sort of thing only happened in stories. It was because their nights together were addictive, hard to give up.

"Let's get back to work then. I have to fly to Brasília this evening to meet with the military. They want to know where we're up to. I'll need that spectrometric analysis."

The following morning, Adimir woke up lying on a thin and lumpy mattress. He was in a small room with cracked walls, and Joana was standing by the window, coughing into a blood stained handkerchief.

When he went to push himself up off the bed, his right hand collapsed, pinched the nerves, and he yelled in pain.

"Come on, Adimir, don't be a baby. Get up. We have to go, we have to get out of here."

He held his hands up and studied them. His fingers were limp strands of seaweed—bivalve poison had dissolved the bones.

Adimir was accustomed to shocks, but the change from São José was so extensive, so complete, that he felt dizzy. He closed his eyes and tried to steady himself, to acclimatize to this new reality and work out what had happened.

He realized in an instant. São José had never been his haven of stability. It wasn't the place at all—it was Danta who'd kept his world stable. When she'd travelled to Brasília, reality's tide had washed him away, back to the south, and he suspected he was in São Paulo.

He took a couple of deep breaths and joined Joana at the window, put his arm with draping fingers around her shoulders.

Outside, Avenida Paulista was obliterated, lined with melted apartment buildings. There were a few people in the street with masks, a few cars passing by, but São Paulo was far worse than he'd imagined. And he could smell it in the air, bitter dust and ashes, the scent of the bivalve's poison.

Danta had been right about one thing at least. This new world wasn't a better place.

"We have to leave. The roads south are going to be jammed."

He knew what Joana was talking about. In São José, he'd heard rumors that Buenos Aires hadn't been hit as hard as São Paulo, that the bivalves didn't like the cold. He would check his diary later, but they must have planned to flee to the south, probably a long way south.

"Okay, let's go."

"Don't forget your precious diary, *amor*."

Joana's left eye was as green as ever. Her right eye was a boiled egg, poisoned by the bivalves. He kissed her. "For good luck," he said.

Joana drove her battered Beetle down the back roads, avoiding the freeways. It wasn't just the traffic or the abandoned vehicles littering the curbside—overpasses had collapsed where the bivalves had fed on the concrete supports.

He read his diary as they travelled. In this world he'd never even been to São José, he'd stayed with Joana. He'd lost his finger bones when a building on Avenida Paulista collapsed and he'd held his arms out to stop a dissolving wall from falling on top of him. Joana had been poisoned by contaminated masonry dust in another collapse.

By nightfall they'd reached Registro in the south, and they slept in an abandoned house on the outskirts. The house was untouched by bivalves, hidden in a yard filled with banana palms.

Day after day, they journeyed southward, but Adimir's journey took much longer than Joana's. Each morning when he woke up he was further north than the day before. For him, it was two steps forward and one step backward.

With strings in loops and Popsicle splints, he'd worked out how to write his diary—Joana called it his exoskeleton— and he knew that in successive days' realities they'd left São Paulo later and later.

As well as the consistent drift northward, there was another, more worrying, aspect to the nocturnal changes. As they travelled, Adimir took stock of the world around him. He counted how many flights of bivalves he glimpsed whirling across the sky, and estimated how many refugees they saw on the roads. He recorded the numbers in his diary.

By morning, the previous day's count of the bivalves had increased and the count of refugees had decreased, and Adimir knew what it meant. His daily worlds were spiraling downward, towards some inner circle of hell.

He couldn't help thinking that the changes were more than coincidence, that something or someone—the universe or god or the devil—didn't want him to travel to Argentina with Joana.

At night they consoled each other, clung to each other, made plans and whispered comforting lies. And whatever anyone or anything else wanted, Adimir knew that his place was beside her.

Outside Florianópolis, just before sunset on the sixth day, Joana ran off the road.

She'd driven into a field of cane stubble, and she recovered easily enough. "Sorry, Addie. It was the glare, the sun was in my eyes."

Adimir knew she was hiding something, and that night when he asked her about it, she admitted the truth. "It's the isomorph poison, it's affected my left eye as well. It started out as floating specks when I looked at the sky. Now they're like shiny snowflakes, they're everywhere."

"I'll drive tomorrow." There was no way Joana could cope with the bright Santa Catarina sunshine.

"You can't hold the steering wheel with Popsicle sticks, *amor*."

"I'll wear gloves. You'll have to tie them tight to the steering wheel."

"And I'll change gears I suppose."

"We're a team, aren't we? It'll be fine."

Apart from a few clashes of gears, leapfrog starts, and the occasional stall, the driving went well enough, as Adimir had predicted.

While he was tied to the steering wheel and otherwise occupied, Joana decided it was time to peek into his diary.

"Well this is boring. Nothing personal at all." She flicked through a few pages, made snoring sounds and tossed it onto the back seat.

"What's that rumbling?"

Joana's hearing had become more acute as her vision faded. Adimir heard nothing.

A moment later, when they passed underneath the Lins Street flyover, he realized where the sound was coming from. A bivalve was dissolving its supports.

He slammed on the brakes, tried to pull the steering wheel, to swerve, but his bloodied hands slipped from the gloves, and the Volkswagen was crushed under the falling roadway.

The next morning, Adimir woke up lying on the floor of small wooden shed, bruised and aching, and alone.

He knew that they'd both died, been buried under tons of rubble, yet here he was. It was an afterlife reality, a fringe benefit of his condition—his second afterlife after the accident at the automotive factory.

But for Joana, it was a different story. She had no possibility of switching worlds overnight.

He opened the door of the rickety shed and looked out over a disused scrap yard. Beyond the piles of rusting metal, he could see the remains of the fallen roadway.

There was no sign of the bivalves, and Adimir wandered around the rubble in a dream, lost in the memories of his pasts with Joana. It was time to say his goodbyes to her, but he still held the faintest hope that somehow she'd survived as well in this new world.

When he glimpsed something red poking out of the debris, that last hope was gone. It was Joana's dirty sneaker. He couldn't unlace it, but he managed to slip it off, and he pulled her sock off between his palms, rested his hand on her cold foot.

—*How much do you love me, Addie? Really. How much?*

He travelled with her, shared her hope and despair. He'd

tried.

"Not enough," he murmured, "I'm sorry, *amor*. I didn't love you enough."

Adimir stayed by her side for an hour. He wanted to be with her, wherever she was, but he had no way of joining her. He was going to spend life after life in hell, in the world of the bivalves. They'd worn his body and mind away, left him numbed and dull, with no reason to live and no way to die.

Would Joana be returned to him? Could she miraculously reappear in the world? He didn't think so. At least not if he continued on the journey to the south that they'd started together, their descent into darkness.

There was really only one place he could go.

Adimir trekked northward for all of the next day, retracing his journey with Joana. Along the way, he tried to find an abandoned car that he could somehow manage with his dangling fingers, but he had no luck.

At sunset, he saw enormous flights of bivalves whirling across the sky, sweeping above him in great curtains, and he knew they were scavenging now, returning to structures that had already disintegrated to look for whatever sustenance they could find.

He chose routes that skirted around industrial sites and urban areas, the ruins of high rises. Adimir knew he couldn't die, but anything short of death was possible, and there were worse injuries than his useless hands.

He stopped for the night in a deserted shanty town outside Florianópolis.

In the morning, Adimir found himself in a farmhouse on the outskirts of São Paulo. During the night, invisible wings had carried him hundreds of miles to the north, but whether those wings were leathery or feathered, he had no idea.

The small holding had belonged to a hobby farmer, and the kitchen was well stocked with food. Adimir managed to make himself breakfast on the kerosene stove before he set out, and with the scent of stale coffee in the air and its warmth in his throat, he found himself wondering whether Brazil could rise again from the dust, whether it was still possible.

Through that day, he only saw one other living person— a truck rattling along a dirt road went past him and the driver waved. For reasons Adimir could only guess at, the flatbed was loaded with mutilated corpses.

By evening, he should have had a clear view of the São Paulo skyline from Cantareira Park, but it wasn't there. The urban cityscape, all its skyscrapers, had dissolved away, and what he'd thought was brown haze blanketing the metropolis was a mist of bivalves.

His stomach felt hollow, and he knew that the old Brazil was gone forever. Reality had travelled too far down this desolate timeline.

Still Adimir would keep heading to the north, to São José. He had no idea what he would find there, whether anything or anyone had escaped the bivalves. But he put one foot in front of the other, listened to his footsteps crunching the gravel, and didn't think about the future.

Adimir bedded down for the night in another shantytown, but the next day he found himself in more luxurious accommodation. The room was small, but the bed was comfortable, and the bedside lamp came on when he pressed the switch with his elbow.

He held up his hands and noticed a slight change—short

foundations on a few fingers before they draped downward, stubs of bone that hadn't dissolved.

From the double glazed window, he looked out across a broken landscape—remains of carpentry, brickwork and rusty iron that wasn't appealing to bivalves. But the building he was in was intact, and outside he could see its buttresses with sunlight glinting off steel cladding.

He knew he had to be at Emit Metrics. Danta had told him about the upgrade for working with semiconductors— the airlocks and ultra-clean environments. But now he couldn't help thinking that the building was a fortress, custom-made to withstand the bivalves.

He was wearing pajamas, and he found fresh clothes neatly folded in a drawer. He suspected that in this reality, he'd been at Emit Metrics for some time, and although his diary had been buried with Joana under the rubble of the overpass, he couldn't stop himself from dreaming that the accident might not have happened in this world, and Joana might still be alive.

He searched in his backpack, in the cupboards and under the bed, but there was no sign of his diary.

"I'm not really sure what's going on here. I've—"

"You're new aren't you? I thought you might be, the way you're staring at me."

Adimir had found Danta's office easily enough, and he suspected that this Danta was the same Danta that knew his secret. He'd decided there was no reason to keep his arrival overnight a secret.

"Yes, I am. I ... lost my diary. I can't even fake it."

She laughed and embraced him. "Well, welcome back. Do you know how to manage a mug?"

"Between my palms."

She pressed a button on her desk. "I think your diary's lying around in my bedroom somewhere. You stopped filling it in, there was no point. I'll tell you what's been happening."

A man in a dark uniform came into the office. Staff in the same uniforms had greeted him in the corridors, and he'd smiled and nodded.

"He'll have an expresso. No sugar, not too hot. Thanks Dario."

Dario nodded and left.

"You're wondering about the uniforms. It's a mark of respect, for all the Brazilians that have been lost."

Danta was dressed the same way, but he guessed she was in charge now.

"Tomorrow will be a big day, the end of the isomorphs, and you're here to see it, darling. You're a hero at Emit Metrics. Everything we've done here, the fight against the isomorphs, it's all thanks to you."

"I'm sorry, I don't understand. What's happening tomorrow? What does it have to do with me?"

"When you first came here and told me about your drifting realities, I knew it could only come from one thing— temporal instability."

Adimir remembered Ernesto talking about time travel when he'd first come to Emit Metrics. "You mean sending information backwards in time. Feedback, when there are paradoxes."

"Yes. It causes ripples, instability in the timeline. I knew it had to be me. I was sending messages back so that Emit Metrics could prepare for the isomorphs, so we'd be ready to fight them. I improved the technique to transmit messages over longer timescales, and I sent them to Benita Silverwood, the woman who started the company. I helped her grow Emit Metrics. I told her about the isomorphs."

Adimir's mouth opened but no words came out. "... My

condition, the nocturnal drifting. That's all down to you."

"I'm so sorry, Adimir, but it was for a good cause. You've survived. The isomorphs have killed countless millions.

Danta was right, so many had died. He suspected that she must have had the same conversation with the other Adimir, a rehearsal.

"Now we have stabilizers, shock absorbers for reality. We just have to send the right messages back. We'll keep sending them even after we've eliminated the isomorphs, and they'll act as a damper on the timeline."

Dario came back with his coffee and Adimir grasped it between his palms.

"It's all going to end tomorrow. We've developed a poison that can be sprayed onto buildings, onto concrete. It's harmless to all carbon-based life, but it will destroy the isomorphs' hydrogen bonding, turn them to sand."

Despite himself, Adimir imagined Brazil as it used to be—a beautiful dream, the Cristo Redentor looking down on Rio de Janeiro, and Joana alive again. "All this—Emit Metrics, your micromessages, it all came out of nothing, it was all created from itself."

"Temporal bootstrapping. You don't think it's possible to create something from nothing? You put a microphone in front of a speaker and you hear a high pitched note— feedback that grows from the faintest sound, from a butterfly flapping its wings."

"And all this time, you've been sending these ... micromessages?"

She nodded. "You've been helping us to tune the process, telling us about the changes in reality you've experienced."

Adimir wondered about his earlier version. How had life treated the other Adimir over the last few weeks?

"Why don't you have a look around? I'll finish off here and see you this evening."

Danta looked over her half-frames and winked, and for a moment, Adimir saw the old Danta, the one who wasn't on a mission to save the world.

Adimir knew where the quantum laboratory was, and he'd managed to find his way there without being seen. The equipment looked a little different, more complex, but he found the turbo pump easily enough, and he remembered what Ernesto had told him about its mounting.

Adimir had no idea what his other self had been thinking, or whether Danta was telling the truth about the previous Adimir. Had he even helped her at all?

What he did know was that Emit Metrics was the problem, not the solution. Danta's messages to the past had made his world drift day by day, and he alone had seen what she'd really done—the oscillations in reality that became wild divergences, until Brazil was so far from the ordinary that the bivalves appeared. She'd tried to correct her mistakes and only made it worse, twisted and warped the timeline until it was broken beyond repair.

There could be no going back, but at least Brazil's slide into darkness could be stopped.

Adimir had strapped a spanner along his arm, and all he needed to do was loosen the bolts at the base of the pump. The vibrations through the quadrupole would misalign the rods, and with any luck he could make it impossible to repair.

When he crouched down with the spanner, strong hands grabbed him by the arms and pulled him backwards.

Danta had always known what he was thinking.

"Oh Adimir. You're so predictable, like a hamster on a treadmill. Why don't you surprise me for once?"

Danta had always been able to read his mind, but he couldn't help but wonder whether there was more to it.

Danta opened her desk drawer and pulled out a syringe. "Take a seat." He didn't move, but his wrists were tied behind his back, and the men who'd brought him to her office forced him into a chair.

Danta was a different person now, cold and callous. He'd only tried to stop Danta once, but what about the other Adimir who'd been here before him? And the Adimirs before that? He imagined himself trying to destroy the quadrupole over and over, a mouse racing around a wheel of time.

"If you die here, close to me, you're going to stay dead, aren't you, darling?" She flicked the syringe. "Just to be sure, I could keep you with me. I could have your bones carved as remembrances—necklaces and bracelets. Maybe even a little furniture."

She saw the look on his face. "Oh lighten up, Adimir. I'm joking ... besides, bone jewelry wouldn't go with my outfit."

She stabbed the point straight through his sweatshirt and injected the milky fluid into his arm. He gasped.

"Don't worry, you're not going to die. It's only a sedative. You'll have a good night's sleep somewhere far away from me."

He tried to speak but he was already dizzy, dark spots were spreading across his vision.

"Dario, could you drive him to Arujá? Take the armored car."

She whispered in his ear. "You're going to wake up in a better world, Adimir, and who knows? We might meet again."

Steve Simpson lives in Sydney, Australia mostly. He has a paid job but the voices at night tell him to write speculative fiction. He thinks it might be the neighbors. His stories have appeared in various magazines and anthologies, and as well as writing, he messes around in clinical neurophysiology, builds time travel machines, and does some digital art. He likes rain, rivers and sky fish. And wood ducks, of course. Everyone likes wood ducks.

Find out more about Steve on his website at inconstantlight.com.

Come One, Come All
K. Kazul Wolf

The illusionist crosses her legs, raising an eyebrow. "So, according to your application, your *talent* is touching your nose with your tongue?"

"Yes ma'am." My cheeks get hot, and I'm happy she can't see the blush with my dark skin. "It's something very few people in the world can do, you know."

She raises an eyebrow. "Wonderful. You'll fit in perfectly to the circus, what with the pyrophobic fire-eater, the narcoleptic tight-rope walker, and the man-eating tiger."

I shift in the leather chair, my jeans making some unfortunate noises on the fabric. "D-do you really have those attractions?"

With a sigh, the circus' illusionist rubs her forehead. "No. We don't. That was the point." She pauses. "Though the tiger *could* be considered a man-eater—but that's a long story."

I glance around the small room, crowded with discarded outfits from performances, trinkets from cities strewn around the room. "So, um, do I get the job?"

"Well, George." She tilts her head. "I have to ask: how many circuses have you applied to so far? You seem a little familiar—have you worked in the industry before? Why this small circus?"

I can't help but grin a little. "I have become rather known for my auditions, though I haven't worked in the industry before. So far, seven venues have witnessed my talents."

"Seven?" Her voice rises a bit too high. "You were refused by *seven* circuses?"

I clear my throat, sit up a bit straighter. I've got this. This circus is my dream circus. It's like it's straight out of a childhood memory, nostalgia and fondness so strong the vendors might as well be selling it. "Yes, ma'am. Though some were carnivals."

"Oh dear."

"Yes, I know. It was rather hard to see why they were so disappointed with my talent. Maybe it's because I've never showed them my full act. Here, I'll need more room. Shall we step outside so I can demonstrate?" I jump up from my seat, grabbing the door handle.

"No, hold on—" She leaps forward from her chair, right as I swing the door open.

And a boy stands in front of me—no, kneels, some wires in his hand, pointed right where the doorknob was. He looks up with wide eyes. "Th-the ringmaster said th-that the room would be empty."

"Him!" The illusionist's voice rises even higher, and I'm surprised there aren't dogs howling in the distance. "He knows better than to mess in my business! I told him it wasn't a trick, but does he believe me? Does anyone?"

The boy and I exchange a glance. Are we supposed to answer, or…?

"Get out!" she hisses, and I glance around to catch her leaning forward, both hands pressed down on the cluttered top of her desk.

"I-I swear, I was only doing as I was told, I didn't think —"

"*Get out!*"

The ground shakes. The walls of the room start to sort of shiver and then… melt. The kid finally turns tail and tries to jump from the step of the trailer but then he stops, form shivering. He looks back, eyes even wider, perfect circles, and he melts too.

And there's just darkness.

A sigh behind nearly makes me jump out of my skin.

Turning slowly, I find her still leaning on the now-nothingness of her desk. "What did you do?" I whisper, wanting to take a step back, but not knowing if the floor would be there.

She closes her eyes. "Are you sure it was me? I'm simply an illusionist. Maybe this was reality all along."

Light flares.

"Don't be dramatic." A new voice. "You can control it, if you try hard enough."

I squeak, stumbling backwards and landing on a couch, right next to a woman. She's plump, with cute, rosy cheeks, dressed in a lacy corset and draping skirts.

She looks at me, blinking and taking a bite of a something chocolate-looking on a stick.

"I-is that a fudgecicle?" God, how is that any sort of important right now?

"No, it's a chocolate-covered corn dog." She takes another bite. "Tastes better than you think. Hey, you look a little pale, want a sip of my milkshake?" She keeps her eyes forward throughout the whole conversation, arm reached out as she offers a milkshake that gives a waft of fresh picked, sun-warmed strawberries. Who knows what the flavor *really* is when in her other hand is a chocolate-covered *corndog*.

"Uh, thank you, but no thank you."

She sighs. "My milkshake doesn't bring any boys to the yard."

I scooch a little ways down the couch, away from milkshake girl.

"George, this is Ana, our flaming sword swallower. She drinks milkshakes to cool down after her act. Ana, this is George. He can touch his nose with the tip of his tongue."

She raises her eyebrows, but says nothing of the matter. In awe, I suspect.

The illusionist takes her hands off the trunk in front of

her, crossing her arms and walking towards the entrance of the cloth room.

"Um, so," I start, rising from my seat in slow motions—don't want another room melting incident, "what's going on?"

She pauses, glancing back at me with eyes that seem too heavy for the bags beneath them. "I don't know."

"Yes you do," Ana cuts in. "Don't try to be vague and mysterious. You're not in the middle of an act, my dear."

The illusionist laughs without humor. "Ah yes, reality is bending out of my control, I understand *exactly* how that works. I just let it grow out of control on purpose, obviously. Let me just explain my entire life story to this random person, see if he can make sense of it."

Ana frowns, reaching out a hand toward the illusionist. "We're here for you, you know. We're your family. No matter what, we're not going to leave you behind."

"You can't say that, not with…. What if I lose control?"

Ana just shakes her head. "You're thick."

The illusionist grins, and opens the door. And her doppelgänger stares at us from the opening.

I take slow steps forward. What…?

Oh. It's her reflection. A hall of mirrors stretch where there used to be a door leading back into the heart of the circus.

She turns back toward me, reaching out a hand. "Come on. We'll get you out of here before you're in too deep."

I think that I would call this more than too deep, but I bite my tongue. I take her hand.

The mirrors glint, shifting and distorting our figures as we move ever deeper. Passing a curve in the tunnel, we plunge into darkness. Flashes of light start to move around us, like how water reflects light onto a ceiling. It moves faster, blowing around me but without any force. Like we're swimming, streaming through the twists and turns even though I can feel my feet hit the floor in even steps. My head swims.

Color bursts into the swirling, rainbows sparkling across the glass, a cyclone turning faster and faster.

Then it stops.

We're in the middle of a circus.

Not like any you'd see nowadays, but how they used to be when I was a kid: magic. The tents were fresh and crisp, so tall they must have brushed the stars. My nose was assaulted with the saltiness of freshly popped corn, and the sweet of the dripping, sticky caramel apples. Jugglers laugh as they waltz and spin, throwing any objects they come across into their tossing—including, not to the owner's amusement, an old man's cane. Men on stilts leap over people, bending down to high-five small children.

The illusionist drags me through the crowds, winding around a candy vendor selling all sorts of swirled sweets and into the big top. We walk between the stands that nearly touch the top rim of the tent. Slowly, the ring opens up to us, showing people twirling and spinning and dancing across ropes through the air. There's no net beneath them, though elephants and their trainers play around the circle beneath. My breath and gut drops to my feet at every leap and tumble.

And then I recognize some faces.

"U-um, is that me on that tightrope? And you jumping across the trapeze?"

She slows down, and then fully stops, staring up with eyes that reflect all the colors and lights, a slight smile across her lips. She looks beautiful.

"Maybe." Her whisper is barely audible above the crowd.

Then it goes quiet. Everyone and everything.

As I turn, I catch sight of a figure tumbling through the air. A figure I recognize. Me.

I hit the ground with a thump. Not a great crash or a

clattering. No cracks or splats. Just a thump, and I don't move any more.

Then the screams start. People stream from their seats, tumbling over the stands, running around us to the entrance. The elephants trumpet, rising above the crowd as they stamp around, maybe on people. All the acrobats are down... except one.

The illusionist sits on the tightrope, staring down. At this distance I can't be sure, but I think I see a tear glimmer on her cheek.

The tent rips. The supports start to fall, everything collapsing in on the people remaining under the cloth. Other than us. We stand in the tear of the tent's fabric. The carnival around us is fire and panic and chaos, not of the normal sort. The carousel next to us has animals that buck and claw and bite on their poles. The Ferris wheel starts spinning, faster and faster and faster until it breaks free from its bearings, spinning madly through the crowd—and straight at us.

But I can't move. I grip her hand tighter, and she squeezes back.

The Ferris wheel is a yard away, the wind of its movement brushing my face—until it shatters the mirrors containing us. We're flung backwards as the world around us turns into darkness and diamonds. We turn and tumble the same as my clone had fallen from that great height, though I can hear the glass ringing against the ground around me. It... it starts to form a melody. Too familiar.

The illusionist tugs at our joined hands, and she comes into focus. She pulls me, twirling and dancing across a sea of stars, a full moon above, and its twin reflected under our feet.

For awhile we turn and dip to the slow rhythm of the tapping dance, stars falling all around us to the other side of the sea. Was that another illusion? Or am I...? Can people be illusions? I let out a breath I didn't know I was holding, trying to focus. All I wanted was a job at this circus, and I got to see my future-self die. Or maybe my past-self.

My breath finally comes back enough to whisper, "This is different."

"Is it?" She meets my eyes, large and dark and so tired. "Has this already happened before? Did this happen yet? Or are you just a figment of my imagination?"

"So, that was real?" I dip her, letting the moonlight trail down her neck.

"As real as anything else here."

I lift her up. The glass melody echoes around us, haunting. "Am I real?"

Her lips purse, and I have a sudden urge to feel them pressed together like that. Touch them with a finger, bridge our distance and touch them with my own.

"One of us is real. The question is…" she leans closer, the melody stopping, the stars blinking out around us until it's so dark that I can't see her, I can't be sure of her breath against my ear, "is it me who made up this world, to see you one more time? Or is it you, that can't accept that I'm the one that fell?"

K. Kazul Wolf (most commonly referred to as Bacon) is a fantasy author and video game writer who spends a lot of her time reading too many books, perfecting her leegndrary typo skills, and being a dragon—though in the latter her interests lean more toward rescuing cats and dogs in distress as opposed to princesses and hoards of gold. She is attempting to conquer the world through culinary and pastry arts, and bouts of obsessive writing. You can find her at her website, kkazulwolf.com.

The Convention
by Rasheedah Phillips

"Moments never last, and yet, there is always one present. Listen, there's a philosopher named Henri Bergson, late 1800s French guy. He distinguished between two types of memories. Memory Type One records the events of our daily lives as they occur in time, assigning a place and a date to each event on our personal timelines. When we want to recall these past moments, we imagine it in our minds, pull it out of our mental filing cabinets so to speak. The imaging of that event, the reconstruction of those recorded images in our mind during memory recall, is what Bergson calls the intellectual recognition of a perception that has already been experienced. These memories are vague, tinted with emotion, subject to our own personal fictions that conform to our worldviews."

- *Dr. Diop Hammond*

"I *said:* can I help you, miss?"

Deenah Lumari blinked at the bellhop standing before her. How long had she been standing here? Better yet, *how* had she gotten here?

Just a moment ago she was sitting in the driver's seat of her car in the parking lot. Now she stood at the lobby doors of the *Walton Hotel.* She distinctly remembered looking at the clock on her dashboard, noting that it was 11:55 AM as she turned off the ignition, feeling anxious about missing even a second of the lecture.

Then... *blank.*

She couldn't remember getting out of her car, grabbing her purse (which she now gripped tightly in her fist), walking through the parking lot, arriving here.

"Oh, I, uh... I'm here for the convention," she managed to stammer.

"Memory Type 2, however, is of a mechanical nature. We employ mechanical memory with every movement we make, in our repetitive actions, in every moment. Remembering to breathe without being conscious of the need, knowing how to put one foot in front of the other when we walk, without having to think about that process as we walk. Reading words without needing to recall learning how to read, that sort of thing.

This memory type—I call it the integrated memory—is dynamic because the memory is constantly in a process of creation at the same time that the memory is being utilized.

Our bodies are taking in new information from the environment every moment and crystallizing it into memory. The body then uses the memories in a feedback loop, much like a cassette tape, to move us through time and space and into the future. And all of this action occurs before we are even conscious of it in thought."

Still feeling a bit disoriented, Deenah mused further about the blank spot in her memory as she moved through the near-deserted hotel lobby, past the concierge, into the Berkeley Ballroom and up to the convention registration table.

A pimply-faced, plump, and bespectacled man-child in what looked to be a two times too small t-shirt sat behind the table, dozing uncomfortably in a metal folding chair.

Her, "Excuse me," jolted him out of his dream. "Registration for PsychCon, please," she said feeling a touch impatient.

His flat gray eyes widened. *"You're* here for PsychCon?" he asked with poorly disguised sarcasm. He studied her freshly twisted locs and rich earth-toned skin as if she were an alien, signaling a simultaneous intrigue and disgust with her body.

"Of course!" she said sharply.

His question seemed like a masked implication that she somehow did not belong here and was unwelcome. It was an implication that she resented above all of the implications leveled at her based on her skin tone, hair texture, gender presentation or any intersections therein.

She'd often encountered these reactions at science conventions, expos, comic cons, and cos cons from jerks, just like this one, who couldn't believe that someone like her would be interested in such things.

Most of them tried to hide their surprise or resentment. Or, perhaps, thinking of themselves as progressives, were unconscious of their own biases. She would catch a twitch in the eye, a crack in the voice, or a feigned smile whenever she stepped into the room. Some of them ignored her presence altogether. Or she would be subjected to questions they would never ask of their white male peers, having to provide proof that she, a woman—and a Black one at that—was an authentic nerd.

But this particular registrant was treating her like an outright invader. His bitterness was nearly as visible as the sweat beaded across his forehead. He sniffed. "That'll be thirty bucks."

"I'm pre-paid. Deenah Lumari."

Deenah held out her hand to receive the name-tag that he plucked out of a stack nearby. But, as if her hand was made of an invisible substance, he completely ignored it; nearly throwing the name-tag across the table toward her.

Locking his cold eyes into an icy stare of her own, a split-second decision arrived now. Should she stoop down to his level, morph into the stereotypical angry Black woman character he likely already thinks her to be, or keep it moving?

She glanced at her watch, felt her heartbeat slow down and synchronize to the tick of the minute hand as it dropped into 11:59 AM, and took a deep breath for composure.

"Determinism does not defeat free will. They co-exist, like the wave-particle duality of light, or the liquid-solid nature of black holes, the electro-magnetic field, or any other number of binaries present in our physical reality. Choice has a duality—free will and destiny. It depends upon the observer, all of it. Unless you act consciously (free will), the next moment will be determined by your integrated memory, memory type II (destiny). So you can either act consciously to create the next moment or you will act automatically and allow stored, integrated memory to determine your next action."

Luckily for him, the watch had chosen her path. It was time to go, and he wasn't worth the couple of seconds.

"What room is the PTSD presentation in?" she asked.

But before he could answer—really, before the question even spilled out of her mouth—the room materialized in her mind's eye in *exact detail.* The room number on the plaque next to the door, a small crowd of people scattered around tables and chairs, a large object humped beneath a black sheet casting a deep shadow, and a man pacing back and forth before it. Deenah thought she could even faintly hear speaking, though there was no one else in the Berkeley Ballroom except her and the rude registrant.

And, although she had never been to this particular hotel before, she felt sure that she knew *exactly* where the room was, and how to get to it... before the registrant lifted his beefy finger to point toward the elevator and mutter the room number.

Yet, the young woman was uneasy about how certain she was of the location, as if the knowledge was not hers to possess. The images of the room in her head were a patched-up snag in the fabric of her memory—like the memory wasn't there from something she herself experienced.

Even as Deenah walked toward the elevators every step she took throbbed familiar, a dragging *déjà vu*. Along with the few seconds she apparently had lost getting from the parking lot to the hotel, the day had been strikingly peculiar so far. She wondered if she wasn't coming down with something.

The presentation was underway as Deenah slipped into the room. Just as in her vision moments ago in the lobby, the small crowd was spread out around tables, hushed with a hum of anxious energy.

What she assumed was the PTSD machine lay ominously in the background beneath a black curtain; Dr. Diop Hammond stood before it at the front of the room explaining the methodology of his research and the engineering behind the machine. Tall and thin with a short salt and pepper Afro and a slight Carribean accent, he occasionally waved his hands excitedly toward the black curtain.

"And then you see, by combining two notable brain stimulation techniques of transcranial direct current stimulation and transcranial magnetic stimulation, the psychotemporal transcranial stimulation device (PTSD) uses a noninvasive method to stimulate several targeted brain regions responsible for memory and time perception," Dr. Hammond said.

"The rest is all very technical, but you can read more about it in the materials I've handed out. The point is, by targeting regions of the brain responsible for short-term and long-term perceptions of time and memory, the first model of the PTSD allows the patient to 'functionally' relive not only their own memories with perfect clarity and consciousness, but also the memories of others, given the massive amounts of collected data that we have synthesized." Dr. Hammond paused for added effect.

"Based upon these essential theories, I submit to you that the ***Psycho-temporal Transcranial Stimulation Device*** is the world's first functional time machine," he announced to the audience.

The audience gasped and bustled and *oohed* and *ahhed*. Even after the discovery of faster-than-light neutrinos and the confirmation of the *Higgs-Boson Particle*, talk of time travel still belonged in the realm of the cautiously possible, but not yet probable.

One of the audience members said just as much: "That's ridiculous! Time travel isn't possible! For starters, it violates laws of causality and—!"

"And I will argue with you that it *is* possible, sir!" Hammond responded. "It holds up theoretically from any number of perspectives. Einstein's equations, for example— as any physicist will tell you—work just as well in whatever direction time is flowing.

"The same equations that describe matter plunging to its death into a singularity at the center of a black hole, can be flipped to describe matter exploding from a singularity and spreading out through space-time to birth a universe! Time is but a feedback loop on the grandest scale, one that can be reversed or played forward. But before you cast your doubts, allow me to explain how it all works." Dr. Hammond pleaded, holding up his hands to tame the crowd.

Deenah had already read all of Dr. Hammond's published papers on the PTSD. Dr. Diop Hammond, a retired NSA analyst for the government, turned psychology professor, researcher, inventor, and lecturer, was a data expert. The key behind his theories was giving the brain direct access to collective memory.

For years, Hammond and his team of researchers at Parallel University had collected information from various databases on people and experiences—pictures, birth dates, stories, videos, astrological birth charts, *YouTube* clips, diaries, statistics, research study results, and social networking profiles.

He then built a machine that used electromagnetic brain stimulation to access the collected data, building in algorithms to choose data and fill in any gaps in perception (memory's blind spots). The algorithms were as simple as the ones used by companies like *Netflix* to recommend movies to watch based on the subscriber's preferences.

The blind spots were filled in for lucid clarity of color, smell, sound, and all other sensory aspects of an experience or memory that were not normally re-experienced upon simply remembering a memory; and those particular smells or sounds that can function to bring a person back to a memory, like Proust's *Madeline Cake*. The body, under the control of the stimulated electrical brain impulses, could not tell the difference.

Dr. Hammond dramatically dropped the curtain under which the PTSD was hidden to reveal a seat attached to a monitor and a helmet connected to the machine via a coiled wire. The *"World's First Known Functional Time Machine"*, as Hammond referred to it, looked a lot like a high-tech version of the race car driving games found in malls across America. Below the monitor was a console with a number of unlabeled buttons spread out on its dashboard.

On either side of the seat, was an armrest with cuffs attached, resembling the blood pressure cuffs used in doctors' offices.

Dr. Hammond flipped through a PowerPoint presentation, which showed a diagram of the head and what parts of the brain were being activated with the PTSD. "When the brain simply thinks about action, the neural synapses are firing in the same cognitive and motor regions that they would if you actually performed the act."

"If you are being guided through a memory of a day at

the beach in the PTSD, for example, not only will you feel the sand upon your skin and the screech of the seagull in your ear, but you will taste the salt water ocean on your tongue."

This was the part of the presentation that Deenah was most interested in. As a clinical therapist, she thought a device like the PTSD had potential therapeutic capabilities for her patients. As a general technology enthusiast, she was also interested in how the device functioned technically.

"And really, the stronger your connection to the memory, the more senses are engaged during the actual experience, and the better you will be able to relive the experience through memory. While in its current phase, the PTSD only allows you to remotely re-experience memories or events without influencing the environment of that event.

With future models of the PTSD you will have the ability to interact with the environment, thus influencing the action," Hammond said.

"This will allow you to make a different decision that can affect your present reality. That's *right* people! You will be able to change the future or the past. Now some of you will continue to scream of these bloody grandfather paradoxes and free will and the like, and I will continue to defeat your logic with just one word: *intention,*" he told them.

Still, Deenah has her doubts about the PTSD, given what she had read. Raising her hand to interrupt, she said: "Dr. Hammond, attempting to exploit the machine's therapeutic capabilities for recollection enhancement in cases of post-traumatic stress disorder, and attempting to progress research on the phenomenon known as post-traumatic slave syndrome, you've performed clinical trials of the PTSD on 100 participants.

"The trials have had varying results, with reported side effects ranging from skin irritation, nausea, headache, fainting, disorientation, minor cognitive changes, dizziness, itching under the electrode and, in extreme cases, seizures, psychiatric symptoms, and temporal disorders; in a rare but significant number of cases," she added.

Dr. Hammond squinted at her nametag before replying. "You've done your homework, Miss Lumari, very good. Many of the trial runs were inconclusive, investigative, or lacking substantive proof. And besides, with any new technology there are bound to be side effects. But, I assure you, it works safely on most participants, and it achieves a level of contact with reality that a virtual-reality game could never touch! In fact, I'd say that temporal disorders are a desired effect of the PTSD," he said, chuckling lightly.

"To describe it best, the experience of sitting in the PTSD is like peeking behind the curtain of your own consciousness, mid-thought, and discovering the wizard—which is you! Really, it is a chance to observe the feedback loop that keeps your conscious awareness functioning, as it is functioning. You get the opportunity to watch the play you are starring in from the audience, as you simultaneously play your role on stage, to parade back through your memory! Now, think of each scene in the play as a slice of time..."

Several hands shot up at once, while the man seated next to Deenah muttered beneath his breath, "I thought this was an emergent technologies in psychology convention, not a freakin' science fiction fair."

A confident man, Dr. Hammond anticipated the reaction of the crowd with an easy smile. "But you didn't just come here for talk, good people! Try it out for yourselves. As you all know, today's presentation is the PTSD's first public show and tell since the patent was approved. Per the terms of the authorization that you signed when registering for my workshop, I have fed the PTSD data of each pre-registered audience member.

"Along with an extensive profile on each audience

member, we have linked the hotel's security cameras to the machine, and thus have looped recordings of each of you from the moment you walked into the building up until this presentation. That is what we will use as our demonstration memory. So, who wants to go first?"

Dr. Hammond looked around the room briefly before his gaze landed squarely on Deenah. "Ms. Lumari. You've expressed a lot of interest in the PTSD. Care to do the first demonstration?"

Deenah felt hesitant. She didn't trust Hammond or his stated intentions. Before she could really think it through, though, she was out of her seat and headed to the front of the room, where Hammond and the PTSD stood. She sat down in the seat in front of the console and slid the helmet on.

A live, real-time feed of her, sitting in the PTSD, flashed up on the monitor before her. She relaxed in the chair as instructed, reclining slightly, pulse slowing, the room around her fading into shadow as she stared at her reflection in the monitor, mirroring her actions in the chair.

Above her, Dr. Hammond's words fell softly into her ears and dissolved like snowflakes, "Close your eyes, Deenah. You see, closing the eyes, immediately activates and enhances alpha wave and theta wave generation in our brains, which is connected to creatively sensing, feeling, and imaging. You are now facilitating a shift from the rational and linear processes of thinking to your more primary and holistic ways of thinking. Let's start off by recalling the moment right before this one...

"Right as I say these words you are becoming conscious of how you are sitting... how you are breathing... where your hands are placed... listen to every word and become conscious of the word and the meaning..."

Deenah wasn't completely relaxed, and shifted

uncomfortably in the chair as she felt a tingling in her head, like tiny bolts of electricity striking at her brain. It didn't hurt, but she was hyper-aware of the sensation, hyper-aware of her brain firing off synapses, hyper aware of one thought leading to the next. Her ears searched for something even slightly familiar, like the sound of Dr. Hammond's voice.

A clock in the corner of the screen counted backward from 12:15:09 PM. For blinking moments, she plunged in and out of an inky black. When she resurfaced, she realized that the scene on the monitor was playing in reverse from the time she sat down in the chair, to the time she entered the room.

On the monitor, she would be back in the elevator soon. "Now, in a quick succession of mental flashes, Deenah, visualize everything you did from the moment you opened your eyes to wake this morning, up to this very moment, up to these very words that are coming out of my mouth..."

Her brain flashed the day through her mind as instructed, until it landed upon the image of her walking off the elevator into the lecture. Even though her brain knew she was still seated in the chair, she felt herself moving backward, as if she was walking too, mimicking her actions on the monitor.

Was she only thinking about the memory, or *is* she *there now*, walking through the lobby back toward the registration table?

"Remember, time flows differently for each of us, friends. Different strokes for different folks, or, as Einstein might put it, different rates of time relative to each person's perception. No two people see the world the same. You can bet, if I were to ask all of you to describe the hallway you had to walk through to get here, or to describe this very room that you are in, you all would have a different answer. Sure, there would be some overlay, but your perspective is uniquely situated in the world, colored by your attitudes, your emotional states, and your world experiences. And

we have a way to recover those experiences—moment for moment, sensation for sensation, memory for memory..."

"Fuck, I'm gonna be *late!"* Deenah yelled, reading the clock on the dashboard: 11:55 AM.

Thankfully she was pre-paid for the convention. As she leaned over to grab her purse from the passenger seat, she became paralyzed by a curious sight just outside the car window.

She sat there in her seat... watching her *self* walking through the parking lot a few feet ahead of her car, puppet-like, as if being tugged by an invisible string.

Rasheedah Phillips, Esq. is the Managing Attorney of the Housing unit at Community Legal Services, a mother, writer, the creator of The AfroFuturist Affair, the co-creator of Black Quantum Futurism multimedia arts collective, and a founding member of Metropolarity Queer SciFi collective. In 2014, she independently published her first speculative fiction collection, Recurrence Plot (and Other Time Travel Tales), and in 2015, an anthology of experimental essays from Black visionary writers called Black Quantum Futurism: Theory & Practice Vol. I. As part of BQF Collective, Phillips was a 2015 Artist-in-Residence at West Philadelphia Neighborhood Time Exchange, is a 2016 A Blade of Grass Fellow, and has exhibited and performed at Temple Contemporary, Stony Island Arts Bank in Chicago, and WORM! Rotterdam, Holland. Phillips has work appearing in the book "Keywords for Radicals: The Contested Vocabulary of Late Capitalist Struggle," The Funambulist Magazine, and "Unveiling Visions: The Alchemy of the Black Imagination" exhibition catalogue, and has had work published in the Temple University Political and Civil Rights Journal, Atlanta Black Star, and other publications.

Visits (with a Stranger)
by Martin L. Shoemaker

Tim was five the first time the stranger saved his life.

It was on a field trip to the local petting zoo. It wasn't what one would usually consider a dangerous circumstance; but Tim had a tendency to wander off on his own and find trouble. His mom always said Tim had inherited his dad's curiosity; but that curiosity didn't extend to the goats. So instead he looked around for something more interesting. When he saw the ice cream cart across the street, Tim snuck away from Mrs. Anders and the class. He never looked for oncoming traffic.

Tim never had a clear picture of what happened next. In later years, he remembered a horn honking and tires screeching; but most of all he remembered the strong arms of a stranger whisking him up and the *clap-clap-clap* of boot heels, running him out of the street just before a big blue van barreled through the intersection. Then the strong arms set him down, and the boots *clap-clap-clapped* away.

Tim was crying (which had the bonus of earning him a free ice cream sandwich) when his teacher ran up to the cart. "What happened? Timothy, are you all right?"

Tim was sobbing too much to respond, so the ice cream girl answered. "He was crossing the street. And there was this van coming. But then his dad pulled him out of the street."

"His dad?" Mrs. Anders looked around. "Mr. Carroll wasn't here with us today."

"Huh. Well, I just assumed. He looked like a relative of some sort."

187

Tim was twelve the second time the stranger saved his life.

It was on a Boy Scout winter campout. After a Saturday morning spent shoveling out from the previous night's blizzard, the leaders split the boys into two groups. The younger boys stayed in the cabin for songs and games and s'mores. The older Scouts packed up tents and knapsacks for an overnight stay up the mountain.

Tim was just too young for the older group. Cousin Mitch was in that group, and Tim didn't like to be left out. If his dad had been on the trip, Scout Master Walters might've made an exception; but his dad had to work in the lab again that weekend, so Tim was stuck with the kids. At his first opportunity, he snuck his backpack and tent out the back window. Then he left for the outhouse; but as soon as the cabin door was closed, he grabbed his gear and set off up the mountain.

At first Tim had an easy trip. The older Scouts had left three hours earlier, and their boots had tramped down the trail so he could move at a fast pace. He was sure he would catch up before they reached the campsite.

But he hadn't accounted for the weather. A half hour up the trail, a squall returned, and soon the air was thick with large flakes, reducing visibility. Slowly the trail faded: clear footprints shrunk to large dimples, and then to a low depressed path through higher snow.

Tim was stubborn. He kept going long after there was no trail to follow. By the time he gave up and admitted that it was gone, it was too late: he turned to follow his own track back down the mountain, but it was gone as well.

Tim's dad had taught him to think through problems. If things got really bad, he had a pack and a tent and an Arctic sleeping bag. He could camp in the shelter of some trees. But it would be better to find his way back down the mountain, face the anger of Mr. Lawrence, and spend the night in the cabin. It wasn't like one of dad's physics problems, after all. How hard could it be? He chewed on his lip as he did when thinking, and he decided there was a simple answer. He just had to go *down*. The mountain told him which way was *up*, so he would just go the other way and watch for familiar landmarks.

But this was more difficult than Tim had planned. *Nothing* was familiar, not with new snow covering everything and more in the air. Plus the storm brought an early twilight. Worse, the snow seemed to be increasing.

Tim picked his way slowly, looking for a path as best he could. He couldn't tell how much he went down and how much he just veered to one side or the other. He tried to make his way from tree to tree, figuring that way he would be unlikely to double back or go in circles.

Ultimately it was the trees that betrayed him. As the night grew darker and the snow heavier, it got harder to see his way to the next tree. Tim found himself under an old pine. The higher branches were needle-filled and bowed with snow, while the lower branches were sparse and dry and made a small shelter from the blowing storm. Tim crawled inside and rested while he looked for another tree as a landmark. It was just too dark and snowy outside this artificial cave. Perhaps he should set up his tent here? No, the branches were too low, the open area too small for the tent. Instead, he gathered his courage, chose a direction, and set back out into the storm—right over the edge of an unseen ravine.

Tim's arms flailed, grasping in vain for a handhold. The slope as a whole was gentle, which probably saved Tim's life: he slid more than he fell. But he also tumbled, twisting his leg with a horrifying *snap* that sent Tim into immediate shock. He was unconscious for the rest of the slide down the ravine.

When Tim awoke, he was warm. Not indoors warm, but warmer than the snowstorm he remembered. Someone was leaning over him, holding a cup to his mouth. "Good, you are awake. Drink this." The voice was muffled by a scarf and masked by the wind. Tim reached for the cup, but then cried out in pain. He was in a sleeping bag, and moving his arms had shifted his leg. It was splinted, but even so the slight movement caused him stabbing pain.

"Here, Timothy." The stranger set down the cup, took off his gloves, and unzipped the sleeping bag to Tim's waist. Tim reached his arms out, and the stranger zipped the bag back up to his armpits. Then he handed Tim the cup. "Your leg is broken in two places, but it shall heal. Drink that. It should raise your temperature and stave off shock and hypothermia."

Tim sipped. Hot cocoa spread sweet, rich warmth through his mouth, down his throat, and through his body. The stranger turned away. Behind him blazed a small fire. The smell of chicken soup came from that direction.

Tim looked around. They were in some sort of small cave in the side of the mountain. The fire and their two bodies were enough to warm up the confined space. Outside the wind still howled. Except for that brief stab of pain, everything looked and felt *fuzzy*, like Tim was watching from a distance.

The stranger turned back to Tim. Between his heavy parka hood, his big scarf, and the backlight from the fire, the stranger's face was completely in shadow. He held out a metal mug full of soup. "Eat this. Then rest. Your body needs energy, but it also needs sleep. How is your leg?"

Tim swallowed some soup. The broth was thick and salty with big chunks of chicken. "Hurts some." He took more soup.

"If it only hurts 'some', then it could be worse. Try not to move too much. I gave you some aspirin while you were semi-conscious, but not enough for a broken leg. The splint will keep it from hurting too badly as long as you stay still."

Tim finally gathered enough wits to ask the question that had eluded him so far: "Who are you?"

Behind the scarf, the stranger was silent for a beat, then another. Finally he answered: "That is unimportant. I am just a hiker who found you in trouble, and I had to help. Now eat, and then get your rest. I shall watch out for you."

Tim nodded. He still felt too fuzzy to argue, and the hot cocoa and hot soup were making him warm and dozy. Eventually he held out the empty soup mug, and the stranger took it. Then the stranger unzipped the sleeping bag again to let Tim put his arms back inside. He arranged an old pair of Tim's jeans as a pillow, and Tim settled back. At first he was afraid that he would shake his leg again and cause more pain; but despite himself, he soon succumbed to sleep.

The next time Tim was conscious, Mr. Lawrence was bending over him. The light in the cave proved that it was daylight outside, and the storm had passed. A much larger fire burned outside the cave, wet green branches snapping and generating a big cloud of smoke.

Mr. Lawrence later explained that it was the smoke that led him and the rescue party to the cave. They had seen no sign of the stranger, but they did find a note explaining the nature and extent of Tim's injuries and what had been done to treat him. They also found boot prints—not hiking boots, more like cowboy boots—that led away from the fire for a few yards before disappearing without a trace.

Tim was nineteen the third time the stranger saved his life.

It was late one night at a bar, one which wasn't too particular about checking IDs. Or to be precise, it was outside the bar as Tim fumbled to try to get his keys into the car lock. Or to be yet more precise—dad always told him to be more precise–Tim was fumbling to get his keys out of his pocket, in preparation for fumbling to get his keys into the car lock. Tim kept sticking his hand in the wrong pocket, the little watch pocket of the jeans where he never kept anything. Then he kept laughing that his hand was in the wrong pocket. Then he kept laughing that his jeans had a useless watch pocket, as if he had one of dad's old pocket watches. Then he kept sticking his hands in the wrong pocket again and laughing again as the –cycle started over.

"Cycles." Tim laughed at that, too. "Cycles, dad. Just like one of your lectures. Around and around, and 'round and 'round and roundroundround... Hand to pocket, wrong pocket, no keys, no watch... No watch, dad, need one a' your watches. No watch, no time! Time to go home! Need my keys! In my pocket, 'round and 'round and 'round time spins. Gonna get me a Nobel prize in keys..."

The cycle ended–and Tim's monologue as well–when Tim heard the sound of hard boots on the pavement behind him as he felt a tap on his shoulder. He laughed one more time, pulled his hand out of the wrong pocket, and turned to see which of his buddies had followed him out to tell him *again* that he was too drunk to drive home. Like he hadn't had enough of that already in the bar, 'round and 'round and 'round. Who did they think they were, his dad? Well, he would give them a piece of his mind for sure, once his eyes managed to focus.

And his eyes *did* focus, just in time for Tim to see the fist rapidly approaching his jaw.

Tim briefly regained consciousness. He couldn't remember how he got there, but he recognized the back seat of his car. He lay across it, knees drawn up, rocking slowly with the motion of the car. His leg ached slightly where the old break had been. This position wasn't comfortable; but soon Tim had a bigger concern than his leg. He managed to lean over the seat edge in time to vomit on the floor instead of the seat. Then, weakened and dizzy, he laid back onto the seat. Soon enough he was unconscious again.

The next time Tim was aware of anything, it was a bright light shining in his face through the rear window. A *very* bright light, and it made his head throb. He closed his eyes, but the pain burned right through the lids. So he turned his head away and buried it in the car seat. He heard voices, one deep and steady from outside the car and one vaguely familiar voice from the driver's seat.

"So who's this, Mr. Carroll?" That was Outside Voice.

"That is my cousin Mitch, officer." That was Front Seat Voice. Tim giggled just a bit. He had a cousin Mitch, just like Front Seat Voice did. His favorite cousin. Bought Tim his first beer. "He called me for a ride. He was in no shape to walk home, and he lost his wallet so he could not call a taxi."

"Lost his wallet, eh?" The light drew closer to the window, and Tim buried his face further. "How old is your cousin?"

"Would it make me a bad cousin if I said I am unsure? Mitch is a few years older than me, I know that."

"Uh-huh. That makes him legal. I guess. Have *you* been drinking, Mr. Carroll?"

"No, officer. I was home watching TV all night. I do not drink much."

"You understand: you're coming from a bar, and your cousin is very drunk. So I have to ask: would you mind taking a breathalyzer test?"

"No, officer, I understand. Drunk driving is... horrible. You have to watch out for it."

"If you could step out of the car please, Mr. Carroll?" The car door opened, and Front Seat Voice got out. There was a jingle like a keychain, and again he heard boots on the pavement. Front Seat Voice didn't close the door. If they were at the side of the road, Tim was sure he would've closed the door. They must've pulled into a parking lot.

After a few minutes, the car shifted slightly as Front Seat Voice got back in and the door closed. Again the chain jingled. Then Outside Voice came back. "Thank you for your cooperation, Tim. You're good to go."

"Thank you," Tim mumbled from the back seat, but he doubted anyone heard him. The car started, the window rolled up, and the car started moving again. The motion quickly rocked Tim back to sleep.

The next time Tim woke up, his little sister Rita was pounding on the car windows, trying to get his attention. Tim looked around and saw that he was parked in mom and dad's driveway, and the sun was up. His dad's car was already gone, probably for some early-morning meeting. No, Tim remembered then, a physics conference in London.

Tim's head spun, his stomach felt like a churn full of sour butter, and his mouth tasted like the sour butter had passed through in both directions; but on the whole, it wasn't the worst morning of Tim's life.

Tim sat up. As he did, something fell off his chest and landed in the tacky, half-dried vomit on the floor. Looking down, he saw that it was his wallet.

Tim was forty the time the stranger *didn't* save his life.

In a run-down motel with cheap weekly rates, Tim chewed on his lip and tried to think of what to do, but he had drunk away all his options. His night in the back of his car hadn't cured Tim of his drinking problem. Flunking out of college hadn't cured him, nor had the breakup of his marriage, the loss of two jobs, nor the fights with his family. Even the fact that his own children wouldn't talk to him didn't faze him.

Cousin Mitch, now an AA fanatic, called Tim a hard case: too smart for their games, too stubborn to accept that anyone else knew what was good for him, and too independent to need anyone. He did what he wanted when he wanted, just as he had his whole life. Sometimes that got a little hairy, but he always scraped by. A little whiskey just made the scraping easier.

The death of his mother had shaken Tim sober. His sister had reached him at the motel with the news. Rita didn't approve of Tim's habits any more than the rest of the family did, but she was soft-hearted. She had never given up hope for Tim, even after most everyone else had. Dad never really gave up, because he never noticed Tim enough to care. He had drifted deeper into his work, and he didn't seem to notice his children any more. Still, he always supported mom when she bailed Tim out of trouble. Maybe he wouldn't, if he knew that Tim had pawned one of his pocket watches to pay his bar bill; but mom bought it back, and she kept the whole thing secret. Even though she still helped Tim out, she had never looked at Tim the same way after that. Tim had planned to somehow get right with her again. But now...

Rita bought a new suit and helped Tim to clean up. Everyone was cordial at the funeral. Marilyn and the kids clustered around him and gave him support. Tim could almost pretend they were still a family, as if the fights and the screams and the divorce had never happened. Mitch had come over and talked, without mentioning AA for once, just Tim's favorite cousin again. With his family's support, Tim kept himself together through the visitation and the service.

That was better than dad, who was numb and weary. Dad accepted sympathy and condolences; but every conversation tailed off into uncomfortable silence. Dad had never been good with people, leaving that to mom. Mom had kept up relations with family and friends, while dad kept up with the Nobel committee. Rita had worried what would happen to dad now without mom, but Tim wasn't worried. Dad would eventually go back to his books and his physics and what he really cared about. He would escape from the world.

And so would Tim. He had a flask hidden in his sock; and at lunch after the service, Tim fell off the wagon again. In his grief and exhaustion, the whiskey hit him hard. By the time they returned to the house, Tim had been sloppy and surly, just as bad as ever. Then he found one of his old stashes, and he only got drunker.

Things fell apart from there. Marilyn and the kids stormed out. Rita's husband Jack tried to take the bottle, and Tim started a fight. It hadn't lasted long, as Tim was close to falling down; but by the time it was over, Rita was in tears. After years of standing as his last defender, Rita finally gave up. She separated the two men, sobbing and pounding on Tim's chest. Finally she slapped his face, stormed out of the living room, and slammed her bedroom door.

For the first time all day, dad spoke without someone speaking to him first. He stood, stared with watery eyes at Tim, and chewed on his lip. Finally he said just one thing: "Your mother would be so disappointed, Timothy." Then he too left the room, boot heels echoing on the polished wooden stairs as he went up to his library and locked the door.

Mitch tried to stop Tim from leaving, but Tim shoved him away and stumbled out of the house. Somehow he found a bus back to the motel.

Now Tim sat alone in the dingy room and stared at the turned off TV, playing a game with himself: *how long before I open the next bottle?* For the first time in his life, Tim really *believed* he might have a problem. He had seen the symptoms for years; but even that had been a way of deluding himself. It just led to another little mental game: *I'm aware of the problem, so it can't be so bad, right?* And after that: *I can postpone drinking, so it can't be so bad, right?* And then inevitably came the *how long* game.

But this time, over top of it all was one recurring thought: *I'm out of control I'm out of control....* After the funeral, the games no longer hid that one ugly fact: *I'm out of control...*

So now what?

And then the stranger spoke from behind Tim. "I give up, Timothy. I cannot help you this time."

"Dad?" But when Tim swiveled the chair and looked, he saw a tall man in his early twenties standing in the bathroom doorway. Tim could muster no stronger reaction. Whether the stranger was a hallucination or a burglar, Tim was too numb to care.

The stranger looked familiar. Tim's face in the mirror looked like an older version of the stranger, but their taste in clothing couldn't have been more different. Tim still wore his suit, but he wore it sloppy. The young man wore jeans and a work shirt and cowboy boots, but he wore them like a uniform: boots shined like wingtips; shirt and jeans crisp and pressed. And the brass watch chain that hung from the belt... *"Dad?"*

The stranger nodded. "Yes, Timothy." Tim looked down at the bottles under the bed, but the stranger drew his attention back. "No, I am no hallucination from your drink. I am Phillip Carroll; and in two years within my timeframe, I shall be your father."

Tim pushed up from the chair and to his feet. He took two unsteady steps to look closely at the stranger. The eyes: younger, no lines, but the same pale blue-gray eyes that zeroed in on physics problems but slid right past his family. The jaw line: the same sharp angles, but the jowls that had sagged over the decades were still firm. There was more hair on the forehead, but with the same lift and shape. The face was unmistakably *dad*.

"How…"

"I could not follow his explanation."

"His?" Tim backed away, his head spinning.

"Mine." Young dad—Tim couldn't think of him that way, it was all too strange. *Phillip* stepped into the room and sat on the unmade bed. "I, your father in your future, tried to explain it to myself, your father in the past." Phillip chewed his lip in thought. Tim knew the family chew. "Timothy, how much do you know about his work?"

Tim collapsed into the chair. "Something about the physics of time. 'Chronal cycles', I know that was in his Nobel citation."

"'Transfer of State Between Chronal Cycles in Superposition.' Do you know what that means?"

"I'm an accountant. What dad calls math and what I call math, they don't even look like the same thing. He said it had to do with information—quantum state—crossing between chronal cycles. Whatever those are, something about time lying upon itself in layers. He said the transfer balanced certain equations and explained discrepancies in certain experiments. Eventually he was able to experimentally measure this transfer. But it never meant much to me as a practical matter. The chronal cycles had fixed lengths. You couldn't affect anything outside of those periods. And he couldn't tell if you could change your own path, or if you merely impacted another you at another part of the cycle. And all you could send were tiny bits of information."

Phillip nodded. "Yes, it started with quantum state. But in your future, I shall perfect macro scale transfers. Timothy, do you remember what happened when you were five?" Tim stared silently. "At the petting zoo?"

"Oh…" Tim hadn't forgotten the incident, but he

seldom thought of it. "The van that almost hit me."

"Yes. And you were rescued by someone who then fled the scene."

"You…"

"And when you were twelve, you fell down a ravine in a storm. And when you were nineteen, when you were too drunk to drive home?"

Tim's brain ached. He was no longer drunk, but he wasn't well. "You were… the driver?"

Phillip leaned forward, just as dad always did when he was explaining something. "I started toying with these ideas just last year, and they will take decades to work through. In my forties I shall work out the basic theory, and I shall continue to work on it long after Grace… after your mother passes away. Passed away. I am sorry, it is difficult to keep tenses and frames of reference straight without mathematics. At some point, I shall travel back across cycles to meet myself and send myself forward to save the life of my accident-prone son. Not once, but four times."

"Why didn't he save me himself?"

Phillip smiled. "Now you are thinking clearly. I asked my future self that. He explained that only a young, healthy person could save you: fast enough to outrun a truck, vigorous enough to survive a blizzard, and strong enough to overpower you. So I shall send me forward to do what I will be unable to do.

"But he never explained why he sent me to *this* cycle. Although I have observed only a little of your life, Timothy, I am sorely disappointed in you."

Phillip stopped as if waiting for Tim to argue; but Tim had heard variations of this lecture for years. He was tired of fighting it, so he silently waited for it.

"Timothy, you are a drunk: a dirty, shabby, broken man. You have disappointed every person who loves you. When I think of what Grace—what your mother must have felt, each time she had to rescue her own son from his vice.... All those times I saved your life, and for what? So you could end up alone in this motel, still tearing your family apart on the day they buried her. Buried... Grace.... Why did I bother?"

Tim felt a tear in one eye. His... father had all but wished him dead three decades ago. And he had made his case with rigor and precision.

But Phillip wasn't finished. "Perhaps... I sent myself here to see the results of my weakness. To see what your mother never could: that your drinking is not like wandering into a street, or falling into a ravine. It is not an incident from which you can be rescued, it is a habit you must unlearn. And you cannot learn without consequences. Sheltering you from consequences only made them worse."

Tim had never won an argument with dad. Of course, they almost never argued, because they were in such different worlds. They were never together enough to argue.

Never together... Cycle after cycle... Tim didn't have an argument, but he saw questions. "How old are you?"

"I am twenty-three, in my first year of graduate school. Grace and I were just married. You shall be born in two years."

"And you won't be there."

"What?"

"Mom told me. She said there was a big conference, and she went into premature labor. You'll miss my birth. Rita's, too."

"Timothy, you are changing the subject."

Tim snarled, "This *is* the subject! You were never there, dad!"

"What?"

Tim leaped out of his chair. "You were never there. Oh, *you* were, the time-traveling stranger; but *where was my dad?*"

"I suppose I shall be working. My work is important, you know."

"I *know*, dad. I've heard it all my life. It *is* important, *but so am I!* So is Rita. And you were never there! You were never on my field trips, you were never on my camping trips. No wonder I got in trouble!"

Phillip leaped up as well, again face to face with Tim. For perhaps the first time ever, Tim saw his father angry. "Is that it? Blame all of your troubles on me, absolve yourself of responsibility? I worked hard, so you are a drunk, is that your excuse?"

Tim was about to argue exactly that; but he realized that an excuse was all it was. Mitch had tried to teach him about excuses. "No, dad, it's a factor, but I made my own choices. Lots of kids with worse parents made smarter choices. That's my fault, not yours."

His father was unmollified. "Then why did you bring it up?"

Tim sighed. He sat. He looked at his feet. Finally he said, "It's not why I drink, but it's still true: I missed you growing up. I didn't understand chronal cycles or quantum state, I just missed my dad."

"So, you are a drunk now because I was not there for you? You got yourself killed at five, and twelve, and nineteen because I was working?"

Killed. Tim really thought about it. There were times in his life where he could've died. Maybe *did* die, if dad had to send himself back to save him. Three times even.

Three times...

"Dad, I know why you sent yourself back here, today. It's not about my drinking."

Phillip's wrath had exhausted itself, and he sat again. "Well, Timothy, I wish you would explain it to me."

"I can, if you can answer one question. Did you tell

yourself about the three times I died all at once? Or one at a time after each incident?"

"I told myself about them all at once, Timothy. All at once... But if..."

"But if I died at five, *who needed to be saved at twelve?* Or at nineteen? How would I be here to talk to you today?"

Phillip chewed his lip. "I was so caught up in so many new ideas... Macro transfer... A family... A son in danger... I never wondered how I could know about multiple threats to your life."

"And you couldn't, dad. If I died at five, there was no one to save at twelve or nineteen. So *my life was never in danger.* Somehow I would've survived."

"But then why did I send myself back?"

"In part for me. I didn't need to be saved, but *I needed my dad.* I was scared, I was hurt, I was stupid, and I needed someone. And you were there. I didn't know it was you, I just thought of you as 'the stranger', but I had what I needed. At the important moments, I had a dad." And then, without thinking, Tim crossed to the bed and embraced his father. "Thank you, dad." At last the tears flowed from his eyes. "I couldn't say it before. Thank you."

Phillip wrapped his arms awkwardly around Tim, patting his back. Then he spoke, a catch in his voice. "I'm... glad I was there. I'm sorry if it sounded like I wasn't." Then he pulled away and looked Tim in the eyes. "But you said 'in part'. I do not believe I sent myself back here so that you could thank me."

Tim shook his head. "Dad, I don't think you're here to save me. You're right, I have to do that for myself. I have to face my consequences. So there has to be another reason you're here *today.* Another reason why *today* is important..."

Phillip swallowed. "Grace's funeral."

Tim nodded. "Mom's funeral. You wanted yourself to

see this day. Dad, you're not here because I need you. You're here because *you* need *us*."

This time it was Phillip who wept. "Your mother... Your... sister, she looks so much like Grace... He knew..."

"He knew that as proud as you will be of your work in physics, someday you'll regret that you didn't have more time with your family. Like me, you made your choices; but you found a loophole, a way to change those choices. You sent yourself forward so that you could see what you were choosing and *not* choosing. If you make different choices, maybe you'll never work out your theory. Maybe you'll work it out later. Or hell, knowing now that it *will* work, maybe you'll work it out *earlier*. And maybe... all of our lives will be different..."

"Timothy, do not get your hopes up. I cannot say whether transfer through the cycles is serial or parallel. I might change things for you, or I might only change them for a you in the next cycle. Or..."

Tim sat on the bed and patted Phillip's hand. "It's okay, dad. This is my life, my mess, the result of my choices. Maybe you can go back and 'fix' me; but maybe I'll be too stubborn, and still end up a drunken loser."

"My son is not a loser!"

"Thanks, dad. You may be right. After today, maybe I can start making some better choices. But you're not here to fix my life. You're here to fix yours."

"For an accountant, that's pretty deep."

"I had a great teacher. When I'd listen." Father and son grinned at each other. "So now what? Do you click your heels together and say, 'There's no place like then'?"

"Heh. No, I have a quantum-entangled trigger."

He pulled out a metal disk, and Tim laughed. "It's one of your pocket watches." In fact, it was the one Tim had once fenced.

"Yes, I shall conceal it in this antique so as to avoid suspicion. But if I twist it right, I will know then, and I shall reverse the cycle gradient."

"Over my head, dad. I'll stick with heel-clicks. So I guess you've done what you need to do here?"

"Yes, I have. Thanks to you, Timothy."

"I'm just returning the favor. I still owe you twice more."

And then father and son stood and embraced again, this time less awkwardly. Phillip stepped back and twisted the rear panel of the watch. And as quickly as that, Tim was alone in the room.

Tim chewed his lip once more and wondered: if dad changed his life, would it happen right away? Would Tim notice? Would things just shift like a scene change in a film? Or would things only change for some parallel Tim?

He couldn't guess, but he knew someone who might. He picked up the phone and dialed. "Hello, dad?"

Tim was forty the time the stranger didn't save his life; but it was also the time Tim saved the stranger's life. And maybe his own.

Martin L. Shoemaker is a programmer who writes on the side... or maybe it's the other way around. Programming pays the bills, but a second place story in the Jim Baen Memorial Writing Contest earned him lunch with Buzz Aldrin. Programming never did that!

His Clarkesworld story "Today I Am Paul" has been reprinted in Year's Best Science Fiction: Thirty-third Annual Edition, The Best Science Fiction of the Year: Volume One, The Year's Best Science Fiction, and The Year's Top Ten Tales of Science Fiction 8. It has been translated into French, Hebrew, Czech, Polish, German, Italian, Chinese, and Hungarian.

If the Stars Reverse their Courses, if the Rivers Run Back from the Sea
by Alter Reiss

The water slapped against the boat as we slipped out of Limien harbor, past driftwood and floating garbage. The boatsman sat huddled in the back, coaxing a few more miles out of a motor as ancient as he was, and I sat up in the front, and watched islands rise out of the cold gray water.

I smoked a post-war cigarette. It was acrid, the tobacco cut and cut again with some local leaf until it was the barest memory, a hint of flavor in a cloud of smoke.

"It's odd, Colonel Andier," hazarded the boatsman, after a while. "Taking a foreigner up to the bay islands."

"New government says it's fine," I replied. It had been years since I had been a colonel, and I was no more a foreigner than he was, but no point in arguing. Time had fixed me as both of those things.

He spat into the gentle swells. "That's for the new government," he said. He spat again. "And that's for the old one."

I had spent the best part of my life fighting against the old government, and I had broken my share of heads during the elections to see the new one safely in. I couldn't argue with either of his evaluations.

"It's just that the Captain had gnats in his eyes about spies up in the islands," continued the boatsman. "Time was, they'd pay me fifty marks for one of you trying to hire a boat to Cavenesis."

"Time was," I said, "little white sailboats would go back and forth across the bay, as fair and as free as birds."

He made a sound somewhere between a grunt and sob,

and looked back at Limien. The Mariners Cathedral had lost its spire in the shelling, and even with the peace, a pair of destroyers was anchored offshore, decks cleared for action. "Long ago," he said. "Long gone."

"So are your fifty marks," I said. "Eight piasters if you pick me up tomorrow morning."

He kept looking at Limien, didn't reply. I took another long drag on my cigarette, flicked it. The glowing red ember described an arc like a barrage flare, snuffed out without even a sizzle when it hit the water.

"Hell with the Captain, anyway," said the boatman. "First he was a traitor, then he was a coward. Eight piasters for tomorrow morning."

My opinions of Cainder Strake, Captain of Limien and Protector of the South, were stronger than those just expressed by the boatman, but I kept them to myself. Cainder had brought war to Limien and his disappearance had lost that war, but he had shone so bright that Limienese would still stab people who insulted their Captain, even when they knew they should hate him.

We passed the rest of the trip in silence. That had been the last of my post-war cigarettes. I had a packet of old eastern cigarettes in the pocket of my forage jacket, but those had cost too much to waste. We got to Cavenesis as the sun burned off the last of the morning clouds.

The boatsman left me at a little wooden pier. There were giant iron caltrops buried in the surf near the old dock, and there were loops of thorn-wire all along the beach where they had pulled up sailboats.

I climbed up past weed-choked gardens, past shattered old trees, past hollyhock and gun emplacements, chamomile and bomb craters, up to the villas. Some were bombed-out shells, but most were still standing. Including the great houses: Dalnan, Coteri, Aminde.

The pillars of Aminde's portico were whole, though toppled; it takes more than an errant bomb to shatter strong-veined Fanerian marble. Inside, the midday sun streamed through empty window frames, giving a hint of grandeur to the few tattered tapestries that remained. There were overturned desks, and wires, and drifts of paperwork in the great hall.

It looked like a signal station. The intelligence boys would have to sort through those papers, see if they could find anything worthwhile in the piles of dross. I left the papers to molder and went down to the basement.

The deeper I went, the less changed the villa was. The light of my electric lantern showed the great casks of the wine cellar standing where they had always stood, and there were even a few bottles left in the racks. I took one, a Coteri red from '08, and went deeper, until I found the loose flagstone.

I put my lantern and my bottle to the side and tried to shift the stone. I was growing old, and it had been a hard climb. Growing old, but not yet old. The stone moved, revealing a narrow staircase. I had put clues together from stray lines in biographies, confused accounts of former servants, and the records of old witch-finders. It seemed that I was on the right track.

At the bottom of the stair was a small stone room, with a single line cut into the floor. That line looped and swirled, turning into all the constellations of the zodiac, linked together by the galaxy snake, with pits to mark the important stars. There was also a corpse. It was wearing the uniform of a captain, and it had been there a long time; five years. It was as dry and as light as a bundle of twigs. Not just a captain. It was wearing the uniform of the Captain of Limien. So far, so good. I kicked it out of the way, sat down where it had rested, and uncorked the bottle of Coteri.

It was a fine old vintage, sharp and flinty. I hadn't

brought a goblet, so I took a long swallow from the bottle. I laid out the things I had brought. The packet of old eastern cigarettes, in its black and gold wrapper. The electric lantern. My old trench knife, its scarred and pitted handle a match for my scarred and pitted self.

There was no need to hurry, but there was also no reason to delay. I drank the wine, to remember, and started smoking the cigarettes. It had been a long time since I had filled my lungs with real tobacco smoke, and it was as sensual a pleasure as any I could name, to run through the packet without any thought of economy. The years rolled off as I breathed it, and soon the light from my little lantern was showing coils of smoke in the close air of the room. It was enough. I took up the knife and opened the vein at my right wrist.

I held my hand out over the carving, so that the blood dripped into the sign of the fox and flowed outward, to the ploughman on one side and to the king on the other, and from them on to the rest of the circle. It hurt, but not badly. The wine of Coteri has many virtues.

My blood spread like oil. It wasn't long before the whole carving was filled with it, from the fox at the top to the ladies at the bottom. I took another puff of my cigarette and watched the room fade, as the smoke filled my eyes.

I was there, and I wasn't there. I could see my body slumped, the bottle of Coteri cradled by my side, the symbols of the zodiac dark red with my blood. Everything else was smoke. I floated up the stairs, a wisp in a cloud.

I floated through a wine cellar that faded in and out of the smoke. When I could see it, it held more bottles than there had been when I came down through the cellars. Up past the kitchens and the servants' rooms, where other wisps bustled to and fro, and then to the ball room.

I only saw glimpses of the mansion. I felt it, I knew it

was there. What I saw was shifting, endless gray. There was a sudden moment of panic; my research had been speculative and incomplete. If I had done something wrong, I might be trapped within that smoke forever. There was the cellar, with me slumped over, bleeding on the floor. I let it go, flowed in with the rest of the smoke in the ballroom, found the pattern of the dance.

The windows were whole, the stars were bright, and when one dance ended, the next began. The Dukes of Aminde were the finest hosts in all the world.

For a timeless time, I swirled with the dancers. There was the faintest of tugs, an inclination to head in one direction. I followed. There. One of the clouds of smoke coming in through the door. We merged, that smoke and I. There was a whirling moment of impossibility. The stone chamber, my blood hot on the floor, the stars above, the scent of lilac perfume on a lady's handkerchief. Then I was a freshly minted lieutenant, attending the graduation ball at the Duke of Aminde's residence.

I hadn't come in alone. There were other academy graduates with me—Kassith, Marn, Cainder, and Sen Loroth—and there were the women with us, wearing silk and velvet. Aletha, Neris, Tirie, and gray-eyed Shirel, heart of my heart.

It was like a dream. I bowed and nodded, and walked out on the floor just as I remembered doing. As in a dream, my feet walked because they knew walking, because they remembered crossing the floor. I was in my body, but it was a mansion I did not fully inhabit. My hand was only real when I thought of it.

A breath, and it became more real. I chose to cough, and I coughed, which I had not done the first time I had passed that way. Kassith blessed my soul, and Neris gave a light laugh. Another breath and my hands were mine, my feet were mine. Slowly, I filled my body from my hair to my toes, old wine in a new bottle.

Cainder gave me a sharp look, which I returned as blandly as possible. Mine was not the only body in that stone room; I was not the only wanderer there that night. The time would come to let Cainder know that I had followed him back, and why. For now, the party was sufficient to my desires.

We swirled out onto the dance floor, Shirel in my arms. It was marvelous to be young and strong, and sure of my youth and strength. The spring in my calves, the easy power in my arms. There was a question in Shirel's eyes when we bowed to each other to finish the dance.

I raised an eyebrow and cocked my head. Shirel gave a low laugh. "It's nothing," she said. "Your promotion seems to have matured you."

"Not too mature, I hope," I said. I might hope it, but I was too mature and beyond. There had been forty years of death at the doorstep of the Aminde villa. Shirel gave a half-smile rather than saying anything, and it melted my heart. Shirel, you were the best of us. Thirty years dead, now alive and young and wearing midnight silk, with a flower on your shoulder. It was enough to make me weep, to make me laugh, to tear my hair like a madman. I did none of those. Instead, we strolled over to the table that Sen Loroth had chosen for us. I had a part to play, before the evening was out.

The floor of the great hall was surfaced with panels of semiprecious stones. Our table was near a section of floor where an onyx-maned lion was pouncing upon a deer of pale jade. Appropriate.

"A marvelous display," said Cainder, just as he had.

"Indeed," I said, just as I had. "And a charming company."

With that, we all raised our goblets and made our toasts.

To the present company; to the Duke of Aminde, who had set so fine a table; to the ladies for their beauty and charm; to the academy, in all its glory; to the army; to the navy; and to all the hosts of heaven, at once and individually.

The wine was not as good as that which I had enjoyed in the ruined villa, or perhaps my palate was cruder. Even if the drinks had been as grand as I remembered them, I had work to do that night which required a clear head. I touched the glass to my lips after each toast, but I did not drain it. Cainder was similarly abstemious, and the ladies, of course, were not expected to drink like soldiers.

We drank our wine, ate from the sweetmeat trays, and watched the dancing. The cut of the clothes and the style of the dance were like memories on old and flickering film, but it was all as real as the fleck of dirt beneath my fingernail, the clatter of silverware as honest as the chatter of a trench gun.

I did not remember everything we said that night, but I am sure that we did not precisely repeat it. My wit had been dulled by long years of little mirth and was not so lubricated as it had been that night.

The words were different but the tune was the same. We had our seats near the balcony, and while the stars through the windows were bright, our futures looked brighter. We talked, we joked, we drank, we danced. Cainder began his game of baiting me. He had done it before, but never so cleverly as he had that night. This time, it did not work as well; I had drunk less, and I was more cautious.

He knew then what I had done, I think. "An exorcism," he called out when I stumbled slightly, returning to my chair. "Our friend Andier is possessed!"

There were laughs at that, and Sen Loroth reached into his vest for his book and blade; he was the barrack priest for our class. As they came out, I could see the stone chamber, the slumped body. "Exorcisms all around," I retorted, sitting myself down. "I fear that we are all filled," I added, and picked up my goblet, "with spirits!"

That got more of a laugh than it deserved. Neris snorted her wine in a most unladylike fashion, sputtering with laughter as Marn clapped her on the back. Neris died when the war was almost over, on learning of the deaths of her sons; Marn lost his legs to a shell and grew bitter, but when I had left Limien he was still living.

"I had not thought," said Cainder, "that the Duke of Aminde would have hired performing bears."

He had said that the last time, and it had been part of his goading. I had taken it, and traded barbs, until I was the one who had said something unforgivable. The others had all thought the fight was my fault. For years afterward, I had thought it was my fault. This time, it was a misstep on his part; he was too anxious to turn the talk away from exorcisms.

I looked back at the dance floor. "Has he?" I replied. "I did not see any."

"Of course," said Cainder. "Not from your point of view."

There were smiles at that, around the table. I was never the most elegant of dancers.

"Oh," I said. "Is that what you meant?"

I picked up my goblet, considered the purple-blue color of the wine as I held it to the light. Then I tossed the wine in Cainder's face.

There was a shocked silence around the table as the wine dripped down his forehead and right cheek, staining the green of his cape, the white of his shirt.

"You have been pushing me for a fight, Cainder Strake," I said. "I do not know what offense I have given you, and I do not care. If you wish—" Shirel laid a hand on my arm, and I shrugged it off. "If you wish satisfaction, I am at your service. If you would rather not face me, crawl off to your kennel and leave us to enjoy our evening."

For a moment, I thought he might actually back down, as if he could hope to hold a commission or return to society after swallowing an insult that clear. Then he saw the others' faces and knew it was impossible. He mopped his cheek with his napkin, and stood.

"You are a peasant and a liar, Andier Evias," said Cainder. "But I praise you overmuch." He turned to the others, gave a short bow. "Gentlemen, ladies; I shan't be but a moment."

The only reply I made to his insult and his boast was to stride out to the balcony and stand, sword in one hand, cape over the other arm.

It was my old sword, the one Cainder had sent spinning off the balcony, down to the sea. Through all the years, I remembered the soft, battered wood of the handle, the delicate ironwork of the hilt, the fine line of the blade. I had used other swords in the years that followed, some better and some worse, but I had never forgotten that one, nor the warm feel of her hilt in my hand.

Duels at these affairs were common enough. A hundred and fifty graduates, proud as peacocks and unaccustomed to fine wines, could scarcely fail to provide a fight or two. As was usual, a crowd grew at the windows as we made our salutes.

The balcony was broad, with wide granite flags. Good, solid footing, and good light from the tall windows. If it were not designed for dueling, it was close enough to it that it made no difference. The air smelled of roses and clean seas, just as it had.

I lunged, he parried, countered. Before that night, I had always thought myself a better fencer than Cainder. He had the reach on me, but he was slower, and less skilled. At least he had been, until that night. That time, he had toyed with me, demonstrating technique after technique, style after style. This time, he came at me full bore, intending the duel to end on the first pass.

It didn't. Perhaps I overcorrected by a hair, unused to a body so strong and so fast. But I had forty years of experience since that night, forty years of hard fighting. His first pass was a saber-man's trick, where the edge cuts inward as the sword withdraws. I had fought with the cavalry during the peninsular campaign. I sidestepped, disengaged, and went after his throat.

I was better than I had been, but Cainder was as good as I remembered. He parried and withdrew, and it was too soon to press.

"It's been a long time," I said.

"Has it?" asked Cainder. "We sparred last week."

"There is a scar over your left eye," I said. "When last we fought, I gave you that." There was no scar, but the muscle near his eyebrow was tensed, as though he had been cut there. He had been better than me, that night, but he had not emerged unmarked.

"Ah," he said. "I guessed that something like this had happened. Do you intend—" and then he lunged suddenly, hoping that I had been distracted.

I had not. I caught the tip of his blade with my cloak and came across with my sword. He moved out of the way, redirected my blade with his hand, and tried to break my nose with his forehead. I stepped away, out of range, brought my sword back into line. There was blood on my blade, and on the palm of his hand.

"—to take my part?" continued Cainder.

"I intend to kill you," I said.

He laughed. "It is good to be ambitious," he said. "But you cannot imagine how skilled I am, how many times I have passed this way."

"Once," I said. "You've been dead five years; not enough time to repeat the trick."

"Wrong," he replied, and attacked, a crescendo of high thrusts. Which meant that he was going to attack low. I kept his blade away, waited. But when the attack did come, it was so pure and fast he nearly skewered my leg.

His cape knocked my counter aside and he was back out, beyond my range. "I lived," he said, "after the first time we attended this ball, and I learned why the Aminde were called the merry suicides. Then I came back, and lived my life through a second time. And what do you think I did, after that? I lived, and came—"

I caught him with a springing, full-out lunge. He had thought my wound worse than it was. I had read that in his stance. He got his cape-hand up, but my blade bit deeply into his arm. "Once or five times," I said. "You will die here."

"Five." He laughed, and his sword was a silver blur. "Five thousand? Countless numbers, different every time, fresh every time. You will never see it, but this endless life is better than you can imagine."

He pressed me hard, almost too hard, but he was quick enough to leap back when I tried a knife-fighter's counter. We stood and faced each other, just as we had. I was facing the dance hall, with the balcony a long, cold drop to my back. There was an excited flush in Tirie's face, and Shirel was standing straight and pale. Kassith was standing next to her, making no attempt to conceal his astonishment. Neither Cainder nor I had been this good before.

"The snake swallowing its tail," I said. "But what happens when you crush the snake?"

"It bites you," he replied, and there was another passage of arms. Neither of us was caught, but it was not so pure as it had been. I was cut in my leg, he was hurt in his arm. I could not say which of us would fail first from those wounds. For the moment, both of our swords were held straight, both our stances loose and strong.

"You don't have to do this," he said. "There are worlds enough for the both of us."

"There is one world," I said. "And you destroyed it."

"Don't be a damned fool," said Cainder, and for the first time there was real emotion in his voice. "There had to be a war so that I could get the mansion. There always has to be a war. Sometimes I'm on one side, sometimes I'm on the other. Once, it only lasted a week. But there has to be a war."

He thrust, I parried, and then he came on like a storm, driving me back towards the edge of the balcony. This time, I noticed a curious hesitation on his part when I had left two possible openings. I didn't think about it long; I stepped out of the way of his blade, and came in with an elegant thrust at the center of his body. It was a hit, a good one, but it was deflected by a rib. He leapt back, gaining a few feet of space.

"Please," he said, and, "You'll see," and, "It's not," all at once.

I saw what was happening; I laughed, and it wasn't a pleasant laugh.

"I broke your circle," I said. "Each time, now, you come up against me and lose. All your futures are collapsing into now."

We had changed our positions during that exchange. Now his back was to the balcony, and mine was to the villa's windows; he inched back, was stopped by the marble balusters.

He tried to reply, but he tried to say so many things that nothing came out. "You know," I said, walking toward him, "it is a long drop from this balcony to the sea. It shattered my leg, and crushed my ribs, but I lived. If you had tried for it sooner, maybe. If you had refrained from baiting me, maybe.

If you had not started the war, maybe you would have found another way into the chamber of the zodiac in the villa of the Dukes of Aminde. In fact, if you hadn't tried so hard to conceal your method, I would not have known where to look. But you held on too tight, and for too long. It all ends now."

Cainder's sword beat at mine, feebly. He was trying to talk, he was trying to thrust, he was trying to throw himself over the balcony, all at once. There was blood coming from his eyes, blood coming from his nose and mouth. He collapsed, his head hitting the balcony railing. I had seen death often enough to know that he was not dead; he was trapped, all the endless copies of Cainder Strake were trapped there, all staring out at me through bloody eyes, trying to do so many things at once that it had broken his body.

I stepped forward and stabbed him through the throat, so that he drowned on his blood. Sen Loroth had died that way, during the first siege of Limien. I looked up as Cainder died. The lights of Limien brightened the horizon, and all across the bay the lanterns of the night fishermen winked in the swell like flowers nodding their heads in a breeze.

Then I turned to face my friends as they came out to the balcony. "What happened?" asked Kassith.

"He tried to fake an epileptic fit," I said, cleaning my sword.

"Really," said Shirel. "What happened? What has been happening all night?"

I could answer. I could lie, or I could tell her the truth. When we grew old, we could find our way back to that secret cellar of the Aminde, and return together to this night. Live eternally, love eternally, through an infinite variation of futures.

I had come back to that night to stop Cainder, to right a wrong. I could not say what would happen if I tried to leave. Perhaps I would vanish like a cloud of smoke when a clean wind blows. Perhaps not. I pulled away, though my body held me tight, despite the joy in tired muscles, the glory of sweat and pain, despite the pale arch of Shirel's shoulders. I saw myself stagger as I left, my friends rushing to my aid. I saw myself stand, shake my head, look dazed.

Then I was smoke amidst smoke as I made my way through the kitchens where the staff were cleaning pots, and chuckling at jokes I could not hear, back down the long road to my other self, who was still bleeding weakly on the floor of the zodiac chamber.

The cut hurt scarcely at all; I put a field dressing on it. A long pull at the wine, to have something red flowing through my veins. The cut didn't hurt, but going back to that old body hurt in ways that I had forgotten. The old scars, the old aches, the hitch in my breathing. I had not vanished. Cainder's corpse was there with me, still wearing the uniform of the Captain of Limien, so it seemed that the world had not changed.

There was one of the old Eastern cigarettes left in the packet. I lit it. It would be some years before we were importing tobacco again, proper tobacco. For the moment, the one I had was enough.

After the cigarette was done, I stood and looked down at the symbols of the constellations, rust-red with my blood and with the other blood that had been spilled into them, each firmly placed in its position in the snake of the galaxy. And there was the Sister Star, a ruby of blood in the galaxy's eye. I flicked my cigarette butt into it and went back up into the ruined villa.

I could have had a sort of eternity. It would have ruined me, as surely as it had ruined Cainder. How long could I keep my friends, if I could see them dead and returned to life, dead and returned to life? How long would it be before I stopped seeing people and started seeing only toys, to be taken out of the box fresh when I wanted to play a new game?

I had hoped to change the past, but I hadn't; the villa was in the same state of ruin as it had been when I came in. I couldn't say what happened to all the other worlds that Cainder Strake had shaped, after I killed him. Perhaps they had fallen apart like dreams upon waking. The one that I returned to was solid enough, so it seemed more likely that they all continued as they were. In each world, Cainder lived, committed suicide in the zodiac chamber, and then died by my blade. Now they were all free to go on as best they could, and Cainder Strake would shape no more worlds.

Somewhere, a younger Andier Evias was trying to explain what he would never be able to explain. I had freed that younger self from the dead hand of Cainder, and from my own scarred and war-weary soul. Best of luck to him, best of luck to Shirel, best of luck to all the young men and women in that villa that night. A man cannot change his past, but I had freed his future. I've done what I could for you, Lieutenant Andier. Live and love, fail and learn, find your own scars. Drink the midnight wine, wherever you are. Smell the clean sea air and roses, look at stars as bright as your future.

It was still a few hours before sundown, so I sat myself beside one of the drifts of paper and started making order of them. When I was done, I'd sleep in the ruins, and I'd meet dawn and the boatsman down by that little wooden quay. The new government had its problems, but I would do what I could for it. I was not yet dead, and I still had work to do.

If the Stars Reverse their Courses, if the Rivers Run Back from the Sea first appeared in The Magazine of Fantasy & Science Fiction in November, 2012.

Alter S. Reiss is an archaeologist and writer who lives in Jerusalem with his wife Naomi and their son Uriel. He likes good books, bad movies, and old time radio shows. His short fiction has appeared in Strange Horizons, Tor.com and elsewhere, and his first longer work, Sunset Mantle, came out from the Tor.com imprint in 2015.

A Switch in Time
by David Steffen

Fred plugged his ears in an attempt to block out the ceaseless noise. An explosion momentarily drowned out the distant chatter of gunfire and shook a fresh cloud of plaster dust from the ceiling inches from Fred's face. Why oh why did he have to choose the top bunk? As he stared up at the ceiling, Fred composed a list of the terrible things he would do to the makers of *Call of Duty* if he ever met them in person.

He pounded the wall three times with his fist, more to vent his anger than in hopes of stopping the noise. Nothing he did ever made any difference. Unlike the stupid sons of bitches next door, he had to go to work in the morning. Running a cash register at the Shell station was unpleasant enough without fighting to stay awake throughout the day. After his shift he had to work on a research paper for Political Science. As if that weren't enough, it was also his first anniversary with Vicki and he'd promised to take her out to eat. Of all days he couldn't afford a nap tomorrow.

The noise disappeared completely, and he wondered for a moment if he'd lost his hearing. But no, a hand against the wall confirmed that there was no rumble. Had they actually listened to him? He glanced at the clock: half past one. If he fell asleep right now, he could get four and a half hours. He closed his eyes and tried to keep his breaths slow and steady despite his pounding heart.

An explosion shattered the silence, louder than ever. His head snapped up, smashing against the ceiling. He put his hand to his forehead, and it came away bloody.

That was the last straw. He would get those bastards to

shut up, no matter what he had to do. He climbed down off the bunk. He was wearing only his boxers and he could feel the blood running down his face, but he didn't care. Maybe the sight of blood would register in their tiny brains where nothing else made any difference. The machine guns began to fire again.

And there was his roommate Stu sprawled over the lower bunk, drool running down his face, oblivious to the noise. How did he sleep through this?

Fred flung his door open, and standing outside, waiting expectantly, was a large balding man in a blue suit. He looked familiar.

"Who the hell are you?" Fred demanded. He could feel his anger ebb away from sheer surprise.

"That's not important right now." The man's voice was smooth and assured, an oily politician voice that raised Fred's hackles. "What is important, no, absolutely vital, is that you do not confront your neighbor."

"What? Why? How do you know about that?"

While Fred reeled in confusion, the man stepped past him into the room. He gently removed Fred's hand from the door and closed it. The room shook with another explosion.

"I know more than you can imagine. I wish I could tell you everything, but that would only make matters worse. But I can tell you this: every action has a reaction, and not always equal and opposite. An avalanche begins with the shift of a single pebble. An empire can crumble under the weight of a song."

"Fine, fine, whatever, I don't care. Just get out of my room!"

The man opened his mouth to speak, but just at that moment, the noise from next door stopped. Fred put up a hand to silence him. Despite the intrusion, he couldn't help grinning like an idiot. "Do you hear that? Finally, I can get some sleep."

The man in the suit opened his mouth to speak again, but the door to the hallway swung open forcefully, knocking him aside. In stepped another man dressed all in black, a ski mask covering his face. He locked the door behind himself.

"Fred?" His voice was gruff, deep. "Thank God I made it in time. Tonight a man in a suit is going to push his way in here. Whatever you do, don't—"

"Who are you?" the man in the suit said.

"Oh shit." The man in black glanced at his watch. "Damned watch stopped again." He gestured at the man in the suit. "Fred, this man is you from the future. He's here to change what happens."

Fred looked more closely at him. So that was why the man looked so familiar. "Is that true?" He'd really let himself go.

The man in the suit said "I can neither confirm nor deny—"

The man in black pushed the man in the suit. "Can it, fatty. Fred, he's here because he's trying to prevent a war."

"What—" Fred began.

"I don't—" the man in the suit tried to cut in.

"He has the right to know!" the man in black shouted at the man in the suit. "If you would've just told me the truth when you came back to change things, maybe everything wouldn't have gone wrong. Fred, this man means well. He is here to prevent World War III, and they've calculated that the trigger point of the war happens at this space and time, when you go next door to confront your neighbor. But he's in over his head. Time machines are still just prototypes and his people are meddling without understanding the consequences."

"A war?" That was ridiculous! Wasn't it?

Fred turned away reflexively from a bright flash of light

in the center of the room. At the same time he heard a sound not unlike a cork popping free of a bottle. When Fred looked again, there was a girl in bright green coveralls staring at him. She looked about twelve years old, with short purple hair that was missing clumps. Her mouth moved constantly, smacking her chewing gum.

"Who the hell are you?" the man in black demanded.

"Let me guess," Fred said. "You're from the future?"

"Yup!" she said, and blew a bubble.

The man in the suit gestured at her hair. "What's wrong in your future? Nuclear fallout?"

She rolled her eyes. "Nope! It's the baffest 'do. If you don't show scalp, you're unworthy to converse, suboptimal to the power of S."

Fred was the first to break the silence. "What do you want then?" he snapped.

"Whoa, Pop! Minus one for brusqueness!" She shouted, her face squinching up with anger. "Jesus on a cracker, I can't believe you spawned me! I'm scratching a paper for history, and I clacked on the title 'My Dad the Hero' but if you're going to be obtuse I'll just go snag Shakespeare like everyone else." She touched hand to wrist and with another pop and a flash she was gone.

They all stood there for a moment, no one speaking a word.

The man in the suit was the first to break the silence. "Fred, I'm sure this is overwhelming for you. Time travel is distressing at the best of times—"

The phone rang. Fred held up his hand to shush them.

"Hello?"

"208, we've received several noise complaints about raised voices coming from your room. We shouldn't have to remind you that this is, first and foremost, an academic institution. You might be here to party, but please respect your more scholarly peers. Understood?"

"Uh... yes."

"If you don't keep it down, there will be consequences. You have been warned."

Fred moved his mouth, but could think of nothing to say that wouldn't involve yelled obscenities. So he hung up. He tried to put the ridiculous phone call out of his mind and turned back to the intruders.

"Why should I listen to you? You broke into my room wearing a ski mask. Why shouldn't I listen to my older self? I must have my best interests in mind."

The man in black sighed. "You're not going to want to see this, but I suppose there's no other way." He pulled the ski mask off, to show another face that he recognized as being a variation of his own, but the nose had flattened against his face and the skin was covered in green scales. His hair only grew in thin, sickly patches, where it hadn't gone away entirely. "This is the result of your changes in the timeline. You prevent international war but end up causing an interstellar war instead. The Krudgegar conquered the Earth in a day, and for the last two years have been turning us into something different. Soon we won't have any trace of humanity left. This was a one way trip using the last of our resources. It was too late to do anything in the future, but if you do exactly as I say, you can prevent it from ever happening."

"How do you know your changes will work any better than mine?" the man in the suit said. "What if you just make things worse?"

"Worse? The future can't get any worse. Humans are extinct! Your wars must be going well for you." He fingered the other man's lapel. "They can certainly afford to dress you up nice."

"This isn't about money!" He shoved the man in black.

"It's about survival!" The man in black shoved him back, both apparently forgetting about Fred.

"It's about–" the man in the suit began, but he was interrupted by a flash of light from the window.

Outside, a small blonde man in a Hawaiian shirt and khaki shorts crouched on the window ledge, peering through at them. He looked at the screen on the back of his camera, and then gave them two thumbs up. And, with no hands left to keep his balance, he tipped, eyes wide, and fell backward off the side of the building.

"Who was that?" Fred asked.

"No clue," the man in black said.

"Time tourist," the man in the suit said. "Time machines must become consumer products some day, at least in some possible future. God help us all."

"I suppose I should make sure he's okay." Fred unlocked the door and opened it.

The moment he opened the door, a loud chatter of voices assaulted him. People packed the hallway from wall to wall. Most of them were alternate future Freds, fat or muscular, pale or tan, old or young. He even saw a robot near the back with an antenna sticking out of its head. They all waved to grab his attention and shouted out their advice.

"Drop out of college!"

"Look both ways before crossing the street!"

"Don't eat pork!"

"Propose to Vicki!"

He slammed the door shut in their faces. "Well, then. I'm going to lay down. It's time for you two to leave."

"But–"

"But–"

Fred was proud at how cool his voice sounded, while his stomach boiled and his heart hammered in his ribcage. "You're going to leave. The hallway's blocked, but the

227

window is free. You can jump, or I can throw you."

The older Freds exchanged a knowing glance. The man in black opened the window and jumped out without another word. The man in the suit straddled the sill clumsily, apparently trying to preserve his dignity even as he made his awkward way out of the window.

"Get out!" Fred yelled, and the man in the suit overbalanced, tumbling out the window. Fred slammed the window shut.

The babble of voices in the hallway continued to rise in volume, growing louder and louder as the night went on. Fists pounded on his door every few seconds, mixed with shouted demands.

Fred stared at the ceiling, willing himself to lose consciousness, but his body stubbornly refused to listen. If only he could sleep through anything like Stu could. Finally the noise died down bit by bit and his eyes slipped shut–just as the alarm clock shrieked out its morning call. He slapped it once. One snooze couldn't hurt.

In what seemed like mere moments later, the alarm blared and he slapped it off again.

"Jesus Christ, will you shut that damned thing off!" Stu's voice called from the lower bunk. "Some of us are trying to get some sleep!"

Grumbling and bleary-eyed, Fred hauled himself out of bed, and got dressed for work. He spent the morning in a sleepy haze, using all of his effort just to keep his eyes open. He downed coffee after coffee and stayed on his feet, hopping from foot to foot.

While he was grabbing a quick bite to eat, the door chimed and he looked up to see the man in black entering, wearing the ski mask again.

"Get out of here!"

"I just want to help."

"I don't care. I'm dead tired and I'm going to fail my test because of your so-called help."

The man in black raised his hands defensively. "You're right, you're right. I'm sorry. I shouldn't have gotten worked up like I did, but that guy just irks me, you know? So self-righteous, so certain his way is the right way. He's the reason I've got scales on my ass. My brain's going next. I saw a gecko the other day and I thought it had a sexy tail. A gecko! Anyway, I'm sorry."

Fred said nothing, hoping he'd go away.

"I shouldn't have come to you. Of all people, I should've known it wouldn't work. But I thought you'd want to know I figured out a way to change things."

Fred's heart raced. "What did you do? Is Vicki okay?"

"Relax, kid. Vicki's fine. I didn't hurt anybody. Well, nobody that exists yet, anyway."

"So what did you do?"

"I said some things to Vicki about you so the two of you won't likely conceive a child tonight."

"What!" Fred spluttered. "We've never–!"

"Well, you would've tonight. It would've been beautiful. And you would've made little baby Brayden, who'd be the lead scientist on the team that sent the signal into space that attracted the Krudgegar. He was a good kid, but a little nutty." The man in black slapped him on the back. "I don't know what your future will be like, kid, but just be happy you won't end up like me."

He turned and walked out of the store. Just as he did, a police car screeched into the lot, lights flashing but no sirens. Three others followed close behind. Half a dozen cops hopped out and aimed their guns at the man in black.

"Freeze!"

After they'd cuffed and hauled away the man in black, one of the officers asked Fred a few questions. He was a tall, thin man with a salt and pepper pushbroom mustache and a deep voice.

"Do you know the suspect?"

"Yeah, I do. Uh, I mean, as well as I could since I just met him last night."

"Did he threaten you or draw a weapon?"

"No."

"He didn't try to rob the store?"

"No, he just wanted to talk."

"About what?"

Fred's mind raced, trying to come up with something, anything, that didn't sound completely insane.

"Well?"

"He just, uh, he just wanted to sell me some timeshares."

The cop's eyes narrowed a bit. "In a ski mask?"

Fred swallowed. "Yeah."

"You're sure that's the statement you want on the record? Whether you're involved or not, your future will be smoother if you tell me the truth."

Fred nodded quickly.

"Uh huh. Mind if I see your ID, and get some contact information? I might need to follow up with you." Fred wrote his phone number on receipt paper and gave it to the cop with his license.

Finally the evening shift arrived just as the cops left. The moment he punched out he dialed Vicki. Straight to voice mail. He left a message, and cursed. He stopped by her apartment. No one answered the door.

He'd told her he'd meet her at their favorite Italian restaurant. It was early, but maybe he'd find her there. He sped across town and arrived forty-five minutes before their reservation. The minutes crawled by, and finally they seated him.

He waited, tapping his foot nervously. And waited. And

waited. He tried her phone twice more, with no better luck. Two hours later he gave up, and went back to the dorm. Stu was leaving, wearing his typical holey jeans and a t-shirt with an ad for The Clash.

"Dude," Stu said, "what did you say to Vicki? She was bawling! I asked her what was wrong, and she just about bit my head off. Said that she hoped you burned in Hell."

Fred felt a rush of relief that she was alive mingled with anger at the Fred in black for screwing everything up. Fred didn't feel up to speaking, so he shrugged and shook his head and headed into the dorm, stumbled in, and climbed up his bunk to collapse. There were two envelopes on his bed, apparently left there by Stu. Fred groaned.

The first one was from the dean of students and marked "Urgent!" He tore the envelope open:

Dear Mr. Frederick Vogel,

We have received reports of loud noise, excessive drinking, suspicious costume play, and rumors of lewd acts being performed in public spaces (that last allegation is admittedly unproven, but combined with the other accusations they paint quite a picture, don't you think?), all associated with your particular dorm room and to your person in particular.

The administration has gone above and beyond the call of duty trying to resolve these conflicts amicably, but it seems that our attempts have fallen on deaf ears. The time has come to escalate our response.

Due to your prolonged incursions with utter disregard to campus peace-keeping provisions, your status as a registered student has been revoked, and you must leave campus within forty-eight hours and never return. You are a destructive presence on campus, not only a danger to yourself, but to everyone around you, and this action is the best consequence for all involved.

We regret to inform you that the final add/drop day has passed so we will be unable to issue you a refund. Rest assured that this decision was reached only after careful thought and deliberation. We tried to give you the benefit of the doubt, but you pushed the boundary one too many times. We have the best interest of all of our students in mind. For the sake of your own future, we advise that you seek professional help.

We cannot in good conscience omit this from your permanent record. Every school has the right to know about this sort of unstable history in students when considering applicants. As they say, one bad apple spoils the bunch! Be advised, as well, that if you choose to reproduce, your offspring had best seek their education elsewhere. One bad apple doesn't fall far from the tree, and suchforth.

We wish you the best in all your future endeavors.

Best wishes,
Samuel Wentworth, Dean of Students

Fred was too exhausted to be surprised or angry, so he looked at the second envelope. This one had no sending or return address marked on it, only one word, written in red marker: "FRED."

Inside was a folded photocopy of a textbook page, showing portraits of all of the Presidents of the United States going from George Washington to the present day and further, to unfamiliar faces with future dates. One of the photos near the bottom was circled in red. It was a photo of Fred with wings of gray at his temples.

Written below the photo: "You can do great things! Stay in school! Sincerely, Fred."

David Steffen is a writer, editor, and publisher. He edits Diabolical Plots and runs The Submission Grinder, a tool for writers, and he is the publisher of the Long List Anthology. You can find his fiction at venues like Escape Pod, Daily Science Fiction, and AE. David suspects that he is the only person who reads author biographies all the way to the end but he is being a sport and writing all the words.

The Time Traveler's Accountant
by John A. Frochio

Every time Andy Freeman came to visit me, he was a different man. Of course, from his point of view, I was a different accountant.

Who really changed? Maybe both of us. Maybe neither. He said that everything was relative. Maybe it was only the world around us that changed.

Of course, this happened only when he traveled to the past. He told me he abhorred traveling into the future. He was afraid that he would learn when he would die, or he would see terrible things that he didn't want to know about. He would try to change things to fix the future and he would only make it worse. It was too unpredictable. It was too frustrating. So he stopped going forward. But he did find he could make little tweaks and adjustments in the past and these changes would be more manageable. So that was how he lived his life, on a pendulum that went back but not forth.

According to Andy, very few had this talent. He personally only knew one other, Fred Dawson. Fred lived on the West Coast, while Andy lived here in Pittsburgh, Pennsylvania. Andy never spoke much about him. I assumed he didn't come in contact with him very often. Or maybe time travelers just didn't like to mingle with one another. Again, I don't know.

I didn't know much about the life of time travelers, and I really didn't want to know. It made my brain hurt to think about it.

Andy once told me about an encounter he had with Fred. When Andy first met Fred, they would hang out in different past eras to share common experiences. But they found they were often critical of one another's experiences. At their last planned meeting, Andy chided Fred for his interference with the development of a popular product of the 1970's. I hadn't heard of it.

"Of course not," Andy told me. "Fred screwed the whole thing up. We had a big fight about it."

Andy said there was no messing around with the past like that! Time travelers knew the potential dangers of their talent. There was an implicit understanding among them that they would keep their interventions to an absolute minimum and only of a personal nature. Fred should have known better! Andy called Fred a fool, a loose cannon, and other less kindly names.

I once asked Andy how his wife handled his journeys through time. I'd met her on a couple of occasions, and she seemed quite pleasant and contented. She was an attractive redhead, tall, slim, well-dressed and soft-spoken.

"It's great with Audrey," he told me. "She understands me. She says it's never boring with me."

He laughed heartily.

I wanted to say, "I find that hard to believe." But I kept it to myself.

On this particular occasion, he visited me late in the afternoon a week before Christmas. It was my last business day before I would be closed for the holidays. As usual, he dropped in unannounced. His hair was dark and a bit shaggy, poured down to his neckline. His skin was deeply tanned–unusual for this time of year. He was uncharacteristically disheveled in a red plaid shirt, worn out jeans and old boots covered with snow, which he proceeded to pound vigorously onto my throw rug.

I looked up from my array of monitors and frowned. "I

don't have much time for you, Andy," I told him. "It's my last day before the holidays and I have to get out of here. We're going away for a couple weeks."

"That's great, Bill. To where am I funding your little getaway?"

"You're not my only client." I didn't have any patience for his humorless, snide remarks. "Anyway, we're going down to Tampa, Florida to spend the holidays with my wife's brother and family."

"It's nice there this time of year. I bet everyone's excited about it – your wife, um, Maggie, and your girls, uh, I forget their names."

"Alicia and Chelsea."

"How old are they now?"

"Twelve and ten."

"Well, I hope you have a great time. Everyone deserves a break from life's relentless and choppy timestream. I just stopped by to check on my accounts real quick. Just in and out. I won't take up much of your time."

I popped up his accounts. He had a mix of IRAs, Roth IRAs, and Annuities, with a healthy balance of Stocks, Bonds and Money Market accounts. Nothing out of the ordinary, nothing too risky. The numbers were significantly higher since the last time I checked. Not surprising for Andy's accounts, however. I read off the bottom line numbers and printed out the summary pages.

He snatched the hardcopies from my printer.

"Thanks, Bill." He stared at them for a moment. Then he jumped as though he had been startled. He looked up at me as though I had just appeared out of nowhere. "Yes, thanks, Bill. I guess I'll see you next year, at tax time."

He left in a hurry.

I didn't think any more about Andy after that. I had a vacation on my mind.

The Christmas and New Year's holidays came and went. We enjoyed the time we spent, but as usual, the time went fast. We returned from vacation completely exhausted.

And now I was back in my office (it seemed like I never left these dismal walls) trying to get myself motivated into reading up on the new tax laws. Every year brought significant and confusing changes.

With no appointments my first day back, I was alone with my tedious reading. Unsurprisingly, my mind began to drift.

In my reverie I was looking into a large, floating mirror, admiring my tall, lean frame, my sharp features, my dark piercing eyes and my infectious (I'm told) tilted smile. For an accountant, frequently bound to his desk and his numbers, I kept myself fairly active and in good physical condition. I observed that my wife and daughters were playing a table game—it was Monopoly. A moment later Chandra—no, not Chandra; no, wait, that's right—began jumping up and down, shouting, "I'm rich! I'm rich!" Then she pounded the table and play money flew everywhere. Pounding and shouting, pounding and shouting...

The pounding roused me from my daydream.

Someone was pounding on my door.

It occurred to me that I had locked my door earlier so I would not be disturbed. This obviously did not dissuade my current visitor.

I got up and opened the door. In walked Andy—who else? He looked more ragged than usual, his normally wavy blonde hair hanging limp, his pale skin covered with grime, his slim frame shaky. He was, ironically, dressed well in a loose, cool blue velvet shirt, neatly pressed black dress pants and polished black dress shoes. When he entered, he looked around like he was searching for something. Or someone.

"What is it, my time wandering friend?"

"Check my accounts, Bill. Check them now!" Then, more meekly, "Please."

He collapsed into a chair.

Wordlessly, I went to my computer and accessed his accounts. My jaw dropped.

"My God, Andy. You're broke. Zero balances everywhere."

"That's what I was afraid of," he said. His voice was calmer now, as though he was completely resigned to his dire situation.

"How could this happen? You were doing so well, extraordinarily well."

"I had plans. Everything was in place. But I didn't expect… my rival, Fred… "

I assumed Andy was referring to Fred Dawson, the "rogue time traveler," as Andy called him. Andy always said Fred had the kind of reputation that gave time travelers a bad name.

"Fred Dawson? What did he do?"

"I think he's been shadowing me for a long time, putting in place those events and people that would cause the right businesses to fail at the right time. The right time for him. The wrong time for me. I should have been more wary of the bastard."

"Well, I better start the bankruptcy procedures."

He stood up, still shaky.

"I can fix this. I can undo the damage."

He went to the door, then stopped and turned. "Just in case I can't fix this, make sure Audrey is taken care of."

He tossed me something. I caught it. I looked it over. It was a very rare gold coin, certainly worth quite a bit.

"Certainly."

"Thanks," he said. He left.

That evening and well into the night, we experienced one of the worst electrical storms I could remember. The lightning strikes were spectacular and frightening. I felt surges of electricity pass through my body. We all huddled in the master bedroom until the storms finally subsided.

Very odd for January in Pennsylvania, I thought. We eventually settled down into a sleep as deep as death.

The next morning, Audrey came into my office to check her accounts. I checked and told her they looked fine. I said there was no need to make any adjustments.

She thanked me. I looked her over. Her long blonde hair and hourglass figure were striking as usual, her voice strong and self-assured.

As she stood to leave, she noticed the new portrait of my family on my desk. The picture was taken over the Christmas holidays when we were in North Carolina with my relatives. She commented on how good-looking my boys were getting.

I asked her how Fred was doing.

"Fine," she said. "Not doing much traveling anymore. Which is fine by me."

Audrey seemed much happier, more content. I was happy for her.

After she left, I opened my desk drawer and picked up the sealed envelope with Audrey's name on it. I again read those mysterious words scrawled in my hand-writing, "For Audrey Dawson in the Event of an Emergency."

I wondered if there would ever come a time when I would need to hand that envelope to her.

John Frochio grew up and still lives among the rolling hills of Western Pennsylvania. For a living, he develops and installs computer automation systems for steel mills. He has had stories published in Triangulation 2003 & Triangulation: Parch (2014), Interstellar Fiction, Beyond Science Fiction, Twilight Times, Aurora Wolf, Liquid Imagination and Kraxon Magazine, as well as general fiction novel Roots of a Priest (with Ken Bowers, 2007, Booklocker) and sf&f collection Large and Small Wonders (2012, Byrne Publishing). His wife Connie, a retired nurse, and his daughter Toni, a flight attendant, have bravely put up with his strange ways for many years.

Absolute Pony
  by Alisa Alering

Marko set the personal intergalactic recreational pod (PIRP) coordinates for Mon-Mon, and switched out of the auto-nav screen. Several kiloparsecs later, he called up the sound library and scrolled his fingers over the screen, looking for just the right song.

Ah, yes—Absolute Pony's "Up Your Neo-Fascist Noodle." Classic, Marko thought. Reena is going to love this one. He hit Play and cranked up the volume.

"Ugh. Not that song again, Marko. Are you trying to drive me crazy?" Reena was sitting at the space-saving dinette at the other end of the PIRP, legs curled under her. She looked up from her computational physics game, a line creasing the skin above her eyes.

"What are you talking about? This is our song. Don't you remember?" Marko sang along, smacking time on his knee with his hand: "*Up your, up your...*"

"No, that's *your* song," Reena said, closing her console. "*My* favorite song is 'Strangers in a Crystal Sea,' by The Dippity Boo."

Marko rolled his eyes. "Analog strings and pretty boys in eyeliner."

"I happen to like strings and pretty boys in eyeliner," Reena said.

Marko whirled around in the captain's chair and mimed strumming a lute. He sang: "*I'm so pretty, so pret-ty. I'm a pretty little boy.*"

Reena shoved away from the table. "There's nothing wrong with The Dippity Boo. You think your music is superior because they build their own instruments out of

241

recycled off-world mining equipment. Very manly. I guess it's no coincidence that they sound like a re-genned mastodon with twelve thousand years of constipation."

"Whoa." Marko held out his hands. "What's got into you?" She had been like this ever since their trip began, and he couldn't understand it.

"Into me?" Reena said.

"You're the one who said we should sell up and go traveling. But you don't seem to be enjoying it. You haven't had a good word to say since we left home."

"I'm sorry," she said. "I'm excited about the trip, just not about revisiting the past at every opportunity."

"You used to love Absolute Pony. I thought it would remind us of the good times."

"They were good times. But I want us to move forward and make new memories."

Marko wondered if she was trying to say that she was bored with him. Twelve years of marriage was a long time. "Like what?"

"Like back when we were at the supply station. I saw that display for Alligator Planet—"

"Alligator Planet is a tourist trap," Marko said.

"See! This is exactly what I'm talking about. I don't care if it's a tourist trap—I wanted to see it."

"But we've dreamed about visiting Mon-Mon for years. We were going to go on our honeymoon, and we couldn't afford it. Don't you want to go anymore?"

"Yes. I just want—"

The ship's alarm blared, cutting through their conversation.

"What's that?" Reena grabbed Marko's hand.

"I'm not sure." Marko swiveled to the controls. "Probably just a false alarm." He wouldn't be surprised if the guy at PIRP World had sold them a lemon. Like that weird upgrade option he had used to sweeten Marko into the sale at the last minute. Wrong Turn Regulator, my left elbow, Marko thought. It was just your usual spatial positioning manifold wrapped in a fancy name. It was a given that all pod salesmen were crooks, but Marko had dismissed that knowledge in his hope that this trip would give him and Reena a chance to rekindle their romance.

"There's nothing to worry about, we're a million miles from...." Marko scanned the security views. That's odd, he thought. Something was blipping on the radar.

Wham! The ship rocked sideways, and Marko fell against the console.

Reena clung to the table. "That felt like an awfully big nothing."

She pulled up the exterior cams on her portable console. "A Narteen pirate ship. They're only supposed to be in the Tilbassian sector - we're miles from...." Reena ran to the captain's console and reached over Marko's shoulder for the navigation, flipping the screens. "Marko, what the hell have you been doing? We're right in the Tilbassian hot zone for pirate attacks."

The ship jolted again as the pirates engaged their boarding mechanism.

"Marko!" Reena shouted.

But Marko wasn't listening. He was on his knees under the captain's console, looking for the Wrong Turn panel. It was pretty much their only hope. He pulled off the factory seal and tried to make sense of the Regulator. It had a flimsy vertical slider, marked in increments, and a big blue button labeled 'CORRECT'. He adjusted the slider, worried that it was going to snap off in his hands. How was he supposed to know how big a correction they needed? He looked over his shoulder. Reena was screaming. The pirates were boarding— he could see the tip of a hairy sword, and the pickle-shaped helmets.

Marko blinked. He was sitting in the captain's chair. His hands were on the controls, flicking through the music files. "Up Your Neo-Fascist Noodle" by Absolute Pony was highlighted. Now, there was a great song, Marko thought. His finger twitched over the screen.

Then he remembered. He spun around in his chair, but Reena was at the dinette, bent over her computations on the portable console, undisturbed. No sign of any pirates. He called the nav screen into the foreground and checked the coordinates. They were headed straight for the Tilbassian sector. The WTR had actually worked—they had escaped the pirates. Marko double-checked the pod's auto-nav against the old-fashioned calculation logs, found the error, manually re-set the course for Mon-Mon, and closed out.

The music library foregrounded again, Absolute Pony highlighted. Reena was wrong, Marko thought. He remembered their meeting clearly: he had been in the Union cafeteria, with his identity set on public, sharing his playlist. Reena had broadcast that she was <really into guys who liked Absolute Pony.> He thought this was meant for him, but he wasn't sure, so he cued another Absolute Pony song—"Neo-Fascist Noodle," in fact—and looked casually around the lounge, hoping that the pretty girl in the manic-chic outfit sitting in the corner was the one who had messaged. And then she got up, and walked towards him.

Reena had loved "Neo-Fascist Noodle" as much as he did. They had listened to Absolute Pony songs almost non-stop the whole first year they were dating. If he told her this whole story, Marko thought, she'd have to admit she remembered. He was so tempted—his fingers hovered over the screen. At the last minute, he scrolled and made a different selection.

Twenty minutes later, the gentle *ba-dum-bim* of a strummed lute drifted gently around the bed.

"That was wonderful, darling." Reena lay back on the pillow, the sheets falling away from her bare shoulder.

Marko kissed her nose.

"Isn't traveling so much fun? I almost don't want to arrive." Reena snuggled against Marko. She hummed along with The Dippity Boo, streaming through the PIRP's embedded speakers on repeat.

"This is the best song ever," she said. "I love 'Strangers in a Crystal Sea.'"

"Me, too," Marko said. His stomach rumbled.

Reena rolled over, her hair tumbling loose around her face. "You hungry, sweetie? How about some scrambled eggs and a bit of coffee cake?"

"Sounds fantastic," Marko agreed.

Reena pulled on her robe and padded over to the little galley.

Marko let a puff of air escape from his lips. They were back on track, he thought. Being squeezed together in the PIRP was a new environment—there was bound to be an adjustment period. He watched Reena open the pod-sized fridge and reach inside. This was his wonderful wife, he thought, and she was his again. He couldn't resist: he got out of bed, naked, and went over and wrapped both arms around her waist.

Reena shrugged him off, holding out a nearly-empty juice cartridge. "What happened to the orange juice? Did you forget to fill it again?"

"What do you mean, 'again'?" It wasn't a good feeling to be criticized when you were naked, Marko thought.

"I mean you always forget the refills. You're so predictable." She turned away, dropping the empty cartridge into the bio-reclamator.

He edged towards the bed, feeling behind him for the edge of the sheet. "Tell me one other thing I do that's so predictable."

She tightened the belt on her robe. "I don't think that's a good idea."

"You can't make claims like that and not back them up. I deserve to know," he said, wrapping the sheet around his waist.

"Fine. You know that thing you do? When you blow on my...." She blushed. "In bed?"

He knew exactly what she was talking about. She loved it.

"I can't stand it when you do that," she said.

"But you always wriggle around!"

"Because it feels weird and I want you to stop."

He couldn't believe it. He had relied on that little move to please her. But if she didn't like it, then.... "You let me keep doing something you hated for twelve years, and you didn't tell me?"

She sat down on the bed. "I didn't want to hurt your feelings."

"So why are you telling me now?"

"Because you asked!"

"I wouldn't have if I had known you were going to rip off my manhood and feed it to the reclamator."

"I'm sorry. I didn't *want* to tell you." She pulled up her knees, and buried her teary face in the pillow.

Marko looked down at his bare feet. That didn't go very well, he thought. And then he remembered the WTR.

Marko's stomach rumbled.

"Hungry, sweetie?" Reena asked. "How about some scrambled eggs and a bit of coffee cake?"

"Sounds fantastic," Marko agreed.

Reena reached for her robe.

"Let me go," Marko said. He scrambled out of bed, pulling on his own robe. He went to the galley and, after some banging around, returned with two trays. "Here we are—bacon, eggs, and coffee cake. And mango juice."

Reena untangled from the sheets and took the glass. "Mmmm, delicious. I love mango juice."

Yes! Marko thought. He had been nervous when he pressed the 'Correct' button but, thank the seven stars of Mon-Mon, it had reset after their romp to The Dippity Boo.

"So clever of you," Reena was saying. "What made you choose mango?"

"Oh—um. I thought you'd like it. Special juice for my special girl." Marko said, climbing back into bed beside her.

Reena's brow wrinkled.

"What's the matter, honeybunch?" Marko said, tucking into his soy bacon.

"I'm trying to remember," she said. "Did you get more orange juice after we stopped at that last supply station? Because..."

Oh no, Marko thought, not the orange juice. He hit the control panel at his side and the projection screen popped up at the foot of the bed. "Why don't we watch the Travel Channel and get inspired?" he suggested, scrolling through the sub-menus.

"Look, a special on Mon-Mon," Reena said.

A suave man in chef's whites stood on a platform at the center of an industrial kitchen, conducting a team of synchronized minions who were painting scenery, roasting pigs, chopping onions, arranging flowers, and decorating multi-story cakes in the shape of pirate ships.

"Chef Alberto!" Marko exclaimed. "He's a total star of extreme cooking. I ordered tickets for his show at the

Gastrodome."

On screen, the chef's eyes flashed as he shouted at an assistant who presented an unflattering costume for his evening performance. A tempestuous black curl tumbled from under Alberto's tall white hat as he cursed the poor man up and down.

"What a diva," Reena said.

Marko stuck a curl of bacon on his forehead and shouted at his scrambled eggs. "Off with their heads!" he declared. Reena giggled. Maybe this PIRP trip could turn out okay after all, Marko thought. That Wrong Turn Regulator was worth its weight in yttrium.

The extreme chef segment ended and the program moved on, panning across the famous pipe organ carved into the face of the rugged Mon-laa cliffs. At its base, an intergalactic delegation of musicians in pastel livery played counterpoint on origami harpsichords.

Reena was fascinated. "So lovely," she murmured. She turned to Marko. "I want to learn to play the harpsichord."

Marko's fork missed his mouth and cake fell into his lap, showering him with streusel. "But you don't like the harpsichord." He distinctly remembered that the girl in the manic-chic ensemble had said the harpsichord was a worn-out bourgeois affectation.

"So now you're an expert on what I like?"

Marko scrabbled in the sheets, clawing at a cinnamon-scented nut lodged somewhere uncomfortable. "I'd like to think I know something about my wife after twelve years."

"Things change, Marko!" Reena pulled the sheets up to her chin. "It's like you don't want me to try anything new."

I don't, Marko thought. I want you to be the same Reena I remember. But he said, "I don't understand where all these things are coming from."

"They're coming from inside me. If you can't understand

that..." she flopped back on the pillow, then sat up again. "What do you mean by *all* these things?"

"Well—" he began, then realized that she didn't remember. To her, this was their first fight.

"Never mind," she said, rubbing her forehead. "I am so tired of this argument, and my head is killing me. I'm going to bed."

Marko knew that what she really meant was that she was tired of him. Marko sighed, and got out of bed. He crouched down under the console and stared at the WTR. He put his hand on the slider and, for a moment, he wondered if it was worth it. It seemed like they were destined to find something to fight about. Maybe he should just leave well enough alone. Then he remembered Reena snuggled up under his arm, warm and smiling...

He pulled the slider, but it didn't budge. He put both hands on it and pulled harder. With a slow grinding, it gave way. He positioned it, and pushed 'CORRECT.'

Reena guided the PIRP into the reserved slot in the orbital dock, and they caught the shuttle down to the surface. As they made their way into the Gastrodome, a trio of tuba, liquid metallophone, and harpsichord played in the lobby. A minion in eyeliner accepted their tickets, informing them that the evening's performance was based upon a Tilbassian pirate attack.

Marko barely heard. He knew Reena didn't remember watching the concert at the Mon-laa Cliffs because, technically, it had never happened. To his relief, Reena didn't seem to notice the harpsichord. They changed into their protective slickers in the lobby, and were handed off to a second minion dressed in elaborate pirate regalia.

"Guess these things are foam and spray paint, eh?"

Marko said, indicating the sword which the minion brandished at their backs as he ushered them to their seats.

"Chef Alberto does not use stage props." The minion sounded offended, even through the grille of his faceplate.

Marko and Reena took their seats in the front row. Chef Alberto sliced, diced, swore, and swaggered, and costumed minions circulated with the first course - savory orange sherbet in a nuevo polymer broth.

"Look," Reena said, pushing back her chair. "Chef is calling for volunteers."

"I'm not sure that's—"

But Reena was already headed for the stage, her plastic shoe covers shuffling on the gleaming floor.

Alberto himself helped Reena onto the platform. "Ah," he said. "Beautiful and brave—what a delightful combination."

The crowd applauded, and Reena beamed. Marko couldn't believe it: the creep was flirting with her.

"Now," Alberto said, "the most important question—are you afraid of pirates?"

"Terrified," Reena said, playing along.

"Wonderful!" Alberto declared. "Show us how you will scream when the pirates attack."

"Aiee!" Reena said.

"Very nice....but perhaps you can do better." Alberto clapped his hands and shouted backstage: "You! Some help with the lady's motivation."

A minion dressed in full Narteen pirate armor, complete with single-bladed gravity skates and pickle-shaped helmet, advanced on Reena, waving his hairy sword. From his seat in the front row, Marko saw the color drain out of Reena's face. She opened her mouth and screamed.

"AAAAIEEEEEEEE—"

"Very convincing," Chef Alberto announced to the

crowd. "This is real talent."

"—EEEEEEEEEEEEEE—" Reena continued. Alberto motioned to the Narteen minion, who stepped back and lowered his sword. It had no effect. All around Marko, diners covered their ears.

The chef harangued his attendants, who tried to usher Reena from the stage, but she was locked in place, rigid with panic, and still shrieking. Marko scrambled out of his seat and leapt onto the stage.

"Reena," he said, grabbing her shoulders. "Oh God, I'm sorry. It's okay." He shook her. "We're at the Gastrodome. There aren't any pirates. There have never been any pirates," he said desperately.

Her scream broke off, and Reena looked around, confused. "Marko?" she said. "What—"

Chef Alberto glared at them from within a huddle of minions. "Get these people out of here!" he hissed.

Marko helped Reena offstage and led her back to their table. She took her glass with a shaky hand, and drained it in one gulp. "I don't know what got into me," she said.

"Let's just go back to the PIRP and forget about this whole Gastrodome thing." Marko started to pull off his slicker. "You were right—Chef Alberto is just a big diva."

"No, I'm fine. I just need a minute." Reena pulled out her chair and sat down. "Let's stay and see the show. We've been looking forward to this for a long time."

Reluctantly, Marko took his seat. "I still think we should go." On stage, Alberto unleashed one of his famous tantrums, hurling expletives and fish heads.

"I'm fine. Really." Reena sampled her broth, then dropped the spoon back into in the bowl. "When did I say Alberto was a diva?"

"I—," Marko began. He was pretty sure she *had* said it, he just couldn't remember in which reality. "I'm sorry," he concluded.

"Why do you keep apologizing?" Reena fished a leg bone out of her broth and laid it on the side of her plate. "Did you know that was going to happen to me? Is that why you didn't want me to volunteer?"

"No!" he blurted. "I just made some...miscalculations."

The Narteen minion skated up to their table with the next course and wobbled to a stop, banging a platter of scent-petrified octopus into the back of Marko's head. He apologized. "New skates," he said, avoiding their eyes. "Chef is making everyone nervous tonight." He withdrew two small hammers from his war apron and placed them on the table next to the platter. "To break the scent crystals," he explained, and skated away.

"Marko, I know a guilty look when I see one." Reena picked up her hammer and smashed the octopus in the face.

Marko stared at the destroyed octopus. It smelled like peppermint. And briny feet. He closed his eyes and sighed. He realized he didn't have the energy to do this anymore. As Reena demolished her octopus, he told her about the WTR.

Reena dropped her hammer. "You have a time machine," she said. Her voice was icy. "That you used to rewrite our history. Without telling me."

"I can explain—"

"No." She held up her hand. "I'm not even having this conversation until you promise me that you will never—*ever*, under any circumstances—use that thing on me again."

"I know, I'm sorry. Of course I promise."

Reena balled her napkin in her fist. He watched her squeeze it as if she wished it were his throat. "I can't believe you would do this to me!" she shouted.

"We can go back to the PIRP and destroy the WTR right now," Marko offered. People were starting to stare at them. On stage, Chef Alberto was building to a frenzy. He frothed and lathered, and the cake galleons fell under the pirate horde.

"That's not the point!" Reena said. "That won't make what you did go away. What have I ever done to you that would make you want to erase me?"

"I didn't erase you, that's not fair. I just...made some changes."

"Says you! How can I believe you when you've already hidden something so big? If you come home and say you just popped out to the store, maybe it's been ten years and you lived a whole other life in between and then just reset it all. How can I believe anything you say ever again?"

"I didn't do it to keep things from you," Marko shouted. "I did it because everything was wrong between us." That, and the pirates, Marko thought.

"Isn't that interesting," Reena said. "*I* thought things were going fine, but since I can't even be trusted with reality, what do I know? I thought our marriage was based on a foundation of trust and mutual respect, but I was obviously wrong about that, too."

"Reena, please try to understand. I did it because I love you and I didn't want to lose you."

She didn't look like she was about to forgive him anytime soon, but at least she seemed willing to look at him again.

The stage show ended, and Alberto swept off his chef's hat and bowed. Marko and Reena stood to join the ovation. "I was desperate," he said, shouting over the thunderous applause. "We've wasted too many nights working late, too many hours on long-distance conference shuttles. We've grown apart. I wanted this trip to be a success."

The pirate-waiters gave a blood-curdling war cry and rushed on the audience, swords and hammers raised.

"I would do anything to keep us together," Marko declared. "I'd climb the Mon-laa cliffs. I'd rescue you from a pirate horde. I'd even march right up there on stage and make that tyrant Alberto eat his own sock-scented squid."

"Oh, Marko," she said. He wasn't sure, but it looked like she might be holding back a laugh. He reached for her hand. She let him take it, but said, "Don't think we're done with this."

The horde reached their table and a Narteen pirate skidded up to them, windmilling out of control. He slammed into Reena, and she caught herself against the back of her chair.

"You okay, Reena?" Marko asked.

She nodded. He looked down and saw the tip of the hairy sword poking through her ribs. She pressed her hand to her side, and her fingers came away red.

"Reena!" he shouted. He brushed away the horrified waiter and swung Reena into his arms. The shuttle took them up to the PIRP, and he carried Reena in and laid her on the floor beside the console. She was pale and sweaty and blood soaked her front. He checked her pulse: weak, but still there. He felt under the console for the WTR. The slider was stuck again. Oh no. This was not how things were going to turn out. Wretched, miserable, neo-fascist, noodling piece of junk, he thought, pounding on the slider with the heel of his palm.

Reena's eyes fluttered open.

"Rest, sweetie, it's all going to be okay," he said, as he grappled with the slider. He needed one more time, one more correction. Just one more. He gave it a final blow, and the slider broke loose, spinning to the bottom of its track.

Reena's eyes seemed to focus, and she took in their surroundings, the WTR and the big button marked 'CORRECT'. "You promised," she said, reaching out for him. "You know it only makes more trouble."

He stroked her fingers. She was right, he had promised.

"You promised," Reena said.

"Huh?" Marko jumped, and banged his knees on the underside of the captain's console.

"Before we left Earth," Reena said. "You promised you'd play my new computational physics game with me. I'm going to kick your butt." She stood up from the space-saving dinette and stretched, her fingertips touching the PIRP's ceiling. "This thing seemed so much bigger at the dealer's," she said. "I hope we're not going to be stepping on each other's toes all the way to Mon-Mon."

"Yeah," Marko agreed. He looked at Reena. She seemed whole and healthy—no blood, no hairy sword. The WTR had set them all the way back to the beginning of the trip, to the supply station just beyond Earth. There was so much he was going to have to remember—again. He ran down the list: orange juice, Tilbassian Sector, Travel Channel, Gastrodome. And—he cringed—he was going to have to come up with something new in bed. He didn't know if he was going to make it.

"You alright, baby?" Reena asked, coming over to the captain's chair where the exterior cams were focused on the robots loading supplies into the cargo hold. "Come on," she coaxed. "Let me beat the pants off you—then you'll feel better."

Marko concentrated on the screen. Once more, Reena didn't seem to remember anything about their experiences before he had used the WTR. And he had saved her life. So why did he feel so guilty?

Reena nudged him with her elbow. "I know you're scared of me," she teased. "But a promise is a promise."

Reena was right, he thought suddenly. He *had* promised. Maybe he could make it up to her.

"Hold on a moment." He reconnected the data link with

the supply station and scanned the inventory lists. Yes, there it was. Exactly what he wanted. "There's just one more thing we need." He relayed the order.

A few moments later, the loading bay lift dinged. Reena opened the hatch.

When she saw what was inside, she gave Marko a puzzled look. "What's this for?"

Marko shrugged, and helped her move the harpsichord into the main space. "I thought you might like it."

Reena ran her fingers over the keys. "I do," she said, testing a note. "I just wonder how you guessed." She turned to him. "I never used to like the harpsichord. I think I even once said it was—"

"—a worn-out, bourgeois affectation. Yes, I remember," Marko said.

Reena tried the keys again. She smiled at Marko, her head tilted, listening carefully to the tones. "Things change, huh?" she said.

She experimented with the notes, sounding out sequences. The harpsichord produced sounds that were old-fashioned, archaic, and difficult—almost not like music at all. Marko watched her, delighted. As she bent over the keys, her hair fell away from her neck. A pair of earrings flashed at her ears.

"Did you just get those at the supply station?" Marko asked.

Reena's fingers slipped on the keys. "These?" Her hands flew to her ears, covering the tiny animatronic alligators. She shook her head and her hair fell back in place. She shrugged. "Oh, I've had them for ages."

"Really? They look just like the ones they're supposed to sell at the gift shop on Alligator Planet. But we've never—"

"You know, I think I'm starting to get the hang of this," she said, sitting down in front of the harpsichord. "Listen.

Tell what you think."

Marko's head ached. He felt vague, as if there were something he just couldn't quite remember. But as Reena pressed the keys, Marko was distracted by the familiar melody.

Reena repeated the notes, and soon Marko was tapping along on his knee, nodding his head as the classic lyrics echoed in his mind: *Up your, up your...*

Alisa Alering was hatched in a secret hollow in the Appalachian mountains of Pennsylvania, where she ran around barefoot and talked to the trees. She now lives, writes, and reads travel blogs in Indiana. Her short fiction has appeared in Podcastle, Clockwork Phoenix 4, and Writers of the Future Vol. 29, among others. She has never been to Mon-Mon—at least, not that she can remember.

I Only Time-Travel During School Hours
by Desmond Warzel

In the present day, the local mall is at the tail end of a slow decline. The busiest store is the Goodwill, and rumor has it even *they* plan on closing up shop and relocating to greener pastures. But the real tragedy lies in the middle section of the building, which in happier times was perfumed by the aromatic bouquet of Roy Rogers fried chicken. Now, it's daily profaned by the diabolical sickly-sweet stench emanating from the Bath & Body Works that has desecrated that space for the last fifteen years.

But at the moment, it's Thursday, September 12, 1991, about one o'clock in the afternoon, and Peterson and I are sitting in that very same Roy Rogers. We're dressed in plain shirts, nondescript jeans, and ordinary loafers, careful not to display any anachronistic logos. Apart from the backpack full of wires, batteries, and iPad viscera that make up my time machine, we've left everything suggestive of the future— wallets, cellphones, car keys—back in 2017. The only thing either of us is carrying is a roll of one-dollar bills.

(I haven't cracked the problem of obtaining large amounts of era-appropriate currency. Ones are the only denomination that looks the same in both times, so I'm stuck using them. Sure, most of the *years* are wrong, but I haven't been found out yet. Who ever looks at the dates on paper money?)

We're probably attracting too much attention. We're the only customers in the place and we've ordered one or two of almost everything on the menu: roast beef sandwiches; cheeseburgers topped with ham (a signature Roy Rogers item); French fries *and* baked potatoes; fried chicken *and*

258

chicken nuggets; biscuits, coleslaw, what-have-you. It's all spread out before us like a Vegas buffet. No doubt the employees feel like footmen serving at Henry VIII's dinner table, but Peterson and I aren't royalty; more like a pair of lost, dehydrated legionnaires reveling in an unexpected oasis. We attack our meal like we're at war with it.

Some thirty minutes later, Peterson finishes up his second baked potato and, finding this a convenient place to pause, interrupts me in mid-debauchery.

"So," he says. "Any good?"

"If we want anything to take back, we'll have to order it," I reply. "There won't be any leftovers."

"This is even more satisfying than killing Hitler." That was Peterson's first proposal upon seeing the machine. When I recommended we recapture small, harmless pleasures from our youth rather than altering history wholesale, he immediately proposed Roy Rogers. I couldn't argue; in 2017 there isn't a Roy Rogers within four hundred miles of us, and I've missed it terribly.

"If we make a habit of this, you're going to need an extension for your black belt. You'll be the laughingstock of the dojo." Peterson operates a chain of karate schools.

"My staff does all the work these days. I show up once a month to distribute colored belts to hyperkinetic grade-schoolers. Still, I'll burn this off by tomorrow afternoon. I've got way more testosterone than you."

Having no useful response to this, I select a drumstick from the fried-chicken container and bite into it. The crunch is satisfying; the flavor is better than I could have imagined. Fast-food fryers use a much less healthy oil here than in the present, and my palate rejoices.

Time passes. As I struggle to consume the last of my fries, Peterson returns from the front counter bearing our final Pepsi refills and, with a grunt, works his way back into our booth.

"Everything everybody ever told me is wrong," he announces. "Not only are things as good as I remember them, they're better. You are wise."

"As, now, are you," I reply.

"Shall we head up to the arcade and celebrate my newfound enlightenment with a game of *Joust*?"

"You'll kill me. We're supposed to work together, but something about riding an ostrich turns you into a homicidal idiot."

"It's not my fault," insists Peterson.

"Why not?"

"It's a *flying ostrich*. An abomination of nature. No mortal man can fully control it."

"*Spy Hunter*, then. We'll take turns." This has appeal; our arcade has the superior seated version of the game, rather than the upright, and after the meal I just ate, prolonged standing isn't in the cards.

"Sure. We have an hour or so left."

"I didn't know we were on a schedule."

"I only time-travel during school hours. I don't want to risk running into my teenage self and rending the fabric of the universe."

"Is that what would happen?"

"I have no idea, but why chance it? Hey, let's stop at the bookstore first. Might as well grab this month's *Omni* while I'm here. I'm rebuilding the collection my mother threw out when I went away to college."

"You should travel back and tell her not to get rid of them," says Peterson in jest.

"I'd have better luck convincing myself not to leave for college in the first place."

The building is a quarter-mile down the road from the house where I grew up. In its heyday, it was Hoover's, a no-frills Dairy Queen analogue beloved by many. In 2017, it sits empty, as it has for years, and there's a bill for thirty-six grand in back taxes taped to the door.

But at the moment, it's Monday, January 19, 1987, one o'clock PM, and Peterson and I are relaxing in Hoover's dining area. The walls and floor are bare concrete. Some might call it tomb-like; I see it as a temple to lost pleasures.

At one end are two narrow windows opening onto the kitchen, for placing and picking up orders. At the other end, two pinball machines. (Five balls for a quarter! Nowadays they want fifty or seventy-five cents for three balls, and that's when you can even *find* a working machine.) Two pool tables occupy the bulk of the remaining space. Shoved against one wall, as if an afterthought, are three wobbly dining tables and a smattering of mismatched chairs. Across the room, a single large window offers a view of the parking lot and admits the grey winter light. It is glorious.

Having spent a week in 2017 recuperating from our first sojourn, we've deemed ourselves fit to tackle Hoover's legendary fish and chips. Seafood was the one glaring absence from our prior bacchanalia, but even Roy Rogers couldn't have measured up to Hoover's in that department. Each of us is well into our second order.

"Not bad," says Peterson. He's spent a week listening to me rave about Hoover's; his faint praise is meant to get a rise out of me. I ignore the bait.

"Every piece of fried fish I've eaten since this place closed, I've compared to what lies before us right now. All have been found wanting. I don't know what they put in this batter. What are you looking at?" Peterson has been glancing over my shoulder during my little soliloquy.

"You really do like this food, don't you?"

"That's the point I was making. Why?"

"Because your thirteen-year-old self just came in and placed an order."

I can't help turning around. The young customer's back is to us. His coat does look familiar, but the clincher is the red bicycle leaning against the outside of the front window. I recognize every scratch and rust spot.

It makes no sense for me to have been here today, but there I am.

"The pinball machines," I whisper. "You play, I'll watch. Let's keep our backs turned; I don't want to make eye contact. Hopefully his order is to go."

"Got a quarter?" asks Peterson.

"I told you to bring some."

"Mine all had states on the backs. I can't spend them here, now can I?"

"Here. Play. And don't make a commotion."

Peterson directs his ball around the machine's Mata Hari-themed playfield with casual brilliance. At any other time, it would be a joy to watch, but I can think only of my 1987 counterpart behind me. I sneak the minutest of glances over my shoulder—just enough to see that he's leaning against the wall next to the pick-up window.

"I thought you said you never skipped school," whispers Peterson.

"I never did."

"Come on, now. Truancy is bad enough; let's not compound the infraction by lying about it."

"I'm honestly at a loss."

"Martin Luther King Day?" suggests Peterson.

"Maybe, but we didn't have it off from school back then. Back now, I mean." I hear the door open and close. From the corner of my eye, I glimpse myself mounting my bike and riding off, steering with one hand and carrying two takeout bags with the other. "He's gone, " I report.

"That's good. Quit leaning on the machine."

Leaving Peterson to his game, I return to our table. I have to think.

Obviously no reality-shattering paradox has transpired, though I was worried for a moment. I take a bite of fish. Even nearly-cold, it's delicious. The possibility of life as I know it coming to an end is evidently insufficient to dampen my appetite.

Life coming to an end...

January 19, 1987...

Suddenly, I have it.

"I'm the worst person in the world," I inform Peterson when he finishes his game.

"You realize both Khomeini and Saddam are still alive right now?" he replies. "Idi Amin, too, I think."

"I remember the day clear as a bell. I just forgot the *date*."

"What are you talking about?"

"January 19, 1987. I'm sitting in Howard's seventh-grade science class—"

"Happy Howard," says Peterson. The nickname was meant ironically; Mr. Howard never once smiled that entire year.

"Happy Howard," I continue. "I got called to the principal's office."

"I remember that. I sat next to you in science. You went to the office and never came back."

"When I saw my mother there, I knew what had happened. It wasn't exactly a surprise. Dad had been in poor health for years. Now he was gone.

"When we got home, we were both starving, but Mom was obviously in no mood to cook, and the parade of casseroles and groceries from friends and neighbors wouldn't begin until that evening. It was cold outside, but pleasant, so I biked up here and got us two orders of fish and chips and two milkshakes.

"Once we finished eating, Mom left me to myself. She knew enough to let me process it in my own way. As I recall, that involved sitting in my room and watching *G.I. Joe*."

"Which episode?"

"The one where Dr. Mindbender invents the mind-control gum."

"That's some memory you have."

"For everything but dates, apparently."

We finish our meals in silence. Now I wish I'd made eye contact with my younger self, and damn the consequences. I really wonder what I would have found there.

I've always told myself that I bore the tragedy well; graciously assuming some household responsibilities, dutifully reporting to Hills Department Store to pick out a dark suit, offering emotional support to various relatives, and most importantly, never crying.

I've always told myself that I held it together and didn't break down once.

I've taken pride in the mature way I handled the situation.

But I remember what kind of kid I was.

I could never have been that strong.

And surely here, in this nearly-empty restaurant, thirteen-year-old me would have risked an unguarded emotional moment. Had I looked, I might have gotten to know myself a little better.

In any case, Peterson and I have allotted ourselves time for pinball before we head back to 2017, and now that the excitement's over, I see no reason not to indulge. I dole out the quarters (all with proper years) and this time I tackle the Mata Hari machine while Peterson plays its neighbor, Eight Ball Deluxe.

"You were quite a trooper," says Peterson, launching his ball. "Real tough kid."

"I always thought so, anyway," I reply, and drop my quarter in the slot.

Dad died on a Monday. The funeral was Thursday, and I was back in school on Friday. Nobody would have blamed me for taking the whole week off, but Dad wouldn't have wanted me to fall behind, and I concurred.

Mom got Father Skinner to do the service. Of all the priests I'd known in my short life, I liked him the best. The inherent awkwardness of funerals means finding yourself in a room full of strangers wearing the faces of your friends and family. But this was ordinary business for Father Skinner, and so he alone spoke and acted as he normally did. It was a great comfort.

It's Thursday, January 22, 1987. I'm attending said funeral for the second time. Nobody recognizes me; I've dyed my hair and taken the time to grow a substantial beard. For that matter, I could have just waited until I was seventy and let nature disguise me.

A time machine removes much of the urgency from life.

(Of course, I may not even *reach* seventy, and I don't dare visit 2043 to find out. To account for planetary motion, time travel requires a "quantum anchor": a unique arrangement of particles existing in both times, such as the big flat boulder in the woods behind my house. But there's no way of knowing if your anchor will still be there in the future, and if it isn't, you've bought yourself a fast, cold death in interstellar space.)

Everyone's attention but mine is on Father Skinner; I'm keeping a close watch on my thirteen-year-old self. I'm determined to speak to him, though I have no idea what to say. Tell him everything's going to be okay? He's heard it fifty times since breakfast. Dispense some self-serving advice, such as, "Major in physics right away instead of wasting two years with philosophy?" I can't do that, any more than I can go kill Hitler. I don't know what will happen if I change this kid's life enough that he never stumbles across time travel. I might cease to exist, or I might return to 2017 and find another one of me already there.

That's the joke of it: the most remarkable invention in history will remain simply a private amusement (at least until someone else discovers the underlying principles, which are astonishingly basic). Just as the serviceable Edwardian-era painter from Austria must become the genocidal German madman, the grieving teenage boy from the Bon Jovi epoch must become the single, childless, forty-three-year-old community-college instructor. To make it otherwise is to risk making everything worse.

The service ends; people mill about. The thirteen-year-old shakes hands with all the men, looking them in the eye and thanking them for coming. Not a tear is shed. He moves to stand beside his father's casket, where he remains, in quiet contemplation. I know he's thinking about the things his father taught him, and that his heart is filled with respect and love, and not a scrap of fear.

I depart. There's nothing I can say to this strong young me. The only lesson I could impart is one that he must learn on his own when he gets older: that things really are as good as you remember them. If not better.

Having proved that thesis to our satisfaction, Peterson and I have moved on to more advanced time travel. Next stop: Wednesday, May 25, 1977, to see the first showing of *Star Wars*. That will take some doing; it only opened in a few dozen theaters nationwide. We might stick around until

Friday and catch the opening of *Smokey and the Bandit*, too.

If that works out, we'll widen the scope. On Saturday, August 9, 1986, Queen will perform the final concert of their Magic Tour at Knebworth Park in England. Peterson and I will be there. It's the last concert the band will ever give before Freddie Mercury dies in 1991, and out of a crowd of 120,000 people, we'll be the only ones who know.

That will be a complicated excursion to plan, obviously, but we have all the time in the world. Most immediately, we need to scrape together a few grand each in cash.

Got any one-dollar bills on you?

Desmond Warzel published his first time travel story in 2007 (rumors that he wrote it in 2030 and sent it back to his younger self are unfounded). Since then, he's published a few dozen short stories in the science fiction, fantasy, and horror genres. These have appeared in nifty magazines like *The Magazine of Fantasy & Science Fiction*, on lovely websites like Tor.com, and on newfangled podcasts like The Drabblecast. He lives in northwestern Pennsylvania.

Not With A Bang
by Rosemary Claire Smith

Julianna shifted her attention from the fluttering monarchs to Marty, while her manicured nails worried a corner of her boarding pass. "You're going *where?*" she asked.

"The Montana seashore. The first manned mission to the Late Cretaceous." He could feel himself grinning like a deranged jackrabbit.

People were giving Marty irritated looks as they wheeled carry-on bags toward the security line. Maybe they didn't care for the hologram butterflies, their blinking orange wings flitting between Marty and Julianna. The monarchs were part of her last-minute preparations for another out-of-town reporting assignment. Green chrysalises dangled from a thicket of milkweeds, which seemed to spring up from the airport's institutional-drab carpet.

Marty continued, "They were looking for a wildlife biologist with pilot training, and wow, I got it!"

"Congratulations. That's wonderful." She didn't look happy.

"Yes, it is. So what's wrong?"

"Well, you can be sure," Julianna said, "that All Science News could never afford to send a science reporter like me to the Cretaceous."

So that was it. She would probably never get to report on living dinosaurs in their prehistoric habitats.

She went on, "You're reaping the rewards of your fifteen minutes of fame in East Africa."

"Don't remind me." It rankled that the publicity from the Jackson Sirloin incident overshadowed Marty's scientific contributions. "The Dinoseum is sending Dr. Derek Dill with me." The Director of the Denver Dinoseum was the world's foremost authority on duckbill dinosaurs.

"He's going with you?" Julianna's green eyes brightened. "My schedule's really jammed, but if I could be the first to do a one-on-one interview with Derek Dill the day you return.... Can you put in a good word for me?"

"Look, I don't know him."

"But you will. When do you two come back to the present—in a week or two?"

"Umm... October first."

"What? That's six months!" She broke off eye contact as she ducked behind a milkweed hologram to examine a pair of black-and-yellow banded caterpillars chewing placidly on leaves.

"The calculations aren't quite as tricky if the jumps backward and forward are for precisely the same amount of time. We need a good six months to survey coastal and upland habitats. If we arrive April first, we can observe key components of the annual cycle. Mating habits, nest building, brooding behavior, eggs hatching, parenting activities..."

He stopped, not wanting to argue when they only had fifteen minutes in O'Hare. That was better than the twelve minutes last week at LaGuardia. Then, she'd been off to interview the marine zoologists who had announced a cure for fibropapillomas in loggerhead turtles off the Florida coast.

"Calendar." Julianna said to the chip implanted in her wrist. "October first."

"Mauna Kea," it replied.

"That's right. I'll be covering the Keck Observatory as they receive higher-resolution images of Earth-like planets."

"Look, I know it's a long trip, but—" Marty hesitated. They had only gone on five dates.

Julianna shook her head. "Neither of us has enough time in our lives for the other."

"We can make the time. I love you." The unfamiliar words tumbled out, startling him, even though they were true. Marty strode through the milkweeds toward Julianna. An all-too-realistic chrysalis dangled an inch from her nose. Ignoring it, he took her in his arms and kissed her lips.

She started to return his kiss, then drew back. "Marty, I don't—"

Her chip interrupted them. "The Smithsonian is calling."

Julianna moved away from Marty. "Gotta take this one. It'll just be a nano-sec."

He watched the caterpillars wink out. The minutes ticked away as she made arrangements for her trip next week to an Andean excavation. Then she was gone, dashing toward Security as the loudspeaker blared boarding calls. Yes, he did love Julianna, even if dating her was like dating a human butterfly.

At the news conference the following month, Marty Zuber and Derek Dill stood in front of the Kennegunky Paleo Trippers Training Facility, named after Amazeballs Media's most famous dinosaur holo-cartoon. The outsized blue and pink globular buildings shimmered like a cluster of bubbles blown by a tipsy god. Marty scanned the sea of reporters for Julianna's face, hoping she would show up.

"Ah... Achoo!" The small explosion shook Dill's body and sent a lock of dark hair tumbling onto his forehead. After the usual chorus of "Bless you" from the tech crew, Dill turned to Marty. "Allergies," he muttered, drawing a capsule from his pill case, breaking it open, and inhaling a leukotriene blocker.

The reporters began peppering Dill with questions. The camera-handsome paleontologist basked in the limelight. That suited Marty, as he didn't have to say much.

"Dr. Dill, aren't you concerned that the comet that wiped out the dinosaurs will hit you, too?"

"I don't lose any sleep over it. We'll arrive millions of years too early."

Marty must have sent Julianna a dozen messages during the month at Kennegunky. Her three brief replies lamented her hectic schedule and said she envied his learning to fly the time jumper.

"Dr. Dill, is there a sound scientific purpose for your trip? Wasn't it determined forty or fifty years ago that an asteroid or comet killed the dinosaurs?"

Dill bristled. "Yes, that's well settled. But I'm more interested in how they lived than in how they died. All species are destined for extinction, one day. We've chosen an era shortly before the mass extinctions, when dinosaurs were likely near their peak in terms of the variety of different species. The Late Cretaceous also saw the highest population figures for dinosaurs."

Julianna wouldn't be here. Two days ago, Marty had glimpsed her on All Science News, reporting live from the Galapagos Islands. An international symposium was being held there to highlight the worsening pollution in the equatorial waters. Like a monarch butterfly, she "migrated" thousands of kilometers every year.

"Can you comment on the rumors that you're secretly planning on launching missiles to knock the comet off course and save the dinosaurs?"

Dill laughed. "That's creative. Also flat wrong. According to our temporal physicists, the Schering-Dyson equations prove you can't change the past. A comet or asteroid hit. Nothing we do will alter that. Let me add that I wouldn't want to change it if I could. Keep in mind, I've loved hadrosaurs and theropods and ceratopsians my whole life."

Marty groaned inwardly. What the paleontologist loved

was to boast about the ten species of duckbills he discovered, and the hardships of fieldwork he endured.

Dill continued, "But if Cretaceous dinosaurs had survived in their prehistoric forms, would our own ancestors ever have had the chance to evolve into something more than nocturnal, insect-eating rodents? There is no place for dinosaurs in our modern world. They're dangerous. We'd need a zoo bigger than this state and how would we keep them inside? I'll step down from my soapbox now."

Off to the side, Marty glimpsed Julianna's shining red hair. She *had* come! All the way from the Galapagos! And looking beautiful and vivacious even after a thirteen hour trip.

"Speaking of danger, aren't you worried about being attacked by a T. rex?"

Marty tried to catch Julianna's eye, but she was whispering to her wrist chip.

"We've estimated that *Tyrannosaurus rex* was extremely rare—maybe one pair in every thousand square miles." True, but Amazeballs would dearly love for them to spot the ultimate paleo-celebrity.

"Any danger from velociraptors?"

"We may come across troödons—first cousins of the velociraptors. That's why we'll be carrying these." Dill gestured to the large tranquilizer guns behind them, which looked more impressive than the tanks of Saur-Away that would serve as their first line of defense. Gesturing to Marty, he continued, "Dr. Zuber, here, is a crack shot, a good man in a crisis. He saved Jackson Sirloin from an enraged rhino."

Marty gave them an "aw, shucks" grin, stuck his hands in his pockets and bowed his head. Jackson Sirloin hadn't asked permission to intrude on Marty's studies in the Sub-Saharan Wildlife Refuge. Sirloin might be the biggest Hollywood star of the decade, but he was also a first-class idiot. Anyone with an ounce of sense knew better than to antagonize a mother rhino by hugging her offspring for a photo op.

Julianna said, "Dr. Dill, how do you feel about having the chance to watch baby duckbills hatch?"

Marty caught her twinge of jealousy at being excluded from the grand adventure. The costs of time jumping were well beyond the reach of news organizations, or for that matter, anyone but a handful of billionaires and an outfit like Amazeballs Media. The company stood to make back its investment through exclusive interactive holo-vids of real dinosaurs.

Marty tried not to grimace. Sixty-seven million years wasn't enough time for him to figure out what he could possibly do about this.

He had a hard time paying attention to the rest of the reporters' questions, and Dill's patient repetitions of what was clearly stated in the press kits. The time jumper, christened the *H.G.Wells*, would touch down in what today was the badlands of eastern Montana. During the Late Cretaceous, it had been a lush, semi-tropical coastal plain bordering a shallow sea.

As the news conference broke up, Dill snaked his way through the crowd toward Julianna. Marty rushed to intercept her. "I didn't know you'd be here," he blurted out, then immediately regretted his words.

Julianna said softly, "How is it that you understand rhino behavior so well, but not mine?"

"People aren't as predictable as rhinos," he protested. "I mean, you're more complicated."

"You say the sweetest things." She flashed him a teasing smile.

Before Marty could reply, another reporter claimed his attention. Then Dill appeared and shook Julianna's hand. Marty watched Dill's fingers linger on her wrist as he smiled at her. In return, Julianna's eyes began to sparkle at Dill the same way they had sparkled at Marty the first time he met her—barely two months ago at Jackson Sirloin's news conference in Kenya.

The *H.G.Wells* folded its wing blades after a text-book smooth touchdown. Marty relaxed, then checked exterior cameras, temperature, pressure, and humidity gauges, and microphones. All were set for continuous recording. The ambient air temperature read 24°C. The cameras showed they were sitting on a thatch of pine needles in the middle of a clearing in a coniferous forest. Clumps of waist-high ferns sprang up everywhere the trees allowed sunlight to reach the forest floor. Overhead, a single pterosaur crossed the brilliant blue sky. Both the motion detectors and the infrared scanners picked up a large biomass, species to be determined, ninety-one meters east-northeast. The external speakers relayed an occasional trumpet-like call coming from almost due south. Readouts popped up on various screens around the cockpit.

"Temporal displacement gauge reads dead on the money," Marty said.

"Hull temperature normal," Dill replied.

Marty verified that the other systems were A-okay. "Let's get to it," he said.

Dill rose from his seat and grasped Marty's arm. "Before we open the hatch, there's another... er... matter to discuss."

Marty waited.

"This will be a historic moment. Our sponsors are expecting me to say, 'That's one small step for a man, one giant leap for Amazeballs Media and the Denver Dinoseum.'" Dill looked uncomfortable.

Marty shook his head. "Gee, that's original." He began pulling gear from the storage bins.

"They think nobody remembers anymore."

They both climbed into their jungle-colored flex-armor. Marty double-checked that their spray tanks of Saur-Away were fully functional. Nobody really knew if the scent would actually repulse the saurians, although it worked wonders on modern-day alligators and birds.

"Probably true," Marty sighed. "But still, we need to say something memorable." If Julianna were here, she would have exactly the right words.

Dill glanced at the readouts flashing across the hatch screen. "We better think fast. The door opens in thirty seconds."

Marty put on his Max-Kevlar helmet and pulled down the visor, covering most of his face. When the hatch slid open, the first thing he noticed was the peculiar tang to the air, followed by the heat and humidity. From the underbrush seventy-five meters away came a faint crash.

Dill began climbing down the ladder.

Marty's heads-up display showed an enormous saurian approaching. "Um... maybe we should wait until—"

"Nonsense. No reason to wait." Dill had raised his visor so the cameras could get a good view of his face, and he couldn't see his heads-up display. The dinosaur had almost reached the clearing. The paleontologist paused on the bottom rung of the ladder, then turned to face one of the cameras. "That's one small step for a—"

"Sauropod!" Marty shouted, pointing over Dill's shoulder at the leathery kneecap of an immense herbivore, now visible through the foliage.

"One small step for a sauropod?" the paleontologist said, stepping onto Mesozoic soil.

"Look over there." Marty pointed. Gripping his tranq gun, he retreated from the landing, into the doorway.

"Hmmm." Dill stared up at the jade-green neck, which arched and waved from side to side as the giant sniffed the treetops. "A titanosaur. Alamosaurus, perhaps. Hadn't expected to find one this far north."

The sauropod began to munch the upper branches of a tree.

Marty whispered, "Either it doesn't see us, or we're too insignificant to bother with."

They carefully circled the enormous creature, then made their way to the aquamarine waters of the sea. As the scientists approached the shoreline, they spotted the inert body of a triceratops. Its head was submerged, with barely six inches of its two brow horns above water. The stench of decomposing flesh wafted toward them. The dinosaur had died while leaning down on its forelimbs so that its gargantuan hind quarters stuck up. The scientists drew closer. Although the triceratops' hide was elephant grey, the bony frill behind its head was white, tinged yellow from a coating of pollen. Its schnoz, as big as Marty's head, rivaled the candy-apple red of Julianna's zipster. The preferred color of sports cars never changed.

Dill frowned deeply. "Looks like it drowned. But it wouldn't deliberately hold its head under water."

"Maybe it did away with itself."

"Dinosaurs don't commit suicide." Dill gave him a contemptuous look. "It must have stumbled and hit its head."

"On what—the water?"

Beneath the aquamarine waves lay nothing but sand, small pebbles, and an occasional ammonite.

"It killed itself," Marty said.

"A word of advice. You may come to regret indulging in unfounded speculation. It's best to leave the assessment of the cause of death to a trained professional like me."

"When did you become a coroner?"

Their dispute was interrupted by an ungodly roar from the forest.

Dill gasped. Marty yanked him back away from the triceratops corpse, then released the safety on his tranq gun. A forty-foot-long dinosaur stomped into view.

The color drained from Dill's face and he began to wheeze. "T. rex," he gasped.

The first one anybody had ever seen alive!

The tyrannosaurus came to an abrupt halt, then swung around to face the two men. Teeth jutted from its closed mouth like yellow daggers. Primal terror roiled Marty's bowels. His hands had a white-knuckled grip on the tranq gun, which suddenly looked puny.

The carnivore opened its mouth, exposing even more yellow knives. Carrion breath engulfed them. Its nostrils flared. Marty raised the gun and sighted on the monster's eye.

"Help," Dill yelped as Marty was about to shoot. Dill darted behind him, accidentally jostling Marty's arm and throwing off his aim. At the same time, the dinosaur opened its mouth wider and waved its forelimbs.

The T. rex issued a massive sneeze. Then another. Its nostrils turned bright red. Its whole body shook and the ground trembled so badly that Marty nearly lost his grip on the gun.

The tyrannosaurus sneezed a third time, expelling a stream of yellow-green snot as long as a man's arm. Marty ducked. The goo landed squarely on Dill's visor and helmet, sending him staggering backwards.

The beast lumbered past the two men toward the triceratops carcass. Marty grabbed the paleontologist's wrist and sprinted toward the forest.

Dill stumbled. "I can't see!" he wheezed.

Marty whirled around and raised Dill's visor. The T. rex braced itself with its miniature forelimbs, and tore a gluttonous hunk of flesh from the dead triceratops's flank. Again, Marty yanked the paleontologist toward cover.

Dill was still shaking when they reached the *H.G.Wells*. Safely inside, he broke open a capsule of inhalant under his nose. The medicine seemed to calm him and to restore his breathing to normal. Tendrils of yellow-green goo streaked down his shoulders and chest.

Marty chuckled. "Amazeballs is going to be pissed. We just proved that the ultimate paleo-celebrity is a scavenger."

Two days after their arrival, the time travelers were awakened at dawn by a cacophony that sounded like an orchestra of leaf blowers and bagpipes. Marty dashed to the cockpit and raised the time jumper's aerial cameras just as a herd of duckbills emerged from behind a hill.

Half dressed, Dill joined him. When the paleontologist activated his main screen, a digital photo popped up in the bottom corner. Julianna. Looking more beautiful than ever.

"Lambeosaurines!" Dill exclaimed. "Probably parasaurolophus." The dinosaurs made straight toward the clearing. "There must be thousands of them." He whistled.

Marty couldn't say a word. The caterwauling outside grew louder.

Dill continued, "Estimated weight is two to three tons apiece." Then he noticed Marty staring at Julianna's image. "Isn't she something? I've only talked to her a few times. Her name's—"

"Julianna Carson."

"You know her?"

"She's seeing someone else, you know." The words came out sharper than Marty intended. He forced himself to look at the aerial images. The striped duckbills reminded him of yellow and brown zebras, except that they ranged upwards of ten meters from nose to tail.

A flicker of alarm crossed Dill's face. He hid it by saying,

"I'm not worried about the competition, whoever he is."

Fists clenched, Marty turned his back on Dill and stared out the window as the first of the lambeosaurines entered the clearing. They loped along on four legs, pausing frequently to chomp any plant in sight, occasionally balancing upright on their hind legs.

The males sported hollow, bony crests curving back a good meter and a half from their heads. The females had shorter crests arching up from their foreheads, over the crown, then down to the nape of the neck, like a bouffant hairdo lacquered in place with hair spray. *Trombone heads*, he thought.

"They really are Mesozoic mowing machines," Dill said. "See that? Not a single plant in their path escapes unscathed. How many acres do you think they could clear in an hour?"

The parasaurolophuses swept past the *H.G.Wells* at a remarkable speed, scarcely glancing at the time jumper. It probably didn't smell like food.

"I'm going to follow them," Marty said, climbing into his flex-armor. He had to get away. "You stay here and keep an eye on the monitors."

Dill frowned. "You're going outside alone? The safety guidelines—"

"Good thing there are no time police." Marty struggled to keep his tone neutral. If the T. rex incident was any indication, he'd be safer without Dill.

The duckbills picked up the pace as they drew close to their nesting grounds. When Marty finally caught up with them hours later, he beheld acres of old nests adjacent to a shallow stream.

The trombone heads ignored him; they were mating. First the females shook their heads from side to side, which evidently enticed the males. When a male approached a female, he would rise up on his hind legs and issue a series of trumpet blasts, each longer, louder, and further off key than the one before. If the female liked what she heard, she led the male off into the forest. If not, the female tilted her head and issued a short honk. The spurned male lowered his head and slunk away, eventually circling back to serenade another female.

Marty's thoughts strayed to Julianna. People *were* more complicated. As he recorded the parasaurolophuses, it surprised him how many females rejected all offers.

He returned to the time jumper to find that their first trans-temporal mail messages—T-mail—had arrived, including vid-notes to each of them from Julianna. Although he couldn't access her message to Dill, Marty could see it was four times longer than the vid-note she sent him, which went on about splicing firefly genes into self-illuminating Christmas trees, but didn't say what he wanted to hear.

Marty groaned inwardly, remembering the monarchs flitting from branch to flower to leaf. By the time he returned to the present, Julianna would have moved on to another exotic interest.

Was he becoming yesterday's leaf?

A large, winged shadow swept across the trampled remains of the parasaurolophuses' migration path. Overhead, a sun-yellow pterosaur made lazy circles, before alighting in a ginkgo tree near the trombone-head rookery. Marty's heads-up display identified the flyer as a pteranodon, on the basis of its toothless beak, elongated head, up-curving saggital crest, and bobbed tail. The creature had a wingspan of almost eight meters. Astounding to realize it must be one of the smaller females.

Marty reached the duckbills' nesting ground and wrinkled his nose as the pungent odor of decomposing plants engulfed him. The duckbills stockpiled enormous amounts of vegetation near their nests, but not so close as to cast shadows on the incubating egg clutches. He frowned when he spotted Dill peering around a rotting pile to count eggs, then lifting his visor to inhale his leukotriene blocker. Could the paleontologist even smell the stench with his nose stopped up?

For Marty, the thing that made the last few weeks bearable was the long hours Dill devoted to observing and quantifying the intimate details of life among the expectant female trombone-heads. That and his allergies, which proved exceptionally resistant to modern medicine. Dill could work like a demon, despite his watery eyes and red nose from too much time amidst the Late Cretaceous angiosperms. The air had grown so thick with yellow pollen that it seemed as though every plant in prehistoric Montana was in flower.

The pteranodon closed its green eyes and shook its head as it preened, reminding Marty of Julianna. Like her, the yellow-winged pteranodon seemed to be in constant motion, hopping from branch to ground to boulder, examining everything that caught its fancy. Infinite curiosity.

Dill waved him over. Marty wasn't about to reveal his own interest in Julianna, not after overhearing her beautiful laugh coming from the cockpit when Dill played the latest vid-note she sent him. At least Dill no longer protested when Marty left him alone to watch the duckbills' behavior—which chiefly consisted of brooding over their eggs and foraging for food.

"See how the ovoid eggs are neatly positioned on end in the nests?" The paleontologist paused while a violent sneezing fit rocked his whole body. So much for the leukotriene blocker.

Dill. Marty shook his head. How could he lose Julianna to someone named after a pickle?

"I've verified that the number of eggs in each nest is consistent with the fossil clutches I discovered at the Little Bighorn sites. But only twenty percent of the female parasaurolophuses are sitting on eggs. Why didn't more females mate?"

Marty shrugged. "Who knows why females..." he left the thought unfinished.

Suddenly, the pteranodon whipped its head around. With a rush of leathery wings and half a dozen powerful strokes, it swept upward to meet another of its kind. The second specimen was larger than the first; its wingspan rivaled that of a Piper Cub. Its upswept crest was an iridescent green and it issued a raucous warble. Must be a male.

The female devoted her complete attention to the male flyer, following him toward the emerald sea. Marty switched to the remote camera shot. A mosasaur rose from the water, driving away a terrified school of prehistoric fish. The female pteranodon issued a shrill cackle while the male dive-bombed the mosasaur. He came within inches of its fang-filled jaws before snatching a fish in his pointy beak.

Why did the male pteranodon take such a crazy chance? Surely it could have caught other fish with less heart-pounding excitement. Then it hit him. The male must be showing off. Was that what the female wanted— a hero?

As soon as he got back to the *H.G.Wells*, Marty sent Julianna T-mail, attaching a holo-clip of the tyrannosaurus incident. Let her see who cowered and stumbled, and whose quick actions saved both of their hides.

Summer's steam-bath humidity embraced Mesozoic Montana. One afternoon, the two scientists were alerted that a squadron of five sickle-clawed troödons was loping through the tall grass toward them. Scrambling up a nearby tree, hearts pounding, they stared down at the leopard-sized carnivores. The troödons looked skinnier than Marty would have expected, and their slack skin was an unhealthy grey-green. Perhaps they'd been searching for a meal for some time.

"Look how scrawny they are," Dill muttered. "You can almost count their ribs." Tears leaked from his puffy eyes, and his nose shone as red as the triceratops'. He had upped his dose of leukotriene blockers, yet again, to counteract the pollen. To no avail.

The hungry carnivores also had watery eyes. Even so, they managed to locate a pack of scruffy mammals, each one no bigger than a rabbit. Not much of a meal for a troödon.

Marty raised the tranq gun and sighted on the nearest carnivore.

Before Marty could shoot, Dill grabbed a tank of Saur-Away. "I'll save them!" Dill sounded like a bad imitation of Jackson Sirloin. He aimed the nozzle and a stream of pink mist shot out.

The troödons ignored it, and began to surround their prey.

"Dammit," Marty said as the wind carried the Saur-Away toward the scientists, and away from the predators, who were closing in. Marty couldn't get a clear shot through the pink cloud.

Then, one of the carnivores sneezed. Seizing their chance, the mammals fled in different directions.

"Yes, go!" Marty cheered them on.

The closest troödons lunged, but were too late.

The carnivores headed down to the sea shore, where they resorted to snatching ammonites that ventured into the shallow waters. Their displeasure at dining on mollusks seemed evident from every tail twitch.

That evening, Marty's good humor at the mammals'

survival evaporated as he perused the latest T-mail from Julianna. He cringed at her worried frown full of concern for Dill's safety. Even worse, the attached holo-clips made Marty look like little more than a beefy bodyguard for the brilliant scientist.

"Maybe we haven't located any ragweed," Dill said, "but I swear we're surrounded by its ancestors." As summer drew to a close, his allergies seemed worse.

Aboard the *H.G.Wells*, the two scientists were watching the duckbills' southward migration. The large males foraged ahead, while the females pushed their offspring to the center of the herd. The big-eyed youngsters, with their shortened snouts, were certainly cuter than birds, except for their sniffles. Their low skulls bore little bumps where the tubular crests would grow.

"At least," Marty said, "we no longer have to watch the mothers pre-chew their babies' food. Those giant gobs were disgusting."

A gaggle of young trombone heads paraded down to a placid pond, choked with vegetation and a couple of floating logs. First one, then the other mothers issued thin, high-pitched squeals. But the juveniles ignored them—acted like they hadn't heard.

Dill laughed. "They're just like my sister's kids at the beach when she says, 'Time to go.' It's amazing how sound simply doesn't carry from a beach chair down to the water's edge."

Suddenly, one of the "floating logs" sprang from the water, snatched a young duckbill in its tooth-filled jaw, and dragged it under. The color drained from the paleontologist's face and he began to wheeze.

As Dill reached for a capsule of inhalant, Marty said,

"The East African crocodiles are just as fast. Just as deadly—" Marty stopped, staring at the allergy medicine. In a hushed voice, he said, "I know what killed the dinosaurs."

"The comet."

Marty shook his head. "Obviously, it hit. But the saurians were dying off before then."

Dill gave him a puzzled look. Had allergies slowed the synapses in Dill's brain?

"Want a hint? Your medication showed me the obvious."

Dill frowned, then raised the capsule to his nose.

Or perhaps the paleontologist's inhalants made him dimwitted. Marty said, "Maybe you should go easy with that stuff."

"Nonsense."

Marty persisted. "Allergies are killing the trombone heads."

"What?"

"The males are too congested to make the proper mating calls. And the mothers can't issue effective warnings to their offspring."

"How about the other extinct saurians?" Dill asked.

"That triceratops didn't *intend* to kill itself. Remember its red nose and the coating of pollen on its neck frill? It stuck its head under water to get relief from an itchy nose. Maybe its front feet sank too far into the sand for it to be able to stand up again."

"And the troödons?"

"The ammonites are not their preferred meal. Allergies are interfering with the troödons' hunting abilities. The flowering plants make them sneeze as they stalk their prey. When they lunge at their victims, their eyes are watering too much to judge distances accurately. In fact, I suspect many doomed species are suffering from allergies."

"Why are prehistoric mammals asymptomatic?" Dill blew

his nose with a loud honk.

"Mammalian allergies must be a later evolutionary development."

"Wait a minute. Flowering plants have existed for at least fifty million years. They mark the boundary between the Jurassic and the Cretaceous."

"Sure," Marty said. "But for much of the Early Cretaceous, the angiosperms weren't present in nearly the quantities surrounding us now."

"True. They had to compete against well-established conifers, ferns, and cycads."

"So, it's only been since their mid-Cretaceous radiation that they've spread their pollen everywhere."

Dill considered. With obvious reluctance, he said, "I suppose you might have something there."

Marty looked at the duckbills again. "Not with a bang, but a sneeze."

A few days before they were slated to go home, the two scientists paid their last visit to the abandoned duckbill rookery. While Marty sat on a broad, flat rock contemplating all they had observed, Dill wandered among the empty nests, pausing now and then to take an occasional measurement, to inhale a leukotriene blocker, or to photograph a nest.

Eventually, the paleontologist came over to Marty. "Never again," he muttered.

"Huh?"

"I never want to see the Cretaceous again," Dill said. "My next paleo trip will be to the Jurassic—a whole world and not one angiosperm anywhere. But that'll have to wait until after my wedding."

"Wedding?" Marty's heart lurched.

"I'm going to propose to Julianna the nano-sec I get

back."

Marty bit back his response.

"Aren't you going to congratulate me?"

That night, while the paleontologist snored, Marty struggled to compose a vid-note to Julianna. On watching the replay, he winced.

"Erase," he commanded.

Dill's snoring continued.

"Begin again." Marty took a deep breath. "Julianna, I have an exclusive for you." This time, Marty detailed his dinosaur extinction hypothesis. He closed with, "I want you to be the one to release the news of my breakthrough to the world."

Before he could change his mind, he pressed Send.

Just after dawn on their last day, a batch of T-mail arrived. Marty paged through the holo-clips from Julianna, growing more excited by the minute. She'd sent him copies of her exclusive report, and her follow-ups on the breaking story. His allergy-extinction hypothesis was electrifying the scientific community. A huge debate had erupted. If there was anything reporters loved, it was controversy.

Marty glanced up to see Dill staring in dismay at his own screen. Wiping his red nose, the paleontologist muttered, "Who knows why females are so unpredictable?" He lurched to his feet. "I'm going for a walk."

Marty waited until Dill was outside before opening Julianna's last holo-clip, which was a personal vid-note. A nuevo-jazz tune played in the background—the same song they'd enjoyed on their second date, when they'd spent their time talking about the far-away places they'd visited. Now, she ran her fingers over a strand of beads around her neck and spoke just eight words. "Hurry home, darling. I've missed you so much." Her eyes sparkled.

"I miss you, too," Marty said to her holo-image.

He replayed Julianna's vid-note a dozen times before turning to the T-mail from Amazeballs. They congratulated him on his allergy hypothesis, and named him to head the second trip to the Cretaceous next April. Even better, he could take whomever he wanted with him!

Marty knew who. "Julianna," he said. He could hardly wait to break the news to her.

Think of it! Six uninterrupted months with Julianna. She'd told him that each spring, huge populations of monarchs migrate thousands of kilometers to mate. Marty laughed. Next spring, it would be just the two of them traveling sixty-seven million years to the Montana sea shore.

Rosemary Claire Smith worked as an archaeologist and a campaign-finance attorney before becoming a full-time fiction writer. Her stories, which have sold to Analog, Fantastic Stories, Stupefying Stories, Digital Science Fiction and elsewhere, showcase her interests in space exploration, sentient aliens, genetic engineering, mythology, and time travel to the heyday of the dinosaurs. She tweets as @RCWordsmith and has been blogging at rosemaryclairesmith.wordpress.com/blogging-the-mesozoic for the last 156 million years.

Further Tales
selected by Zach Chapman

Still looking for more time travel? I assume you've already watched *Back to the Future* and *Looper*, that you've already read Jack Finney's *Time and Again* and David Gerrold's *The Man who Folded Himself*. That's probably what brought you to this anthology. If you haven't read those stories, you should get on that. Read Heinlein's —*All You Zombies*— for good measure too. Now, for those of you who have read the classics (Hey, Finney's *The Body Snatchers* is better than *Time and Again*), I've decided to point out some great tales in other mediums instead of retreading stuff you've already discovered and love.

Video games. Time travel could be considered a trope in late 80s, early 90s video games, a crutch for developers, a reason to have different backgrounds and enemy variation in side scrollers; I'm looking at you, *Turtles in Time*. In the late 1990s, it evolved from an aesthetic trope into puzzle mechanics. Think *Zelda*. Plant the magic beans as a kid, so you'll have access to that floating Heart Container when you travel into the future, Link! Mid 2000s saw time manipulation form as a gameplay element. About to fall on a spiky deathtrap? Rewind. Enemies spraying bullets at you? Toss a temporal grenade. And the 2030s? Well traveler, you tell me what kind of time travel games they have. I'm dying to know.

Here's a list of what I think are standout time travel video games:

Ape Escape. 1999. PlayStation, PSP.
Blinx (series). 2000-2004. Xbox.

Braid. 2008. Xbox 360, Windows Max, Linux.

Chrono Trigger*. 1995. Super NES, PlayStation, Nintendo DS, iOS, Android.

Daikatana. 2000. Windows, Nintendo 64, Game Boy Color.

EarthBound (and Mother 3). 1994. Super NES, Game Boy Advance.

Fire Emblem: Awakening. 2013. 3DS.

Life Is Strange. 2015. PlayStation 3, PlayStation 4, Xbox 360, Xbox One, Windows.

The Legend of Zelda: Ocarina of Time*. 1998. Nintendo 64, GameCube, Nintendo 3DS.

The Legend of Zelda: Oracle of Ages. 2001. Game Boy Color.

Maniac Mansion II: Day of the Tentacle. 1993. Mac Os, MS-DOS.

Mario & Luigi: Partners in Time. 2005. Nintendo DS.

Prince of Persia: The Sands of Time (series). 2003-2005.PlayStation 2, Xbox, GameCube, Windows, PSP.

Quantum Break. 2016. Xbox One, Windows.

Radiant Historia. 2010. Nintendo 3DS.

Rachet and Clank Future: A Crack In Time. 2009. PlayStation 3.

Singularity. 2010. Windows, PlayStation 3, Xbox 360.

Sly Cooper: Thieves in Time. 2013. PlayStation 3.

Sonic Generations. 2011. PlayStation 3, Xbox 360, Nintendo 3DS.

Spider-Man: Edge of Time. 2011. Wii, PlayStation 3, Xbox 360, Nintendo 3DS.

Star Ocean. 1996. Super Famicom, PSP.

Tales of Phantasia. 1995. Super Famicomm Game Boy Advance, PlayStation, PSP.

Teenage Mutant Ninja Turtles: Turtles in Time. 1991. Arcade, Super NES.

TimeSplitters (series). 2000. PlayStation 2, GameCube, Xbox.

So you say video games aren't for you? Holding a controller hurts your fingers and you're too lazy to travel into 2030 where all these games are playable in VR? Fine. Check out these comic books instead:

Aetheric Mechanics by Warren Ellis. Avatar Press.
All-Star Superman (issue #6) by Grant Morrison. DC.
Batman: The Return of Bruce Wayne by Grant Morrison. DC.
Black Science by Rick Remender and Matteo Scalera. Image.
Booster Gold by Dan Jurgens. DC.
The Bunker by Joshua Hale Fialkov and Joe Infrurnari. Oni.
Chrononauts by Mark Millar and Sean Murphy. Image.
Crisis on Infinite Earths by Marv Wolfman. DC.
Days of Future Past by Chris Claremont. Marvel.
Flashpoint* by Geoff Johns. DC.
Patience by Daniel Clowes. Fantagraphics.
Paper Girls by Brian K. Vaughan. Image.
Pax Romana* by Jonathan Hickman. Image.
DC Universe: Rebirth Special #1 by Geoff Johns. DC.
Red Wing by Jonathan Hickman and Nick Pitarra. Image.
Trillium by Jeff Lemire. Vertigo.
Valérian and Laureline by Pierre Christin and Jean-Claude
Mézières. Dargaud. Cinebook.

In Superhero comics, we see many books with heroes
and villains coming from the future to save or destroy the
past. Cable, Rip Hunter, Booster Gold, Abra Kadabra, Per
Degaton, Kal Kent, Professor Zoom, Kang, Mordu the
Merciless, Iron Lad, Waverider to name a few. Many of these
heroes and villains were written during The Silver Age of
Comic Books. Later, time travel was used as an easy access
reset button for convoluted continuity. So while the DC
classic Crisis on Infinite Earths functioned as a time travel
story, it's main purpose was to wipe the awkward continuity
and give DC a clean slate to work with. DC has reached for
the easy time travel reset several times since Crisis on Infinite
Earths, including in this year's DCU reboot Rebirth. If you
don't look at The Big Two, you'll notice several great indie,

creator-owned time travel comics. These are true time travel stories, as fantastic and varied as the stories you read in this anthology. Image has a gold mine of titles, some currently being published monthly, some complete, weighing in at several volumes. Have fun reading.

ACKNOWLEDGEMENTS

Many thanks to: Daniel Shallue and Nick Tchan for helping me traverse the time travel slush pile. Taylor Fox for putting up with me as I worked on this project and for her contributions copy editing. Oh, and for contributing a copy of Quantum Break... for the project... for studying! Dan Chapman, Michele Petty, Daniel José Older, Kyle Shepherd, Lou J Berger, Alex Shvartsman for their support. Dan McCarthy for the stellar cover art. And every author who subbed to my call for submissions

ABOUT THE EDITOR

Zach Chapman lives in Austin, Texas with his librarian wife Taylor, a cat, a rabbit and a lazy eyed dog named Dingo. When his ADD isn't compelling him to check his phone, he writes, edits, and games. And does day job stuff too. His fiction has appeared in the anthologies *Writers of the Future volume 31*, *Futuristica volume 2*, *Steampunk Universe* and *Chilling Ghost Short Stories*. Check out his publishing adventures at chappyfiction.com or on Twitter @chappyzach

www.ingramcontent.com/pod-product-compliance
Lightning Source LLC
Chambersburg PA
CBHW060539180626
46817CB00002B/640